BUFFALO WEST WING

A WHITE HOUSE CHEF MYSTERY

BUFFALO WEST WING

JULIE HYZY

WHEELER
CHIVERS

This Large Print edition is published by Wheeler Publishing, Waterville, Maine, USA and by AudioGO Ltd, Bath, England.
Wheeler Publishing, a part of Gale, Cengage Learning.
A White House Chef Mystery.

The text of this Large Print edition is unabridged.
Other aspects of the book may vary from the original edition.
Set in 16 pt. Plantin.

LIBRARY OF CONGRESS CATALOGING-IN-PUBLICATION DATA

Hyzy, Julie A.
  Buffalo west wing / by Julie Hyzy.
    p. cm. — (A White house chef mystery) (Wheeler
  Publishing large print cozy mystery)
  ISBN-13: 978-1-4104-3688-7 (pbk.)
  ISBN-10: 1-4104-3688-8 (pbk.)
    1. White House (Washington, D.C.)—Fiction. 2. Women
  cooks—Fiction. 3. Large type books. I. Title.
  PS3608.Y98B84 2011
  813'.6—dc22   2011001520

BRITISH LIBRARY CATALOGUING-IN-PUBLICATION DATA AVAILABLE

Published in 2011 in the U.S. by arrangement with The Berkley Publishing Group, a member of Penguin Group (USA) Inc.
Published in 2011 in the U.K. by arrangement with The Berkley Publishing Group, a division of Penguin Group (USA) Inc.

U.K. Hardcover: 978 1 445 83734 5 (Chivers Large Print)
U.K. Softcover: 978 1 445 83735 2 (Camden Large Print)

Printed in the United States of America
1 2 3 4 5 6 7 15 14 13 12 11

To everyone from Bouchercon 2009

ACKNOWLEDGMENTS

A big shout-out to Margie McGuire, who suggested this book's title during one of our famous Blackberry Breakfasts. Thanks, Margie! And to Rene Baumgartner, whose famous chocolate chip cookies morphed into wings for this story.

Special thanks to my wonderful editor, Natalee Rosenstein, as well as Michelle Vega, Megan Swartz, Kaitlyn Kennedy, and Erica Rose at Berkley Prime Crime. Thanks also to the folks at Tekno, especially Marty Greenberg and John Helfers. I owe a great debt to the incomparable Denise Little, who keeps Ollie cookin'.

Every writer needs support and I'm incredibly fortunate to have my blog-sisters at MysteryLoversKitchen.com, and my cozy-mates at KillerCharacters.com to rely on for both morale-boosting and cheerleading. I'm very lucky to be friends with these amazing writers.

I would be nowhere without my family. It's impossible to put into words how much they mean to me, but I know they know, so it's all good. Love you, Curt, Robyn, Sara, Biz, Paul, Mitch, Grandma, Auntie Claudia, Kitka, and Violet. We miss you, K'Ehleyr.

Thanks to Mystery Writers of America, Sisters in Crime, and Thriller Writers of America for camaraderie and support, and thanks especially to readers who are willing to take a chance on new authors. You're the best!

CHAPTER 1

Inauguration Day

"Hurry up, Ollie. It's almost time," Cyan called from the center hall.

"Go ahead, I'll meet you there!" I shouted back. I placed my inelegant creation on the oven's center rack, gave it a final critical glance, and reminded myself there was a first time for everything. Especially in the White House. Shutting the oven door, I quickly washed and dried my hands, then hurried to join Cyan.

The musty fragrance of old papers, books, photos, and historic paraphernalia hit me the moment I stepped into the curator's office. That familiar "library smell" mingling with the delicious aroma of fresh coffee caused me to slow down and take an appreciative breath. This was a room where I could get lost for hours at a time.

Like I'd ever have that luxury.

Stocky and bearded, our curator, John

Weaver, maintained his office with loving efficiency. Archived materials were kept off-site, but in here he crammed as much as he could into every available nook. He was extraordinarily well organized; I'd seen him produce obscure artifacts within moments of a president's request.

Right now, however, his office swarmed with people. Huddled around a tiny television, staffers jockeyed for position. I caught sight of Cyan's red ponytail — she'd managed to claim a spot up front. My second in command, Bucky, stood directly behind her. Among the others present were our florist, Kendra, her assistant, and several new people. I was the last to arrive and stood on my toes, hoping for a glimpse of the TV screen. But everyone clustered in front of me was too tall.

John noticed. "Olivia," he said, gesturing me forward, "you can't possibly see anything from there."

"I'm fine," I said, but by the time I'd gotten the words out, everyone had shifted to make room for me. I removed my toque and took a position next to Cyan, turning to face the group that had closed in behind me. "Can everybody see okay?"

"There's no problem seeing over you." Bucky said, not unkindly. "You're short enough."

We were stealing precious minutes here. At our stations before dawn, every one of us had been rushing nonstop from the moment we'd arrived. Just as soon as our new president was sworn in, we would hurry back to resume today's crazed timetable. Of all the busy days at the White House — and there were many — this was by far the busiest. Thank goodness it only occurred once every four or eight years.

From the instant President and Mrs. Campbell stepped out the south portico door this morning to head to the Capitol until our new president arrived here later in "The Beast," his brand-new custom-fitted limousine, we would be hard at work, changing everything in the mansion to accommodate its new residents.

Housekeeping had swiftly transported all the Campbells' personal items: pictures, notes, books, colognes, dresses, suits, and socks into moving vans, and were now in the process of scouring the already gleaming home before bringing in all new belongings and favorites to replace the old. Different sizes, colors, preferences.

Everything changed in what appeared to the outside world to take no longer than whispering "abracadabra." But it was the

11

endless rehearsals, the thick binders filled with detailed instructions, reams of notes, and the tireless work of ninety staffers that made the switchover look like magic.

"You're just in time," Cyan whispered.

One of the new Secret Service agents, Bost, shushed her. "Quiet," he said. "The chief justice is about to administer the oath of office."

Cyan rolled her eyes but returned her attention to the television where we all watched the young and handsome Parker Hyden become the new president of the United States. His lovely wife, Denise, held the Bible upon which he set his left hand. Accompanying them before an audience of millions — if you included those gathered in front of the Capitol building and everyone watching from home — were their two children, Abigail, thirteen, and Joshua, nine. The Hydens were a handsome family, bright with hope and determination.

What would the future hold, for him, for them, for us? As the oath was completed and President Hyden stepped to the microphone to deliver his first speech as commander in chief, I wrestled with the sadness I'd been fighting these past few weeks. I liked our new president very much. I liked what he stood for. But for the past four years, I had served at the pleasure of President and Mrs. Campbell, and I missed them already.

A bond forms between the White House staff and the First Family. It's an unusual bond because it is, by definition, temporary. Every four or eight years the residents change, but the staffers largely remain the same. I had come to treasure my time with Mrs. Campbell.

With a new family moving in, I had no idea what the days ahead held for me or for others in key positions on staff. For those of us in the most visible posts, continued employment was not a given. So far, the Hyden family seemed willing to keep me around. After all, I was the first female in the role of White House executive chef, and it wouldn't look good to cut me from the staff without giving me a chance to prove myself. But there were no assurances they would like my style. No guarantee I would bond with them the way I had with the Campbells.

President Campbell had served only one term and had not run for reelection due to health issues that threatened to hamper his ability to serve. After the news broke that he would not seek a second term, entertaining at the White House was severely curtailed. President Campbell had finished out his presidency in relative quiet.

By contrast, Parker Hyden, a junior senator from a Midwestern state, had taken the world by storm and had won the election over President Campbell's former veep by a landslide. The new president promised to continue promoting a platform of unity. I was glad. But when it came time for the final good-byes in the Entrance Hall, I'd gotten choked up when Mrs. Campbell leaned forward to hug me. She'd whispered in my ear, "Life was never boring with you in charge of our kitchen. I hope you take as good care of the Hydens as you did of us."

John interrupted my reverie as he stepped away from the television. "The next few weeks ought to be interesting," he said. "Now that the election hoopla is over, the media will hound our new president relentlessly, hoping for an early misstep to get everybody all fired up again. Be on your guard, everyone."

His warning was appreciated, but unnecessary. With the exception of the new people, everyone gathered here had weathered more media blitzkriegs than we could count. "Good reminder, John," I said. "Thanks."

The group around the television dispersed. Cyan, Bucky, and I followed the new staffers out the door with Kendra and her assistant close behind. As much as we would have liked to stay to hear what President Hyden had to say, we couldn't afford the time. I planned to catch his speech online later.

Passing the kitchen, one of the new agents, Gardez, sniffed the air. "What's that? It's so familiar." His faint Spanish accent and height — over six feet tall — combined to make for one very attractive Secret Service agent.

Cyan laughed before I could answer. "Bet it smells like home, doesn't it?"

"Come on, Gardez. We don't have time for this." In contrast to his companion, Bost was muscular and trim, with a blond buzz cut, and an acne-pitted complexion. He fisted his companion's arm. "We have to report in to MacKenzie in five."

My heart gave an extra beat. MacKenzie. Tom. I hadn't seen him very much since his promotion to head of the Presidential Protective Division. We crossed paths now and then — and worked together when situations required us to do so — but we hadn't yet reached the level of friendship that had been lost when we'd ended our romantic relationship. It had been over a year now. I

15

wondered if we would ever get back to that place.

Cyan waved to Gardez as the two agents headed toward the West Wing and I spotted a hopeful glint in her eyes. I wasn't the only one suffering from a nonexistent love life these days. She and Rafe, one of our SBA chefs, had been an "item" in the kitchen until six months ago when Rafe had accepted a position as executive chef at a prestigious New York hotel. Like me, Cyan was "single" again. Unlike me, however, Cyan was ready for a rebound. I was happy to immerse myself in my job and forget about relationships for a while. Life was so much simpler that way.

At least that's what I kept telling myself.

Bucky led us into the kitchen, talking over his shoulder. "You didn't tell Gardez what you were making in here. Why not? Too embarrassed to admit it?"

"Hardly," I said. "Did you get a look at the other guy, Bost? He was ready to deck Cyan for continuing the conversation. I'm surprised he even took time to watch the inauguration." I shrugged. "But then again, I suppose we were all like that when we were new: anxious about making a good impression."

Cyan laughed. I wasn't quite sure why,

16

but I had too much work to do to bother finding out. Bucky headed into the refrigeration area, and I went to check on my "masterpiece." Some accomplishment: mac and cheese with green beans. I shook my head. This dish was on Abigail and Joshua Hyden's list of homemade favorites. In addition to the tacos, minipizzas, and salad that we planned to serve our young guests tonight, we would also feature make-your-own sundaes, and Marcel's famous brownies.

Even though Marcel was the only one of us with the freedom to whip up an original creation tonight, I wasn't jealous. The event we were organizing was no less important than the parties our new president and his wife would enjoy as they were fêted all over town. My team was charged with providing dinner for the new First Kids and their friends who had been invited to tonight's sleepover.

I missed Marguerite, Mrs. Campbell's social secretary. She had been replaced by Valerie Peacock, who had arranged the evening's festivities. While Valerie wouldn't be here in person to oversee the show — she would be attending all the gala events around D.C. tonight with her boss — she had left detailed instructions with her staff.

Valerie had set up a scavenger hunt for the youngsters' entertainment. Designed not only to be fun, the race around the White House would help familiarize the Hyden kids with their new home.

Part of their game would bring them to the kitchen, and I was looking forward to that. I'd met the children briefly during their initial visit, but I wanted them both to know we were here for them, ready to prepare whatever they wanted — assuming their mother approved. We hadn't had school-age children in the White House for a long time. I knew things would be different. Just how different remained to be seen.

"What kind of pizzas are we making tonight?" Cyan asked, scratching her head. "I know it changed."

"We're adding spinach pizzas in addition to the pepperoni," I said. "They invited a couple more kids and one of them is vegetarian," I started to question where my assistant's mind was today. I'd answered that question for her at least twice already. I finished checking on the cheesy green bean casserole and came around to continue. That's when I spotted an out-of-place box on the countertop behind her. "What's that?" I asked, pointing.

She twisted to look as I made my way over.

18

The box was about twelve inches square and about eight inches deep. Bright red in color, it bore the familiar Rene's Wings logo. Rene's was a well-known national barbecue/chicken wing chain. An oval sticker read "Garlic and Green Pepper."

"I'd guess it's an appetizer."

Wondering how Cyan had missed seeing it, I lifted the lid of the box to find exactly what we expected: a plastic-covered take-out container jammed with sauced chicken wings. What we didn't expect to see was the bright yellow note taped to the inside of the lid.

"For Abby and Josh," Cyan read aloud.

"Where did it come from?"

She shrugged. "No idea."

At that moment, Bucky returned, carrying two trays of freshly washed cooking utensils. "Who left these wings here?" I asked him.

Dropping the utensils on the countertop, he peered into the box. "Don't know, but they look delicious. What kind are they?"

I told him.

"Mmm. Good choice."

I stared at the note again. "Whoever left this clearly intended for the Hyden kids to have it."

"You use your finely honed deductive skills to figure that one out?" Bucky asked.

I shot him a glare but ignored the jab. Although Bucky was always sarcastic, I couldn't ask for a better chef in the position of first assistant. He and I had an unspoken agreement: He would do his best to keep the sarcasm to a minimum, and I would try to overlook it when he slipped. Most of the time it worked. Bucky had even learned to apologize — occasionally — when he was really out of line.

I tapped the box. "My point is that whoever left this here must be new."

Bucky raised his eyebrows. "And . . . ?"

"I can't serve these to the kids until I find out where they came from."

Cyan laughed. "Why not?"

Was she kidding? "You know how it works. Nothing gets served to the First Family unless it comes through proper channels."

"But it must have come from someone who works here. The only people in the White House today are official personnel." She shrugged again. "And everyone here is cleared."

"Yeah," I said under my breath, "until they're not." I'd had enough run-ins with people who *should have been* trustworthy, but who'd proved to be anything but. "I'll talk with the Secret Service. In the meantime, I'll store this in the refrigerator until we find out who left it here."

Cyan grinned. "Careful. If you leave the box in there too long, those wings might start flying off. That's their most popular flavor and my all-time favorite."

"I wouldn't let you eat any of these either," I said. "Not until we figure out what it's doing here. This is very odd."

I picked up the box and headed toward the refrigeration area. Just as I reached for one of the stainless steel handles, I sensed a presence in the doorway.

"Good afternoon, Ms. Paras."

Peter Everett Sargeant didn't smile when he delivered his greeting. So I didn't smile when I responded. "What can I do for you, Peter?"

He stepped closer. Dressed impeccably, he wore a custom suit and perfectly coordinated tie, and, as always, the crisp, folded edges of a matching handkerchief peeked out from his breast pocket. His undisguised curiosity skimmed the box in my hands before he answered. "Today," he said, speaking softly, "is a new day."

"It seems most of the world would agree with you."

"You don't?"

I did, but I wasn't about to get pulled into a political discussion with Sargeant. White

House staffers knew that it was our job to take care of the First Family. Just as important was leaving our own politics at the door — every single day. While I was as happy as the next guy to see Parker Hyden as the new leader of the free world, I wasn't about to chitchat about it with our sensitivity director.

Sensitivity director. Talk about a walking contradiction in terms.

"Today is a day to celebrate," I said, and with what I hoped was finality, placed the wings on an empty shelf and shut the refrigerator door. "Which is why I need everyone *out* of my kitchen except essential personnel. What was it you said you needed?"

"Why do you have store-bought chicken wings?" he asked, avoiding my question. "Aren't you up to preparing that level of delicacy?"

I wanted to say that it was none of Sargeant's business, but I took the high road instead. "I didn't buy these. And, to be frank, I don't know where they came from. The box was here when I got back from watching the inauguration in the curator's office."

His hands came up, clutching one another as though seeking to grasp my meaning.

"What?" He blinked several times. "You're telling me you have a secret admirer?"

"Apparently it's for the children. There's a note inside. But until I figure out who left it here and why, I'm keeping it refrigerated and out of sight."

"Clearly, the snack was intended as a gift for the new First Son and Daughter."

"And just as clearly, I will not serve anything to anyone in this home unless I can be absolutely certain that it's safe."

He scoffed, frowning in that condescending way of his. "Well, of course it's safe. It couldn't get inside the White House if it wasn't."

I was about to remind him of other confections we believed had been "safe," but he must have anticipated my reply because he backed up a step and raised his hands. "Have it your way," he said. "The reason I came down here was to let you know that I will be keeping close tabs on the children for the first weeks while they settle in."

My face must have betrayed my skepticism because he continued. "Although I am generally in charge of making sure the White House is sensitive to social and religious mores when entertaining guests, I have taken it upon myself to expand my responsibilities to ensure the new First Family is made to feel welcome in their new home."

That was the job we *all* shared. Rather than point this out, however, I asked, "Do you have kids?"

He blinked. "No, why?"

"I don't either," I said, "so I'm not speaking from experience. But they're going through a major upheaval in their lives right now."

He waggled his head. "Upheaval? You make it sound so negative. They're the new American royalty. They will have everything they want. And then some."

"They've left their home and friends, and they will be living in a fishbowl from now on. With everything changing around them, I have to believe the new First Children will be most comfortable interacting with adults they already know." If I could keep this tedious little man away from the kids, I would be doing a very good deed. "Their grandmother will be in residence. If you intend to plan anything, I suggest you make arrangements through Grandma Marty first."

Sargeant didn't care for my advice. I could see it in the precise way he steepled his fingers near his chest and tapped them together. "You've been lucky, Ms. Paras. I'll give you that. But the Hydens are not the

Campbells and while you may have fooled Mrs. Campbell, I suspect our new First Lady will not be such a pushover." A tiny smile curled up one corner of his mouth as he took his leave. "It's about time the First Family sees my worth rather than be dazzled by the stunts you pull. I'm looking forward to the next several weeks."

I glared after him, knowing in my heart he was wrong, but knowing just as clearly that he would never admit it. My "stunts" had saved the White House — and its staff — from several embarrassing incidents. Was it too much to ask for a little respect from our sensitivity director?

At the door, he turned back. "Finally, after all your shenanigans, it's my time now."

I shook my head. I guess it *was* too much to ask.

CHAPTER 2

I got my first chance to talk with the kids when the social secretary's assistant, Carol, accompanied them to the kitchen that evening during their scavenger hunt. Bucky, Cyan, and I knew exactly what role we were expected to play when the troops swarmed us, and so were prepared for the ruckus that rolled our way just before 10 P.M.

Eight kids arrived, laughing and talking, consulting hint sheets and arguing over who'd spotted which clue first. Both First Kids had invited three friends each, and the noise from their chatter was louder and more boisterous than we'd heard in our halls since Mrs. Campbell had organized the Mother's Luncheon a couple years back. Several Secret Service agents accompanied the young crowd. I recognized Agent Gardez and was introduced to Agent Nourie, who nodded hello. Before the kids were allowed in, the two men scoped out the entire kitchen and then remained to guard the kids during the visit.

Thirteen-year-old Abigail was all gangly legs and arms. Tall and slim like her parents, she wore her dark hair to her shoulders and her nervousness on her sleeve. She stayed close to one particular girl and they giggled every couple of moments. I liked her immediately. Abigail had a quick, genuine smile; just from the looks of her, I could tell she was a cheerful kid.

"Hello," I said, and introduced the staff.

Abigail solemnly shook my hand and thanked us for dinner. "The green bean casserole was very delicious," she said.

"I'm glad you enjoyed it."

Her younger brother shoved at the three boys who had been jostling with him since they arrived. Joshua was a full head shorter than his sister, carrying the tiniest remainder of baby fat. He had wide brown eyes and deep dimples. "Come on, Abby," Joshua finally said. "We're supposed to be looking for clues, remember?"

The social secretary's assistant, Carol, cleared her throat. "Josh . . ."

The boy's shoulders drooped. He stepped forward, shook my hand, and thanked me for dinner. "Sorry," Josh said. "I forgot."

"No problem," I said. "I want to welcome

you all to the main White House kitchen. In here we can prepare anything you like to eat . . . providing your mom gives us the okay."

"Can you make ice cream?" one of Josh's friends asked.

"We can," I said. "But my friend Marcel, the pastry chef, usually makes the desserts. What kind of ice cream do you like?"

He was overridden by Josh. "Can you make crab cakes?"

That took me aback. "We make great crab cakes."

I was about to say more, but one of Josh's friends pulled at him. Abigail had begun to search the kitchen for the planted clues. Our job was to offer hints only as a last resort. The object of the game was not to rush through the scavenger hunt, but to allow the kids to become comfortable in all areas of the huge home.

"Your sister is beating us," the friend said. And with that, they both took off, ice cream and crab cakes forgotten. Although there was little to fear in the White House itself, agents Nourie and Gardez watched over the kids with eagle eyes. Hands at his sides, posture erect, Nourie was as tall as Gardez, and just as handsome. Soft-spoken, he reminded me of Matt Damon, but with dark eyes. Where were they growing these Secret Service agents these days?

Cyan had noticed him, too. "Help yourself," she said, pointing to the bite-sized portions of fresh fruit, veggies, and cheese we'd set out. "Would you like something to drink?"

"No, thank you," Nourie said. When he broke his focus long enough to smile at her, she blushed. I remembered Cyan's reaction to Gardez earlier. She was definitely ready for a new relationship.

Apparently satisfied that the kids were safe in the kitchen, Nourie and Gardez excused themselves and said they would wait in the hall.

Abigail and her friends were much more polite about rummaging around the kitchen than Josh and his troop. The girls made a methodical search of the area, scribbling answers on their sheets of paper, and whispering as they compared notes. Josh and the three boys ran from cabinet to cabinet, opening and slamming them one after the other. They missed at least two clues.

Josh disappeared around the corner into the refrigerated area. There were no clues there — we'd decided to keep that area off-limits — and I followed to let him know. Just as I turned the corner, I heard him exclaim, "Hey!"

There was Josh, on tiptoes, pulling the box of chicken wings from the refrigerator shelf. If I would have set the box just six inches farther back when I'd put it away, he probably wouldn't have been able to see it. "Look at what I found!"

Next to him in a heartbeat, I tried to peel the box from his hands. "I'm so sorry, Josh," I said. "This isn't for you."

But he'd already opened the lid. "No, see. It *is* for us," he shouted happily. "Abby, come here. See what I found!" Beaming, he looked up at me. "These are our all-time favorite. Abby and I even agree on that. Thank you for such a nice surprise."

Of course he believed the wings had been left there as part of the scavenger hunt. Of course.

"I'm very sorry," I repeated. I tried to close the lid, shaking my head as everyone else gathered in the cramped area. The kids surrounded me and Cyan stood behind them, her eyes chastising me for what she knew I was about to say. I swallowed. "This really isn't for you," I began, doing my best to explain. "I know what the note says, but here in the White House we have certain rules."

Okay, bad choice of words. I realized it

the instant they left my mouth.

Abigail stepped closer. She shifted her weight in a gesture I recognized. I'd used it when I was her age and didn't agree with what I'd been told. "But it has our names on it," she said politely. She pointed.

"I know." Blowing out a breath, I watched Cyan wag her hands as though she wanted no part of this. Bucky wore a smirk that told me he wondered how I would try to talk my way out of this one. I finally succeeded in shutting the lid and held the box close to my chest. I felt like an idiot standing in front of them all, like a kid refusing to share. Josh was clearly displeased, his eyes piercing me with accusation.

"Carol will know what I'm talking about," I said, hoping to heaven she would. "Here in the White House, we cannot ever serve food that comes to us suspiciously."

Carol, for her part, looked as confused as the kids.

Then — just what I needed — Peter Sargeant, strode in. He cleared his throat and everyone turned.

"Hello there, kids. I came to see how the scavenger hunt was progressing. But what is going on here?" He pointed to the box in my hands. "Ms. Paras, have you been able to determine where that came from?"

"No." I wished he would just stay out of this. "I'm actually trying to explain right now, how we take precautions to keep the White House food safe."

The kids grumbled, and Sargeant stepped into their midst. They gave him a wide berth. Chalk one up for kids' impressions. "You're disappointed, aren't you?" He didn't wait for them to answer. "I had this exact same conversation with our executive chef earlier today —"

"And I told you then," I interrupted, "that unless we know exactly where food comes from, we cannot serve it to anyone in the First Family." I met Abigail's skeptical stare because it was easier to face than Josh's quivering lip. "Listen," I said. "If I knew who left this here, I would be delighted to serve it." I thought about a way to make Josh understand. "It's a mystery. Until we know who brought this, we can't serve these. But if you can find out who bought this at the store and left it in the kitchen, I'll be more than happy to talk with them. As soon as this gets cleared up, we're all set."

Abigail asked, "Can't you just, like, look at some tapes to see who was carrying the box when they came in?"

Sharp girl. "I've talked with the Secret

Service about this," I said. "They're already checking. That's how important this is."

Josh made a face and turned away. I thought I heard one of Abigail's friends whisper, "It's just some stupid wings. Your chef back home would never take those away from you."

Sargeant, never one to miss an opportunity to rub salt in the wound, held up his hands. "I'm so sorry, children, but this is Ms. Paras's kitchen and these are her rules."

"No," I corrected him, "these are all our rules."

"Would you be willing to send someone out to the nearest Rene's Wings and pick up replacements?" he asked. "That would satisfy you, wouldn't it? As long as no one knows it's being purchased for White House consumption, it's considered safe, no?"

"Yes," I began, hating the quick brightness I saw in Josh's eyes. I knew I was about to disappoint him again. "But I'm sure none of them are open. It's well after ten."

Sargeant made a show of looking at his watch. "So it is."

Josh no longer looked like he was about to cry. At this point he was angry, and bored of the conversation. He jabbed the box with his finger. "I want these wings. Abby does, too." Glancing back over his shoulder, he asked, "Right, Abby?"

His sister shrugged. "Just forget about it, Josh. We'll tell Mom later."

Sargeant added unnecessarily, "I'm so sorry, but Ms. Paras is quite strong-minded and we don't want to get her angry."

"That's not the issue," I said under my breath.

Carol had begun gathering the kids. "I think we've found all we need in here," she said. "Let's move on to the Map Room." She met my eyes and I hoped to detect some friendliness, some measure of understanding there. Instead I found only sparks of anger.

They left quietly. Sargeant followed.

Bucky patted me on the shoulder. "Way to go, Ace."

CHAPTER 3

Two hours later, I had rehashed every moment of the kids' disastrous first visit to the kitchen a hundred times. No matter how you cut the cheesecake, there was no way I could have served those wings. If I had to do it again, I would still refuse. What I *should* have done was dump the whole box in the garbage as soon as I'd made my decision. But I had harbored hope that the beneficiary would make himself or herself known. I'd *wanted* to be able to let the kids have the treat.

I'd made a serious tactical error and there was no way to predict how much I'd hurt myself. If the kids didn't like me — and they clearly were not pleased — it would be a hard path to their mother's heart. I knew very well that if a First Lady didn't like her executive chef, that chef was toast.

Cyan and I cleaned up and prepared for the next day's meal. Bucky had gone home earlier and now the kitchen was quiet and tidy. Paul Vasquez, the chief usher, had informed us that the president and his wife would be back much later, so the butlers shuttled food upstairs to the residence just in case they happened to be hungry when they returned. Cyan and I could go home. I gave the room's center countertop a final disinfecting swipe and realized that I needed to be back in less than five hours. I was grateful Inauguration Day didn't come around too often.

Just before leaving, I headed to the refrigerator to discard the controversial chicken wings once and for all. After the commotion, I'd placed the logoed box into a large unmarked bag and shoved the whole thing into the back of the farthest unit. This way, no one else would find it until it was time for me to go home and I could personally see to the wings' disposal. Part of me was still hoping someone would come forward and claim it. But no one had.

I opened the fridge door and reached in. The box was gone. I scanned up and down through the grated shelves to check if someone might have moved it. Nothing.

I opened the next refrigerator, and the next, even though I knew the search would be futile. I'd put the box in the *last* fridge.

Bucky and Cyan would have had no reason to move it — unless they had taken it upon themselves to throw it out. Other staff members occasionally used these refrigerators, but no one ever took anything that didn't belong to them without asking.

Where could it be?

Clinging to the belief that perhaps Bucky had taken it to throw away when he left, I called Cyan over. "The chicken wings are missing."

She didn't react. That was my first inkling that something was wrong.

"Cyan?"

She laughed, but nothing was funny.

"What happened to them?"

"Quit worrying," she said, "Everything is fine."

Now I really started to get concerned.

Talking fast, she said, "I get that we can't serve anything weird to the First Family. But that was a *huge* order of wings. I mean, I think that size goes for like fifty dollars. It seemed like such a shame to waste them."

"You ate them?"

She laughed again just as nervously. "Of course not. But I knew we weren't going to find out who left the box here, so about an hour ago I walked it down to the laundry department. Because of the inauguration and all the extra work, there are a bunch of women working late. I thought they could use a treat."

"What?" I started for the laundry room. Maybe I could —

Cyan grabbed my arm. "Ollie, they're all gone."

"What do you mean, they're gone? The staff?"

"The wings. Lisa and SueJean shared them with the other women and a couple of the butlers," she said. "I went back to grab some for myself but they were gone. In like ten minutes."

"Cyan," I said striving for control of my temper, "you should *not* have done that." It wasn't often I got angry with her. In fact, I couldn't remember ever having done so. But right now I couldn't believe she had been so careless. "Do you realize what you've done?"

She laid a hand on my arm. "Ollie, you know as well as I do that the wings were fine. They were store-bought, for crying out loud. If they were homemade cookies or muffins I would be on your side, but . . ." She shrugged away any remorse. "I think you made a mistake by not letting the kids have them. You let your imagination run away with you this time. And I couldn't let good food go to waste. I'm only sorry I didn't get any."

"I'm the one who's sorry," I said. "I'm going to have to write you up."

"What?"

"You defied a direct order."

"Direct order? Ollie, this isn't the army, this is the kitchen. You always tell us you don't want mindless minions. You claim you want people working who are strong enough to think for themselves. Well, I did think for myself, and this time I decided you were wrong."

I wasn't wrong, and her logic was flawed. Sure, I wanted my people to take responsibility for their own decisions, but she knew — clearly — where I stood when it came to safety. And at least as far as this kitchen was concerned, I was supposed to have the last word. "Maybe I have made a big deal about nothing," I said. "Maybe I'm all wrong and you're right. I hope to God you are. But this is a security breach, Cyan, and I can't let it go without documenting."

"You really believe there's something wrong with those wings?" she asked.

"That's not the point."

"But that's the question I'm asking you. Do you really believe there was anything wrong with them?"

"What I believe is immaterial."

She threw up her hands. "Then why do you have to write me up? It's not like I force-fed them to the laundry ladies. I just thought it was something nice we could do. Show we appreciate them. Okay?"

I couldn't agree. "The reason we have these rules in place is because . . ."

"Yeah, I know," she said. "You don't have to quote me chapter and verse. I apologize. Does that make things better? I'm sorry I gave the wings to the laundry department. Okay?"

"It's not a case of being sorry . . ."

"You're still going to write me up, aren't you?"

I didn't answer, but she must have read my expression.

Her gaze grew hard and her jaw set. "I understand," she said, though she obviously did not. She grabbed her coat from a nearby chair and looked ready to spout something else. Changing her mind, she said, "I'm going home now," and left without a backward glance.

Since I'd moved to Washington, D. C., I hadn't had a lot of time to make friends. I counted Cyan among my closest and it hurt me to reprimand her. She knew as well as I did that we were the last line of defense

40

before food was served here. There was no margin for error. None. Cyan had been wrong, clearly.

So why did I feel so miserable?

I took care of a few last-minute updates on the computer, trying to convince myself everything would eventually be okay. When I looked up at the clock, I realized I had already missed the last Metro train of the night. I called a cab. I couldn't wait to get home, get to sleep, and wake up to a brand-new day.

CHAPTER 4

The first morning with our new president started off with a bang. The problem is, in the White House, we usually try to avoid things that go *bang!*

The First Family chose to have breakfast in the family residence dining room on the second floor. Also known as the Prince of Wales Room because said titled royal stayed there in 1860, the converted bedroom was spacious and bright. A wonderful choice for creating memories of a key family moment. The kids wouldn't start their new schools for another day, and Mrs. Hyden had requested an elaborate meal that the family could enjoy together on their first full day in their new home.

There is nothing more fun than preparing great food for eager diners. Here was our chance to shine. With Virginia ham and spinach omelets, as well as simple scrambled eggs, Henry's famous hash browns, pancakes, bacon, scones, fresh fruit, and cinnamon toast, this would be a breakfast they would never forget.

Well, I probably got that part right.

Cyan, Bucky, and I had everything ready to go at exactly 7:00 in the morning — the time the First Lady had requested we serve. We stood in the dining room's adjacent kitchen to wait, surrounded by the heady smells of fresh coffee; sizzling bacon; and hot, yeasty bread. My stomach growled.

At 7:05, Mrs. Hyden was ushered into the dining room. The butlers, perplexed by her solo arrival were quickly informed that the kids were sleeping in and that President Hyden had gotten up extra early to run the Ellipse. He requested coffee and wheat toast be delivered to the West Wing. Bucky jumped on that task immediately.

I overheard Mrs. Hyden speaking to one of the butlers. "Please tell the kitchen staff that I'm sorry if they went to any undue trouble."

I shouldn't have been annoyed, but I was. Just a little bit. I was used to Mrs. Campbell talking to us directly. Although there was no way for me to connect with the new First Lady unless she initiated a relationship, I felt slightly put out. Swallowing my disappointment, and noting that Cyan's and

Bucky's expressions wore the same sentiment I was feeling, we plated our offerings and prepared to return to the downstairs kitchen to await further instructions.

"Mom!" Still in his pajamas, Josh appeared in the dining room. With matted hair and one side of his face bright red from what looked like a hard night's sleep, he looked forlornly around the room. "I'm hungry."

Accustomed as we were to shifting gears quickly, we stopped cleaning and began to assemble a sampling of all of Josh's favorite breakfasts: a portion of scrambled eggs with bits of ham mixed in, golden pancakes, milk, a cut-up banana, and fresh strawberries.

As soon as the eggs were done, we plated his meal and handed it to Theo to serve.

Theo didn't notice Josh racing along the room's perimeter, making jet-engine noises. The butler crossed through the doorway just as Josh rounded the curved wall, barreling directly into Theo's path. "Watch out," I yelled.

Too late. Theo bellowed as his tray upended, sending pancakes flying forward. China crashed to the floor, exploding into little pieces. A surviving saucer rolled and rotated like a spinning quarter. Josh cried out, his bedhead doused with cold milk. He ran, dripping, to his mother. I grabbed a terry towel from the kitchen and hurried in to hand it to the First Lady. She dried Josh's head, chastising him for running. "Calm down, honey, it's just milk. You needed to take a shower anyway."

Cyan and I helped pick up the broken china and tried to scrape scrambled eggs bits from the area rug. Two members of the wait staff rushed in to help.

On my way back to the kitchen, I spotted a large chunk of a broken tumbler that had skidded across the floor's wood perimeter. As I bent to reach the errant glass, my right foot slipped on a slick pat of butter, sending me sprawling. I yelped in a very unladylike way. I'm sure I looked a lot like the tray must have, when Theo shot it into the air.

I broke my fall with my knees and palms, which is to say I smacked the floor hard. I was just happy that my right hand hadn't landed on another piece of broken glass — I'd avoided gashing it by mere millimeters.

The First Lady was on her feet immediately. "Are you all right?"

Embarrassed beyond belief, I righted myself and apologized for the fuss. "I'm fine," I said, although my dignity had suffered a mighty blow. Leaning down — careful to watch my footing this time — I picked up the glass and tried to make light of it. "This piece was out to get me, I guess."

The First Lady had turned back to Josh and was trying to get him settled into one of the side chairs. A butler had hurried to replace the boy's milk and brought fresh squeezed orange juice with it. "See," Mrs. Hyden was saying, "have a little sip and you'll feel much better."

I returned to the kitchen, my face burning. I noticed that Bucky and Cyan were taking pains to avoid looking at me. "It's no biggie," I said, sounding unconvinced. "At least she won't forget my face, right?"

They both chuckled politely.

Once everyone was resettled, I consulted with Theo, letting him know that whenever Abigail awoke, we would be more than happy to prepare whatever breakfast she desired. But right now we were returning to our ground-floor kitchen as soon as we cleaned up.

Cyan said, "I sure hope this morning isn't an omen of things to come."

"It's a good omen," I said with forced cheer. "We managed to get rid of all the negativity in one fell swoop. We got it out of the way up front on the first day. From here it will be a piece of cake."

"Piece of cake, huh?" Bucky smirked as he peeled pancake fragments from the back of a broken dish. "Like these?"

Sargeant was waiting for us when we arrived downstairs. "The First Lady is none too pleased with your decision to withhold the gift from her kids."

"*She* bought the wings?" I felt all the blood race from my head to my feet. "Oh my gosh, was she the one who had the box delivered?" My words came out fast as I realized what a major faux pas I'd committed. "Why didn't anyone tell me? Of course I would have served them if I had known."

I held my breath, envisioning her anger and disappointment in me. No wonder she'd been so cool this morning.

But Sargeant was shaking his head. "No, no, no." Stepping closer to me, he continued, his voice soft, "We still don't know who sent it, but it doesn't matter. You stood by your convictions and now you get to deal with the consequences of your decision. The First Lady is most certainly aware that this was all your doing."

"With help from you, no doubt."

Sargeant affected an innocent look. "When I am questioned, especially by a member of the First Family, I always strive to give the best, most truthful answer I can. I'm sorry if that bothers you."

"What bothers me —"

Before I could finish, John Weaver came running into the kitchen. His eyes were wide and his forehead damp with sweat. "There's a siege going on at Lyman Hall Hospital," he said, pointing toward his office. "Right now. Just happening now. It's terrible. Terrible."

"What sort of siege?" Sargeant asked him.

He held up both hands, palms upward. "Three people have been shot. That's all I know."

Bucky, Cyan, and I raced to John's office with Sargeant bringing up the rear. Three agents stood in front of the little TV, which was blaring the news. An announcer's voice tried to rise above the cacophony of screams and shouts behind him to let the audience know what was going on, but I could barely make out what he was saying. I scooted between agents Bost and Nourie to see better. Bedlam reigned at Lyman Hall Hospital. Handheld cameras tried to capture everything but shifted focus so fast they wound up catching nothing at all. I heard the announcer say, "Five White House employees . . ." and ". . . taken hostage."

"What? Who?" I turned to the agents

behind me as though expecting them to have answers. But these guys were part of the PPD, Presidential Protective Detail, and as such would be stationed here to keep the residents of the White House safe. The third agent, Gardez, stepped away from the group to listen closely to his microphone. Nourie joined him.

Bost lifted his gaze long enough to make eye contact with his colleagues, then returned his attention to the television.

"We are as surprised as you are," he said to no one in particular. "This is the first we're hearing."

At a signal from Nourie, he nodded. "The White House is officially on lockdown until we can understand what's going on."

"What hostages are they talking about?" I asked.

"Don't know," he said over his shoulder as he joined the two other agents. The three huddled together, listening intently to their microphones, all looking ready to spring should the order be given. I saw the intensity in their faces and it scared me. Lyman Hall Hospital wasn't more than three miles away from the White House. Threats to the hospital were threats to our security as well.

And what did the television announcer mean by "Five White House employees?"

The agents broke apart as I approached them. "The First Family is covered by a contingent upstairs," Bost said. "The president is being moved to a more interior location. The White House is secure. Those of us on this level are to remain here until further notice. Everyone on staff is to return to his or her station." He pointed toward the kitchen. "We will update you there."

Thus dismissed, Bucky, Cyan, and I started for the door. John's phone rang. He hurried to answer it.

The last of our party, Sargeant, stood in the doorway. His shoulders were pulled so far back it had to hurt. "My office is not in this part of the building," he said to Bost. "Am I to remain here as well?"

Bost nodded. "Either here or in the kitchen. Take your pick."

"Here, of course."

My relief at being free of the little man was short-lived because John held up his hands. "Paul is on his way down to talk with you, Olivia. I told him you'd be in the kitchen."

Sargeant's impatient eyes lit up. "Excellent. I need to speak with Paul as well." Turning to Bost, he pointed west. "I'll be with them."

The four of us trooped to the kitchen,

discussing the siege, wondering what was going on, and why. Cyan looked at her watch. "It's still pretty early. Why would anyone plan to attack a hospital during the day? Does that make sense?"

"I'm sure we'll know more soon," I said.

Bucky didn't chime in, but his face wore an expression of concern.

"What's wrong, Buck?" I asked.

He shook his head and made his way across the kitchen without another word.

"Such a temperamental fellow," Sargeant said. "I'm surprised you keep him on."

I shot him a deadpan look. He missed it. "Why don't you sit right there, Peter." I pointed to the stool I kept in front of the workstation that served as my desk. My computer was on and connected to the Internet. "If you want to check for news updates while we wait for Paul, the rest of us can get lunch started. I'd really like to know what that announcer was saying about the White House. It sounded important."

"Everything about the White House is important," Sargeant said. Having successfully one-upped me — which probably made his day — he pulled himself onto the stool and fidgeted until he was comfortable. I watched him grab the mouse, his attention focused completely on the screen, and

I knew we were good to go.

I stared at the list we'd prepared for today's lunch, but couldn't concentrate. I was aware of reading the first line twice, but, too worried about what was going on at the hospital and how the White House might be involved, I simply could not force my brain to pay attention.

Just as I started reading for a third time, Paul Vasquez came in. "Good morning, everyone," he said, startling Sargeant. "You've all heard?"

"Not enough," I said. "We're still pretty much in the dark."

Bucky returned from the other room and Sargeant wiggled off the stool to stand next to me. "When you're done here, Paul, I have a matter to discuss with you."

"Okay," Paul said, then turned to face the rest of us. "First: Our regular morning meeting is canceled until further notice. Here's what's up: I don't understand it, and I don't know what the connection is, but we could be facing a significant threat."

Not one of us said a word as he explained, "Three women from our laundry room and two butlers were rushed to Lyman Hall Hospital early this morning. Two others were sent home due to illness."

Laundry women? Butlers?

I glanced at Cyan. She'd gone completely still. Neither of us spoke while Paul continued.

"The five who were hospitalized were complaining of violent stomach pain and vomiting. Some experienced other intense symptoms." He made eye contact with each of us as he spoke. "We believe several butlers were in the laundry room late last night, and we have a team down there right now, scouring the place and looking for what might have caused so many to get sick all at once."

Cyan sat straight down on the floor and placed her head in her hands.

Paul glanced at her, then at me.

"Paul," I said. "We need to talk."

CHAPTER 5

Paul alerted Secret Service immediately, and told them to search the laundry area for any remnants of the mysterious chicken wings and the box they had come in. Cyan remained cross-legged on the floor, holding her head, little moans escaping from time to time as the weight of the situation crashed down on her. Bucky kept a hand on her shoulder and crouched next to her, speaking softly.

We didn't know for sure that the wings were the culprit, but the circumstantial evidence mounted. Cyan identified which butlers had been in the laundry room the night before when she'd delivered the wings. They were — to the man — the same individuals who had been stricken with this inexplicable illness.

Sargeant nodded at me, a strange smile on his face. Acknowledgment for being right, perhaps? I didn't know and it didn't matter. Right now I needed to make myself available to help wherever I could. I turned to him. "You may want to hold off talking with Paul about your 'other matter' for a little while."

Clearly stunned, Sargeant nodded again, and started for the door. "I will be in the curator's office if anyone needs me."

Paul peppered us with questions until the Secret Service swarmed in. Bucky, Cyan, and I were questioned separately. Bost and another agent pulled Bucky toward the giant mixer for his interview. Gardez and Nourie took Cyan into the refrigeration room, and as executive chef, I was blessed with Tom.

"Why, Ollie?" he asked in a low voice. "Why is it always you?"

I thought for a moment about Special Agent in Charge Leonard Gavin. Higher ranking than Tom, he and I had butted heads a few years ago when we'd first met, but we had eventually become friends. He'd once explained to me exactly *why* it was always me. After knowing me for just a week, Gav had understood me better than my then-boyfriend Tom had.

This close, I probably should have felt the familiar zing that often accompanied my interactions with my former love, but this time his question left me cold. "Because I notice things, Tom," I said. "And once you hear the whole story, you might not be so quick to find me guilty of interfering. In fact, this time you might even thank me."

He started to reply — probably how he wouldn't count on it — but Paul rejoined us. "You two okay?" he asked. Paul had been one of the few people on staff aware of our relationship — such as it was — while it was in full bloom. Some people change. Others don't. Our bond had suffered for that difference.

"I think it would be better if *you* explained everything that happened yesterday, Paul," I said.

Paul nodded and began. When he got to the part about the chicken wing box bearing the message that it was for the children, Tom stiffened. "If we discover that food was tainted," Paul said, "this will have very serious repercussions."

Tom listened to the rest of the story then asked why he hadn't been notified.

I reminded him that he had. "I called your office yesterday to ask about the delivery, remember?"

He shook his head.

"I left a detailed message about checking the tapes . . ."

Recollection hit him. I saw it in his eyes. "I did get that message," he said. "I had my guys follow up and check for what you were looking for, but we came up empty. We believed the situation had been handled. I planned to talk with you this morning, to follow up."

I couldn't stop myself from asking, "Why didn't you call me back last night yourself?"

His eyes met mine. No anger there. Resignation, maybe. "We followed up. We ran down every delivery of every box that matched the size and shape you described. Our search was exhaustive. I can tell you with certainty, that the box didn't arrive yesterday." He pursed his lips. "Unless," he said, "it was hidden in the Hydens' belongings."

Tom seemed to forget we were there. He started to sprint away, then turned back. "That may be it. I'll be in touch. Keep your eyes open." And with that he was gone.

The agents with Bucky listened and nodded, taking notes. Bucky's hands gesticulated wildly as he answered their questions — a clear sign of nervousness. All I could see of Gardez and Nourie were the broad backs of their suit coats. Between them, facing me and looking very small, was Cyan. Her eyes, rimmed red, were a stark contrast to the frighteningly bright blue of her contacts. Always cheery and rarely emotional, Cyan shifted from foot to foot. Her lip quivered. I couldn't hear what she was saying, but when she vehemently shook her head, I thought I read her lips: "I never would have . . ."

Paul watched them, too. I asked him, "What do we do?"

He took a breath and let it out before answering. "Cyan's breach was serious, Ollie. I don't know if she'll make it through this." He looked at me. "I don't know if she should."

"I understand." And as much as I didn't want to, I did.

"There will be an emergency meeting shortly. Select staff members only. Put Bucky in charge of lunch and send Cyan home for the day."

I took another look at my employee. Tears flowing down the sides of her cheeks, she seemed to have shrunk even smaller than from a minute ago. "I'm not sure if that's a good idea," I said. "She's pretty fragile."

Paul gave me a look that said Cyan should have thought of that before doling out suspicious food, but I knew he was a compassionate man and Cyan needed support to get through this. "You and Bucky handle the food until further notice. I know Cyan is trustworthy but we have to follow the proper protocols. Have her reorganize your cabinets . . . or . . ." he looked around the room, ". . . clean up that desk area," he said, pointing to the computer station Sargeant had vacated. That was my mess. I couldn't inflict that pain on anyone.

Still, I understood his meaning. "Got it."

"And Ollie?"

"Yes?"

"I know I don't have to remind you to keep all this quiet for now," he said. "But I feel it necessary to mention that the Hydens are not the Campbells. You are a valuable employee, a talented and creative chef, but you don't have the same capital with this new family. I'm in the exact same position. They don't know either of us yet. And if you get into trouble again, I don't know that there will be anything I can do to protect you."

His warning brought back this morning's fiasco. I couldn't afford a misstep right now. "Gotcha," I said.

On that happy note, I slipped next to Bucky, whose interrogators were just leaving. I leaned close and whispered. "Paul is calling a meeting soon. You've got lunch on your own."

To his credit, Bucky didn't even raise an eyebrow. "Figured. What about Cyan? She's in it deep, isn't she?"

I nodded. "I managed to talk Paul into letting her stay, but she's got to be on scut duty. She can wash dishes, clean cabinets, but no contact with food."

Bucky sighed deeply — for all his flintiness, I knew he liked working with Cyan. "Better than being canned."

"For now," I said.

Nourie and Gardez escorted Cyan out of the kitchen, with no explanation as to where they were going. I wished there was something I could do to fix this. Bucky must have read the expression on my face, because he patted my shoulder. "Nobody else might have the guts to say this, Ollie, but you did good yesterday. You probably saved those kids."

I appreciated him very much at that moment. "We can't breathe a word about this to anyone."

With a shrug, he moved toward the center island and grabbed a shallow pan from overhead. "So what else is new?"

When I left the kitchen for Paul's meeting, Cyan still wasn't back. Despite the fact that I had been in the right in this situation and no one was disputing that didn't make me worry any less. Cyan had been wrong to give the wings away, but I hated to think what might happen if I were to lose her in the kitchen. Being fired for such an infraction would be a significant mark on her otherwise stellar record. Finding another position with that stigma attached to her name would be nearly impossible. I trudged up the stairs to the Ushers' Office, wondering how this would all shake out.

Paul greeted me when I arrived, as did agents Gardez, Nourie, and Bost. Sargeant was there as well. He'd snagged the chair closest to Paul's desk. I saw how quickly this little room could get cramped.

As if in answer to my unspoken question, Paul said, "Excuse the close quarters, but I didn't want to take over one of the main rooms. I prefer to keep this as quiet as possible. Too many questions."

I wondered why was there such a need for secrecy. It seemed to me that the faster we disseminated the information we had, the sooner we might be able to determine who had purchased the wings and how the box had been smuggled in.

"Have a seat, Ollie," Paul said, gesturing to the other empty chair. The three Secret Service agents remained standing, hands clasped behind their backs, staring off into a middle distance as though waiting to be spoken to.

I sat down, and Tom came in. "I just got off the phone," he said, shutting the door. "Remnants of the wings we found in the garbage are being analyzed, but we're pretty sure we're looking at a massive arsenic poisoning here." He held up his hand. "Let me brief you on what we know so far, and what we require from all of you."

Paul was seated at his desk, and Tom moved to stand behind him, his back to the window. "As you all know, a box of chicken wings appeared in the kitchen yesterday. We have no indication of how it got there, or who delivered it. We've checked all surveillance tapes from all deliveries. No leads. The only thing we can deduce now is that the box was secreted with the Hydens' personal belongings. Whoever placed it there either removed it, or had an accomplice remove it from the storage units when they were unloaded. This person then brought it to the kitchen."

Tom took a breath and glanced around the room. "We are currently investigating everyone who had access to the Hydens' property before, during, and after its arrival here. We are also questioning every Rene's

Wings franchise in both the Hydens' home city and here in D.C. This is a monumental task and will take a great deal of time. Unfortunately, we do not have that luxury. We must operate under the assumption that the chicken wings were intended to harm the president's children. That, in itself, is bad enough. We also believe that, had the children been stricken, they would have been immediately transported to Lyman Hall Hospital."

He stopped long enough to let his words sink in. Our staff members had been taken to Lyman Hall. That's where the siege was going on.

"You believe whoever did this planned to take the kids hostage?" I asked.

Tom took a deep breath. "This is one of the reasons you've been included in this meeting, Ollie," he said. "We view this as the most serious of threats. An attack like the one going on at Lyman Hospital cannot be pulled off by one individual. This is a well-orchestrated assault. A surgical strike." He pointed to me. "You and your staff must be on guard against further attempts on any members of the First Family."

I sat up a little straighter. "Of course."

"What we know," he continued to the entire gathering, "is that at this point, the group taking responsibility for this attack is unknown. They've yet to name themselves or to profess allegiance to any of our enemies."

"Do we have plans in place to get our people — and the other hospital hostages — out safely?" Paul asked.

"In the works, but we are not at liberty to share any information at the moment. Suffice it to say that we believe that the strategy these terrorists employed was planned for weeks, if not longer. It is our belief that these individuals expected to use the president's kids as hostages, but had to settle for members of the White House staff when their plan was thwarted by Ollie here."

Sargeant sniffed. "Lucky."

"Not luck," Tom said. "Ollie did what we are all charged to do — protect the First Family. I'm just sorry her assistant, Cyan, wasn't as careful."

"Do we have any idea what they want?" Paul asked turning the subject back to the terrorists.

Tom shook his head. "Not yet. We've got several contacts inside the hospital who are trying to keep us apprised of the hostages' condition. If we are dealing with arsenic, as we suspect, the victims will require treatment."

One of the agents cleared his throat. Tom shot him a look that expressed thanks for being reminded, but held a touch of annoyance just the same. "We're short on time, so I'll cut to the chase. You are all being briefed because we need to enlist your cooperation. No one is to be told about the possibility that the wings were tainted. We are not releasing that information to the public and we need to keep it from everyone, including the First Lady."

"What?" I exclaimed. "You're not going to tell her that her kids were threatened?"

Tom stepped toward me and lowered his voice. "We can't risk it. At this point, we don't know that the wings actually *were* tainted, nor that the kids were the original target. That's just the theory we're working with right now, and we don't have any solid evidence to back it up at this point. There is no reason to get Mrs. Hyden unduly worked up at this point."

I disagreed. The kids' mother should most certainly be told, and I said so.

"You have to trust us at this point, Ollie." Tom's voice strained with patience. "We know what we're doing."

"What about Valerie's assistant, Carol?" I asked. "She was right there when I refused to give the wings to Josh. Don't you think

65

she told Valerie? She would definitely tell Mrs. Hyden."

Tom nodded as though he'd expected the question. "This is why we are not mentioning the wings at all. Not to the First Family, not to the media, not to any other members of the staff. Bucky and Cyan have been ordered to keep what they know to themselves. No one is to know about the connection between the chicken wings and our staff at the hospital. Not until we believe the time is right."

I didn't say anything.

Tom pointed to two of the agents. "From here on out, agents Gardez and Nourie are assigned to the kitchen. They will be working in close proximity with you, and both will sample all the foods you plan to serve to the First Family."

"Taste-testers? Like in a king's court?" I asked, highly annoyed by the fact that this development indicated a lack of faith in my kitchen. "To make sure His Majesty doesn't get poisoned?"

Tom's jaw was tight. "Something like that." He pointed again. "Agent Bost will assign extra people to the kids. We're lucky they start school tomorrow. The added coverage won't be noticed. We will make it appear as though this is all just standard procedure." He looked around the room. "Any questions?"

I had one. "Has President Hyden been fully briefed?"

Tom held up a hand. "You don't need to know."

CHAPTER 6

Cyan's eyes, still bright red, were swollen. She kept her head down, looking up only briefly when I walked in. "Hey," I said.

She swallowed and looked up again. "I'm so sorry. I should have listened to you." Her voice cracked and the tears flowed. "Did you see the news? They won't give us updates on the hostages. What if they die? It's all my fault. I wish . . ." She snuffled. ". . . I wish I would have eaten the wings. Then I would be there, too. It would at least be fair."

Bucky worked at the computer across the room. His back was to us, but I could see his head tilt to hear better. "Cyan," I said, "this is serious. Very serious. You broke the rules because you thought you knew better. We've all been guilty of that at one time or another." I knew I had. "Let's hope for the best for all of us." I patted her shoulder, both grateful and sorry for the look she fixed on me. So full of hope and so miserable all at once.

I raised my voice. "Bucky, have you said anything to anyone about the chicken wings?"

He turned to answer. "Other than the Secret Service guys this morning, no."

"You didn't mention the box's mysterious appearance and Cyan sharing the wings with the staff?"

"No. And before you ask me a third time, no, I didn't even mention it to Brandy. She got in late last night and I was already asleep."

"Thanks."

He turned his back again, but I heard him mutter. "Give me a little credit."

"It's my job to double-check," I said.

He nodded, but didn't answer.

"What about you, Cyan?"

"I told my mom, but she's not going to say anything."

I groaned and started for the telephone. "I'll have to tell Tom and Paul."

"No, you don't understand," Cyan said, stopping me. "My mom isn't . . . She isn't well. She's got a lot of problems and doesn't talk much anymore." I watched my assistant's eyes well up yet again. "At home sometimes I talk with her for company. But she doesn't understand. Last night was one of her bad nights and I just, you know, yakked to have someone to talk to. She stared at the TV the whole time. There's no way she's a security risk. Even when she talks, she doesn't make sense. Nobody listens. Not anymore."

I placed a hand on her arm. "I didn't know that about your mom," I said. "How come you never said anything?"

"It's really . . . hard," she said. Cyan was clearly losing the battle to maintain composure. "You don't know how hard it is."

She was right. I didn't. "I'm sorry," I said, because I couldn't think of anything else to say.

Dinner that evening went better than breakfast, thank goodness. Although Bucky and I worked short-staffed with Cyan relegated to reorganizing the storage room, and our every move was scrutinized by Secret Service agents, we served a wonderfully fresh dinner of salmon Oscar, new potatoes, and grilled asparagus, right on time.

Official kitchen observer, Agent Nourie, did the taste-testing honors. He lifted a forkful of salmon and sniffed at it. When he took his first bite, his face broke into a huge smile. The effect was transforming. I'd considered Nourie handsome from the start. When he loosened up enough to smile, he was downright gorgeous. Cyan blinked up at him from her spot on the floor where she was digging out old pans from a bottom cabinet. For the first time all day, I saw brightness in her eyes. I think Nourie saw it, too, because he looked down at her and winked.

Cyan returned to her task. Her shoulders lifted just a little.

Dinner was plated and handed off to the butlers to serve. We started in on our cleanup and preparations for the morning. When word came down from two floors above that the First Family had enjoyed dinner very much and sent their regards to the kitchen, we breathed a collective sigh of relief. Finally a success with the new family.

We called it a night around 7:00, after ensuring there were plenty of snackable items in the ground-floor kitchen and the one upstairs. It would take a little while before we became entirely comfortable with the new family's rhythms, but until we did, we made sure to keep all their professed favorites available to them around the clock.

Gardez and Nourie waited with us until I shut off the lights. "What's next for you?" I asked them. "Do you get to go home now?"

Gardez spoke softly. "Yes," he said in that soft Spanish accent. I could listen to this man recite the phone book and enjoy it. "What time will you return in the morning?"

I laughed. "I'm usually here before five. Sometimes earlier."

"I will be here before you," he said with a grin. "I guarantee it."

Now I understood why Secret Service agents rarely smiled. It ruined their image of tough, no-nonsense brutes. Gardez's grin nearly took my breath away.

I smiled back. "We'll see."

At home, I curled up on the sofa to watch updates on the standoff at Lyman Hall Hospital. Reports came in that one of the hostages was about to be freed with a message for the government. Camera crews stood by, eager to record the captive's release. I worried about the laundry ladies, some of whom I considered good friends. Had they recovered from whatever had sent them there? They had to be terribly frightened. I pulled my butterfly afghan tighter around me. What were the hostages thinking right this minute while I sat here, safe and warm?

I flipped channels, gathering different bits

of information from each news source. The first channel claimed that one of the captors had been identified as a disgruntled hospital employee — a former security guard who had lost his job six weeks earlier. They posted his face on screen.

In a too-close shot that made his nose look superwide, the gray-haired, sixty-year-old Ernie Spokes seemed more like a grandfather than a terrorist. Rumors were swirling that he'd been recruited to assist in the siege by two other as yet-unnamed employees who had also been recently fired.

I wondered, not for the first time, if the hospital drama and the mystery at the White House might be unrelated. They kept the photo of Ernie Spokes on screen, high over the anchorwoman's shoulder, for a full minute. This man didn't look capable of infiltrating the White House. I knew better than most that looks could be deceiving, but still . . .

The next channel had continuing coverage as well. They referred to Ernie Spokes as well, but claimed that rumors connecting the siege to him were now being disputed. They didn't offer other explanations, but suggested everyone stay tuned.

The final channel I watched was the most interesting. One of their correspondents spoke into a microphone, but not in front of the hospital. This fellow stood in front of the White House, wearing a black wool coat with an upturned collar. "Sources inside remain tight-lipped," the reporter said as the brisk January wind lifted his hair and caused him to blink. "No one at the White House will comment on what sent so many employees to the hospital at the same time. President Hyden has been in office for less than twenty-four hours and is already facing a possible crisis at home."

"Oh, no," I said.

The reporter didn't mention chicken wings. Instead, he said, "Because the affected individuals came from two different departments in the president's residence, experts are speculating that whatever illness brought them here most likely is airborne."

The anchorman at the desk interrupted. "Are you saying that we can expect more White House staff members to become affected? What about the First Family? Are they in danger as well?"

Nodding solemnly, the shivering reporter answered, "As I said, Rick, we do not know exactly what we're dealing with. But experts I've talked to hypothesize that there may be more casualties of this virus — or possible airborne pathogen — soon. Keep in mind,

Rick, White House staff members are citizens of the Washington, D.C., area at large. They work, live, shop, and commute among us. We must all be on our guard against contamination. Later in this broadcast we will offer suggestions for preventive care." With an even more serious look, he added, "Needless to say, anyone experiencing symptoms will not be taken to Lyman Hall Hospital. All streets surrounding the area have been closed to traffic."

I turned the television off. Over the past several years, I'd had enough dealings with the media to know that stations got their jollies — and high ratings — from terrorizing the public. I'd heard the old adage that if it bleeds, it leads, but wondered if their motto should be "Never let the facts stand in the way of a good story." The threat of a potentially deadly airborne virus would be enough to wreak havoc on the city for weeks.

I set my alarm for 3:30 and hoped tomorrow would be a better day.

The kids got off to their first day at their new schools after lots of last-minute crises. I wasn't upstairs in the residence for most of it, thank goodness, but the butlers carried stories down, warning us that the breakfast we'd prepared had gone largely untouched.

Not yet used to their new environment, the kids took much longer than anticipated to get ready for school. The family believed they were prepared for the cascade of photographers descending upon them to chronicle this first-day milestone, but every "just one more photo" and each reporter's burning question, stole precious minutes. The kids would be late.

The schools the Hydens had chosen for their kids would, no doubt, tolerate tardiness from their high-profile pupils on this first day. According to the butlers' reports, however, Mrs. Hyden was doing her utmost to explain to her children why it was important to plan ahead and stick to a schedule. I wished her luck.

Tom called another meeting, again in the Ushers' Office. Sargeant and Paul were already there, but this time agents Nourie and Gardez stayed back at their kitchen-sentry posts. Bost was also missing, probably herding the kids to their classrooms. I was the last to arrive.

Sargeant looked at his watch. "Can we get started now?"

I shut the door behind me.

"We've gotten an update," Tom began without preamble. "Demands have been presented. The president is consulting with members of Congress and hostage negotiators." He held up his hands as though expecting us to interrupt. "Before I go on, let me reiterate that nothing leaves this room. The following information has not been distributed to any media sources."

We all nodded. He continued.

"Tests on the remnants of chicken wings have confirmed arsenic poisoning."

I gasped. "How bad is it?"

Tom's face was unreadable. "That may depend on how much each individual ingested. The hostage-takers are most likely responsible for the poisoning, but just in case the incidents are unrelated, we have taken the precaution of communicating with the offenders the need for treatment for our people. It is our hope that they will allow doctors to administer to our stricken staff members. If any of them die of poisoning, the situation will escalate quickly. It is in everyone's best interest to ensure that does not happen."

I said a silent prayer for my friends being held. "What kind of demands are they making?" I asked.

Tom graced me with a weary look, but said, "A convicted terrorist from Armustan by the name of Farbod Ansari is being held at the federal penitentiary in Wisconsin where terrorists are held. Cenga Prison is just outside the town of La Crosse."

"I didn't realize there was a prison there," Paul said.

"Very few people do." Tom took a deep breath. "The hostage-takers at the hospital are demanding Farbod's immediate release and safe passage out of the country."

"To where?" I asked.

"Armustan, of course, although they refuse to provide a precise destination until after the plane is in the air. What I can tell you is that Congresswoman Sandy Sechrest will be handling negotiations."

Sargeant blurted, "She's a hostage negotiator?"

"She is, as a matter of fact. Thirty years' experience. We're very fortunate in that regard." Tom frowned. "Cenga Prison is in her jurisdiction. The kidnappers at the Lyman Hall Hospital have demanded we involve Wisconsin's senators. We are choosing to involve Congresswoman Sechrest as well."

This was a twist I hadn't expected. "Is she here in D.C.?"

Paul answered that one. "She's meeting with President Hyden as we speak. Went home to Wisconsin after the inauguration and flew back early this morning. She'll be making a statement later today."

"Have you told Mrs. Hyden about all this yet?" I asked. "About the fact that these were the chicken wings intended for the kids?"

Tom and Paul exchanged a glance. "Not yet."

"It's going to come out sooner or later."

"Preferably later," Tom said with finality. "We need to be able to control what is released to the media. The longer we can prevent the public — and the First Lady — from knowing that the kids were targeted, the safer they will be."

I didn't follow his logic, and opened my mouth to argue, but Tom held up a hand. "Don't."

Irked, both because he knew me well enough to anticipate me, and because I was powerless to fight an edict from the head of the PPD, I changed my approach. "Any update on the condition of our staff members?"

"To the best of our knowledge, they are all still alive. At least that's what we've been told."

I turned to Paul. "What about Cyan?"

The look on Paul's face turned my stomach to stone. "We are not emotionless bureaucrats in this house, Ollie, but what Cyan did was irresponsible. She demonstrated an incredible lack of attentiveness to her duty. She should be fired."

Should be? I held my breath, then asked. "Do I sense a 'however'?"

Paul gave me a piercing look. "Cyan has been a valued member of staff for several years and she's never once caused the sort of trouble we've experienced with others — others who remain on staff."

No one in the room missed his meaning, but it was Sargeant who piped up, of course. "Because you haven't fired this 'other individual' for *her* misconduct, I assume you intend to give yet another kitchen staff member a second chance. Is that it?"

Paul ignored him. "Ollie, perhaps it would be better if you and I discussed this privately."

Tom cleared his throat. "As much as I like Cyan personally, I am recommending she be fired. I am extremely uncomfortable with the fact that she hasn't been relieved of duty already."

Sargeant adopted a smug expression as he shifted in his chair. He didn't say anything, but his wordless chuckle was as clear as "I told you so."

Tom added, "I think it is appropriate to

discuss this right now." Holding both hands up against any objections, he said, "I advocate taking this action immediately."

Panicked, I looked to Paul, who said, "Tom, I understand your position and I will note Cyan's record to reflect your concerns. But firing her now would require we divulge the reason for her dismissal. If I understand you correctly, we are to tell no one about the tainted chicken wings at this time. Any report about Cyan would naturally expose our reasons, and I believe there's a good argument — in the interests of security — that we keep her on. For now."

I could have kissed Paul right then.

Tom flexed his jaw.

I wanted to chime in, but I knew what was coming next, and I also knew Tom would take it better from the chief usher than he would from me. "Everyone in this room knows that Cyan is no threat to the First Family," Paul continued. "Keeping her on staff is not posing a risk to anyone. She made a mistake. One that I'm certain she will never make again. In fact, I would like to direct Ollie to allow Cyan full kitchen access again."

Clearly unhappy, Tom gave him a brisk nod. "I see your point." Turning to me, he said, "Going forward, I will hold you personally responsible for Cyan. Is that understood?"

Anyone seeing us now would never believe that Tom and I used to sprawl across my couch together, laughing as we watched old black-and-white movies into the wee hours of the night. Those days were long gone. Nope, anyone present now would think we were two people who barely tolerated one another.

I stood. "Yes, sir. And I am only too happy to express confidence in my employee by taking full responsibility for her." I glanced at the others in the room. "Is there anything else?"

Tom shook his head.

"Thank you for the update," I said. "If you need anything further, you know where to find me."

CHAPTER 7

I let my staff and the Secret Service agents assigned to us know that Cyan's job was safe for now. I didn't give them a word-for-word accounting of the meeting, but I didn't need to. Cyan and Bucky were sharp enough to read between the lines. "I know you both understand how important this is, but it's my job to remind you that we are not to breathe one word about the chicken wing situation to anyone."

Cyan wore an expression of fearful anticipation. "So they know for sure that the chicken wings were poisoned?"

"I can't discuss it," I said.

Cyan's head dropped and tears started again, full force. "Oh, why didn't I listen to you in the first place, Ollie? I'm so sorry. So very sorry."

I put my arm around her. "The kids are okay, and that's important. Let's focus on what we can do to move forward, okay?"

She nodded, but I knew it was more her attempt to end the conversation than it was genuine agreement.

Standing in the doorway, Gardez shifted and looked away. Nourie wore a thoughtful expression. As soon as I moved away from Cyan, he approached her. "Listen," he said softly, "if I get any updates I can share with you, I will."

Cyan looked torn between a polite response and wanting to hide her freshly blotched face from him. "Thanks," she said between ragged breaths. "I feel so stupid."

Nourie looked ready to pat her on the shoulder, but he restrained himself. Instead, he said, "Everybody makes mistakes. Let's just hope things get better from here."

Cyan didn't smile, but I could tell his words had helped. Good. We had a lot to do today and the sooner we got busy, the easier it would be to start focusing on the positive. Bucky had taken care of lunch preparations and with three of us working on dinner, we were in good shape.

I had offered to bring chairs in for Agents Gardez and Nourie, but both men declined. "Don't you get tired standing all day?" Cyan asked.

Nourie shrugged. "We alternate taking breaks, so that helps. But think about it: If anything were to happen, isn't it better if we're standing? Ready to move? Sitting invites complacence. That's not how we were trained."

Looking up from slicing carrots, I smiled. "Be honest with us: What do you really expect to happen in the kitchen? If anything were to show up suspiciously like the chicken wings did, you know we would alert you."

"Better to be safe," Gardez said with a stern look. "And remember, we will still be taste-testing."

"Lucky us," Nourie said.

Cyan smiled up at him.

Sensing I'd ruffled Gardez's feathers, I sought to clarify. "What I mean is, aren't you bored in here?"

I must have hit a nerve because Gardez frowned and didn't answer.

"I've seen a couple of those cooking shows on TV," Nourie said. "I like them. I think it's fun. Watching other people in the kitchen helps me relax."

Gardez cleared his throat. "Agent Nourie does not intend to suggest that he is relaxed in his duty here."

Nourie's lips tightened. "No, of course not."

Any lightness that had momentarily

graced our group vaporized with Gardez's remonstrance. "I understood what you meant," I said to Nourie. Returning to slicing my carrots, I wondered how long it would be before we had our kitchen to ourselves again.

"Understood what who meant?" Sargeant appeared from behind Gardez and scooted past the tall agent. For the first time since I'd met him, Sargeant's face was creased into a smile. "Not that it matters," he said, still grinning. "Ms. Paras, may I see you a moment?"

Next to me, Bucky gave a low groan. "What now?"

"I'm about to find out." I washed and dried my hands. When I realized Sargeant was ushering me out into the hall, I untied my soiled apron and tossed it into the bin by the door. Seeing the pileup of dirty aprons made me think again about our laundry ladies being held hostage at the hospital. What I wouldn't give to replay the events of Inauguration Day. The minute those chicken wings appeared in the kitchen, I should have immediately sent them to the Secret Service. But I hadn't wanted to hurt the gift giver's feelings, if indeed the benefactor had turned out to be a friend. Because of my concerns, I'd hesitated. Although I'd never intended for anyone to touch the food, I felt as guilty as Cyan for not taking a more proactive approach.

I followed Sargeant's mincing gait across the hall to the China Room. I used to love the China Room, but over the past few years I'd been pulled in here too often for Secret Service interrogations. These days, it was difficult for me to feel anything but trepidation when I walked through its door. Not for the first time, I focused on the china patterns to quell my antsy nerves. My gaze came to rest on a large platter.

Sargeant noticed. "Is that from the Coolidge era?"

I shook my head. "Hayes." The meat platter was rectangular with curled-up corners. But its most notable attribute was its depiction of a wild turkey. With its head held high and chest thrust forward, the bird stood tall on spindly legs. This turkey reminded me — very much — of the self-satisfied egotist in front of me.

"A handsome bird, isn't he?" Sargeant asked.

I smiled. "I'd like him better skewered and roasted over an open flame."

Sargeant gave me a peculiar look. "Yes, well." He pulled himself up to his maximum height and said, "I did not call you in here to discuss the china."

"Of course not." I had my back to the magnificent painting of Grace Coolidge in her bright red dress, and I hoped to convey some of the serenity she exhibited in her colorful portrait. It wasn't easy. Whatever Sargeant had on his mind was making him very happy. That couldn't bode well for me.

"Because you and I have worked together for these past few years," he began, "I feel it is my duty to give you fair warning."

Rocks rattled around my stomach, bouncing like sharp-edged Ping-Pong balls, but I was unwilling to reveal my disquiet. Tilting my head quizzically, as he so often did, I asked, "What's on your mind, Peter?"

I watched him struggle to tamp down his enthusiasm. He lost. "I have it on good authority that you are on your way out."

Speechless, I waited.

"Out of the White House," he said, as though the statement needed clarification.

I fought to affect a look of indifference. "And who is this 'good authority'?"

He wagged a finger in front of me. "Ah, ah, ah. Not so fast. You will be notified in good time."

"You're telling me that I'm about to be fired?"

For the first time, his smile faded. "Not

quite. You occupy a unique position here. Up until now, that has worked in your favor. My intention today is to inform you that I've become aware of certain privileged information. There's a change in store for you. Be prepared. When it happens, I guarantee your days will be numbered."

His happy smirk returned and he minced back out of the China Room without another word.

I stared at the empty doorway for a long moment. "Gee, thanks, Peter."

Agents Bost and Zeller were waiting for me in the kitchen when I returned and they gestured me back out into the hall. What now? Zeller was as tall as many of the male agents and just as athletic. Her mouth turned upward as though she was trying to smile, but her eyes were cold. "Ms. Paras," she said. "A minute of your time?"

I made sure Bucky and Cyan had everything under control then followed the agents out. I was fully prepared to return to the China Room, but they surprised me by leading me to the small Secret Service office just a few steps east of the kitchen. I didn't usually have any reason to come in here, nor did I often visit the larger Secret Service office in the West Wing, but once in a while we brought treats to the agents. These two, however, were too new to know that.

The office was small, not much bigger than our refrigeration room. Several of the agents nodded a greeting and Zeller led me to an even smaller office in back, where she offered me a chair. "Would you like some water?" she asked as I sat.

Bost pulled the door closed behind him, closing off all sound and life from the rest of the area. Now it was just the three of us. Two tough agents, a tight office, and me. I began to feel a little claustrophobic. "That depends. How long am I going to be here?" I asked.

Expressionless, Bost said, "As long as it takes."

Before I could ask "As long as *what* takes?" Zeller moved to stand next to Bost. The two of them effectively blocked the door. Both of these agents were brand-new to the PPD, and although they carried a lot of weight, I wasn't frightened. Clearly, however, intimidation was their intent.

"Ms. Paras —" Zeller began.

"Call me Ollie. We'll get along much better that way."

"I'll get right to it, Ms. Paras." She pursed her lips. "If you suspected there was something wrong with the chicken wings, why did you not alert us?"

I sat back. "Are you kidding?"

With his blond buzz and linebacker shoulders, Bost looked like a giant square. "We never kid."

That I believed.

Zeller's turn. "Ms. Paras," she said, "we only want to ask you a few questions about the sudden appearance of the box of wings, and your decision not to bring it to our attention."

Our attention? Did they mean the attention of the Secret Service — because if they did, they were sadly misinformed. That had been one of my first orders of business. If they meant that I should have notified the two of them — and I couldn't imagine why they would — we had a problem.

"Why are you asking me?"

"Why, do you have something to hide?" Bost asked.

"Of course not. But I find this questioning peculiar."

"Peculiar?" Zeller repeated. "And why is that?"

"Does Agent MacKenzie know I'm down here?"

"That's not important right now," Bost said.

"It most certainly is important," I said, standing. "I'm willing to help this investigation in any way I can, but it seems to me that you ought to clear it with him before you start personally interrogating staff members."

"Sit down."

"Agent Bost," I said, refusing to sit, "You were in that first meeting in Paul's office. You know as well as I do that we are not to discuss this matter with anyone who was not included in that meeting." I shot a pointed look at Zeller. "If Tom . . . er . . . Agent MacKenzie wants to bring others up to date, then he should be the one to do it."

"Are you willing to risk the children's safety?"

"Of course not." I looked from one to the other. Both towered over me, but I was too angry to be nervous. "It sounds to me as though you are questioning Agent Mac-Kenzie's orders. You're both new here, and maybe you think you can make a name for yourselves by working behind his back. You go right ahead and do that. See where it gets you. But don't involve me."

They didn't budge.

"If you'll excuse me, I have work to do in the kitchen."

Zeller looked to Bost, who still stared

down at me. "No one is questioning Agent MacKenzie," he said quietly. "I want to be very clear on that point."

The look in Bost's eyes was downright murderous. If I were the First Lady, I might be thrilled to have such a scary guy protecting my kids, but I would certainly limit their interaction with him. He would give me nightmares.

"Got it. Very clear. Can I go now?"

He hesitated just one moment more before stepping aside. Zeller moved away too, granting me access to the door. "Have a lovely afternoon," I said. "It's been nice talking with you."

It wasn't until I got back into the hall that my heart started to speed-beat, its staccato palpitations quickening my pace. What had that been about?

I'd gotten about twenty feet into the hallway when I heard my name called. I turned. Bost stood in the doorway of the Secret Service office with a finger raised. "I expect you to keep information about this meeting quiet."

Uh-huh. Right.

"What's wrong?" Cyan asked when I got back.

I waved her off. "Nothing really."

"What were they asking about? Are you in trouble because of me? I'm so sorry."

"Cyan," I said, shaking my head, "really, it was nothing. I think they're just a couple of goons who think that if they do an end-run around Tom, they'll be on the fast track for promotion."

"Don't they know this is just about as high as you can get in the Secret Service?"

"I'm sure they do, but they also know that they report to Tom. I can't understand what they're up to."

Cyan tilted her head. "What did they ask you?"

I didn't want to get into it. There was no way to express my thoughts on the subject without divulging things Tom and Paul had expressly asked us not to share. "I think the two of them are headed for trouble, that's all."

Cyan bit her lip. "Speaking of headed for trouble . . ."

"What happened?"

Her hands came up. "No, nothing here. I just was wondering if you might have some time tonight?"

"You mean after work?"

Hesitant at first, her words came out in a rush. "I've got a lot going on right now and you're always so sure of yourself. I need

94

some advice, I guess. Or maybe just some-one willing to listen. I thought maybe you and I could go for coffee, or a drink, or something."

Startled by her comment about me always being so sure of myself, I took a couple seconds to answer. "Sure, I'd love to."

"Thanks, Ollie," she said with such a look of relief that I got the impression an enormous weight had been lifted from her shoulders. I felt almost guilty for having obviously missed signals and not suggesting the idea myself.

Changing the subject, I asked, "Any updates on the hostage situation?"

Cyan had her back to the computer monitor and now turned and clicked the mouse to bring up a news website we used to keep tabs on what was happening at Lyman Hall Hospital. "I checked a few minutes ago and Congresswoman Sechrest had just arrived on the scene." She spoke over her shoulder. "I'm so worried, I want to sit here and watch this all day, but that won't help anybody."

I came to stand next to her. "We've got a few minutes now."

She relinquished the mouse and I used it to turn up the volume. The most recent news upload was of Sandy Sechrest, flanked by SWAT team escorts, being led into a trailer that had been positioned just across the street from the hospital's main entrance. The legislator was a petite woman, no taller than five foot three. Surrounded as she was by tall, muscular men, she looked even tinier by comparison. The camera following her showed us only her back. Sechrest wore a dark coat and gloves but no hat, even though the weather was frigid. Her short, white hair fluttered in the January wind.

News crews chased the congresswoman as she and her bodyguards navigated the police-established perimeter. One of the reporters shouted, "Congresswoman! Congresswoman! What do you hope to accomplish here?"

She turned to face the pack of paparazzi and microphones. I couldn't see them, but I could picture them falling over one another in an effort to get to her first.

Her bright blue eyes flashed with anger, but she spoke kindly. "To end this siege with the safe release of all the hostages, of course," she said. "Why are *you* here?"

She didn't wait for an answer, but turned away again and made it into the beige trailer without another comment.

"I like her," I said.

"Do you think she'll do any good?"

I thought about the laundry ladies — my friends — SueJean, Lisa, and the others who probably had no idea of what was going on outside the hospital. Those people were probably doing their best just to stay alive right now. "Let's hope so."

CHAPTER 8

That evening, Cyan and I relaxed at the upscale bar, Fizz, just across Lafayette Park. Set in the basement of one of D.C.'s premier hotels, it was the perfect place to have a private conversation without fear of distraction. With expensive drinks and a hard-to-find location, this particular bar eschewed easy popularity, preferring to lure patrons in with its traditional décor and old-fashioned class. With heavy furnishings, an ornately carved ceiling, and soft instrumental background music, Fizz hadn't changed much from its original design. Except for Wi-Fi capabilities and the flat-screen TV above the bar, patrons might have felt magically transported back to the 1920s.

Billy, the bartender, waved hello and indicated for us to take any open table. I chose one near the center of the room and across from the bar, because the tables immediately flanking it were empty. I sensed

Cyan wanted as much privacy as possible. I scooched into the booth side with my back to the red-cushioned wall. Cyan took the matching wing chair facing me. A moment later, Billy appeared at our table. Bald, tall, and quick with a smile, he placed cocktail napkins on the table before us. "I haven't seen you two for a while. Busy with the new boss, I'll bet. You heard anything else about your people being held hostage?"

"Nothing but what they're showing on TV," I said.

He knew we couldn't share any privileged information, but I appreciated his attempts to make conversation nonetheless. "How's business?" I asked.

Billy grinned. "Hopping," he said. And indeed it was. The bar was busier than I'd seen it before, filled with recognizable movers and shakers interspersed with tourists who could afford this exclusive hotel's rates. We made a little small talk, and placed our drink orders.

While he was gone, Cyan took a slow look around the room and commented on a couple of senators having a quiet but heated discussion in the corner. "Wonder what's up with them."

"I'm wondering what's up with you," I said.

She met my gaze, then let hers fall to the table, where she made little circles with her finger on the glossy wood. "I can't believe I made such a stupid mistake," she said finally.

"Let's not dwell on it," I said. "The situation is in good hands, and for now at least, your job is safe."

"For now," she repeated.

"You've got more on your mind, haven't you?"

Cyan's eyes teared up. She glanced from side to side and hunched her shoulders. Her voice cracked, but she tried to smile. "Good thing I have my back to the room, huh?" She shook her head. "What is wrong with me? It seems all I ever do these days is cry."

Billy returned with my gewürztraminer and Cyan's merlot. He started to chitchat. "You ladies have been through a lot these past few days. Tonight's on me. Order something from the kitchen. I know our chef would appreciate the opportunity to test some of his new creations on you two." At that point, Billy noticed Cyan's face and took a step back. "Like I said, everything is on the house tonight. Just signal if you need me."

I thanked him and promised we would and he left us. "What's going on, Cyan? Is it Rafe?"

She nodded, then shook her head. Taking a moment to compose herself, she said, "I know Saturday is your day off, but can I trade with you? I've got . . ."

Her composure crumbled.

I reached across to squeeze her hand. "What's wrong?"

She squeezed back, then pulled away to cover her face. "This is so embarrassing," she whispered. "Is anyone looking at me?"

Worry bubbled up inside me. "You know this place. Nobody pays attention to anyone else." She seemed unconvinced, so I added, "Nobody is looking."

She bit her lip, then began to talk. "I told you about my mom the other day," she said. "What I didn't tell you was how bad it really is. She was diagnosed with Alzheimer's — over a year ago — and she's not safe by herself anymore. I've had to hire people to come stay with her while I'm at work, but even so, she came close to starting a fire in the kitchen. She just doesn't understand things anymore."

"I had no idea."

"I didn't want anyone to know. I mean, you never come in and share any problems you're facing, unless it has something to do with the White House. Neither does Bucky.

101

I didn't want to bring my family problems into the kitchen. I didn't want you to think I might make mistakes because my mind was elsewhere. But it looks like that's exactly what I did."

As much as I wanted to disagree, I couldn't.

"I've been dealing with my mom for a while now. It's getting to be too much for me to handle on my own."

I waited.

"I found a nursing home that will take her. It's wildly expensive, but comes highly recommended. I'm supposed to bring her there on Saturday. That's why I can't work."

"I understand. No problem. I don't have any plans that day. You take as much time as you need for your mom."

She sniffed. "Thanks, Ollie. I knew you'd understand."

I waited. "There's more, isn't there?"

It took her another long moment to answer and when she finally did, her words came out fast and breathless as though she'd harbored so much for so long and was finally able to release. "I keep thinking about Rafe and how much fun he's having in New York. I mean, he's getting all sorts of exposure in newspapers and magazines. Maybe he made the right move." Her face was tight with misery. "Maybe it's stupid for me to stay here. What if they let me go? Wouldn't it be better for me to leave before they fire me? Maybe Rafe could get me in at his hotel." Her eyes brightened slightly, then immediately dimmed. "But I can't leave my mom."

I decided to tread carefully. "I thought you said things had changed between you and Rafe now that he's getting so much press. Didn't you tell me he's not even returning your texts anymore?"

"He asked me to go with him when he first got offered the job."

I knew that. But I also knew that had been more than six months ago and from what I could tell, Rafe had moved on. "Cyan," I began, "you had no interest in moving to New York until all this hit. You said you couldn't be happy in that environment. Don't you think you should ride out the storm and see what happens first?"

She wrinkled her nose, and I recognized it as her attempt to keep tears from starting up again. "It's just that now, with all this going on at the White House and with my mom . . . I don't feel like I belong anywhere anymore."

I understood. "You know I'll do my best

to keep you in the kitchen. I depend on you."

"Oh, Ollie, of course I know that." She tried to smile as she wiped her eyes. "Maybe I just need to stop feeling sorry for myself, huh?"

"Maybe you just need a break. And a shot of good news."

"A shot of good news?" She took a sip of her merlot. "I guess I should have ordered that instead of this."

"A couple of our new agents are kinda cute. We've got Bost . . ."

She wrinkled her nose. "You mean Mister Stuck on Himself?"

"What about Gardez? That Spanish accent makes me weak in the knees."

She laughed. "You? I thought you were sworn off men since you broke up with Tom."

I held up a finger. "I'm not ready for a relationship," I said, "but that doesn't mean I don't notice the cuties. And speaking of noticing, don't think I missed you flirting with Gardez and Nourie."

For the first time all night, Cyan's mood lightened. "Aha! I knew it. You have your eye on one of them, don't you?"

I laughed. "Not a chance. But they are both really good-looking. Any idea if they're married?"

She shrugged. "Matthew isn't. Alberto might be. Haven't found out yet, but I'm working on it."

"Matthew?" I asked. "Alberto?"

Cyan's cheeks went pink and it wasn't from the merlot. "Their first names. Alberto — that's Gardez — is so sexy, but doesn't even know I exist. I like Matthew — Agent Nourie — better. He at least seems willing to hold a conversation."

I thought about Tom. He and I used to talk all the time before we started going out. Now, we barely spoke. "I envy you," I said. "You're open to a new romance and that's fun. I just . . . don't have time for anything like that."

"Only because you don't want to."

"My career is too important —"

"Careers aren't everything," she said. In her effort to help me with the problems she perceived I had, she had temporarily forgotten her own. "I don't think it would hurt you to flirt a little."

"With Nourie and Gardez?" I asked. "No thanks. I've had enough with Secret Service agents."

She leaned close and lowered her voice. "How about with the guy sitting to your far right? He's been watching you since we sat down."

Instinctively, I glanced over to see a forty-something man in a business suit looking right at me. Carrying about thirty extra pounds, he had bushier eyebrows and slightly bigger ears than his head warranted, but his dark hair and five o'clock shadow combined to form a handsome enough package. I would probably refer to him as cute.

Instead of averting his gaze, he smiled and lifted his glass in a silent toast. He was about three tables away, too far to start a conversation. I didn't know what to do, so I lifted my glass of wine in response and turned back to Cyan, who was suddenly cheerful. "See?" she said. "I think he wants to meet you."

I didn't want to make it look as though we were talking about him, so I kept a smile on my face and said, "No way."

"Why not?"

"I'm not about to introduce myself to a man in a bar, okay?"

"This is not your ordinary pick-up bar."

That I knew. "Which is why I don't think he's being anything more than friendly."

"You are so naïve."

Cyan was younger than me by a couple of

years. Having her tell me I was naïve made me laugh. In my peripheral vision I saw the mystery man stand up and make his way over to the bar, where he spoke with Billy. "He's probably settling his bill and leaving, so we can just forget about him," I said.

Just as I predicted, he left.

Billy came to our table a moment later with a tray of fresh drinks. "From an admirer," he said, winking at me.

Cyan sat up. "The guy who just left?"

Billy nodded. "He knew who you two were, and asked me to extend his compliments to both chefs."

"Who was he?" I asked.

Billy shook his head. "Never saw him before. But he seemed to be paying particular attention to you, Ollie."

Cyan tapped my arm. "See, I bet he wanted to ask you out."

Billy lowered his voice. "I've been a bartender for a long time," he said. "No offense, Ollie, but I don't think he was eyeing you for a date. He seemed interested in you in a completely different way."

"Different how?"

"Don't know. Just different. Like he was studying you."

"Did he say anything unusual?"

"Just that he was a great fan of yours."

"Wonderful," I said, making light of it. "Instead of a suitor, I've got a stalker."

Billy shrugged. "He seemed harmless enough. But if he comes back, I'll try to find out more."

"Is he staying at the hotel?"

"Don't know. He didn't charge anything to a room."

"Thanks, Billy," I said. "Nice to know you're watching out for us."

Cyan beamed as Billy left us to our fresh drinks and further conversation. "You really need to start thinking about getting out again," she said. "If you don't make some progress soon, I'm going to start setting you up."

It was an empty threat, and we both knew it. But I was grateful to see Cyan cheerful again. I was about to ask who her first choice would be when a scene on the TV caught my eye. A bearded man struggled to break free from the four policemen holding him. Close-captioning allowed me to read his shouts: "This is not over! We will prevail!"

I recognized the background. Hurrying to the bar, I said, "Turn that up."

"What is it?" Billy asked.

Cyan had followed me. "It's the hospital," she said.

Billy turned up the TV's volume. A few other patrons came to stand next to us and watch.

A news reporter spoke solemnly. "Again, we repeat: The Lyman Hall Hospital stand-off is over. The siege has ended and we are now waiting for word on the hostages' condition. Updates should be coming very soon."

An anchorwoman chimed in from off-screen. "Allen, do we know yet if this result is due to the efforts of Congresswoman Sechrest?"

The on-scene reporter nodded. "I am hearing that if it weren't for her efforts, lives may have been lost. As it stands, the Armustan terrorists are now being taken into custody. Congresswoman Sechrest negotiated this stand-down and we hope to hear soon that —" He stopped talking, pressed a finger to his ear, and then continued, "The hostages are safe." He stopped long enough to listen more, then added, "Everyone is reported in stable or good condition. Still no word on what hospitalized the White House staff in the first place, or if these events are at all connected."

"Have you been able to speak with any of the hostages yet?"

"No." The reporter's eyebrows came

together as he listened to whoever was feeding him information. "The hostages will remain here, under care, until they are able to be released. The White House will issue a statement later this evening, but the president has expressed his gratitude to Congresswoman Sechrest for her intervention." He was jostled from behind by a police officer. "We are being asked to leave, so I'll give it back to you in the station, Meredith. This has been Allen Pernott with the latest in the news from Lyman Hall Hospital."

As the scene switched, I turned to Cyan, grabbing her into a bear hug. "They're okay," I said. "They're okay."

For the third time that night, Cyan broke into tears.

Mrs. Wentworth peered out her apartment door when I got off the elevator. My elderly neighbor waved hello.

"How are you?" I asked.

"We're doing great, Ollie," she said, referring to herself and longtime boyfriend Stan. "Pretty late night for you, isn't it?"

Always aware of my comings and goings, Mrs. Wentworth was a good watchdog as well as a friend. "Yep," I said.

"I'm real happy for those hostages," she said. "Glad they're safe. You tell them that when they come back to work, will you?"

"I promise," I said.

"Good night, Ollie."

"See you tomorrow."

I let myself in and threw my keys on the nearby table. As soon as I got myself settled, I decided to call Tom. Although it was extremely unlikely that other Metro riders had any interest in my conversation, I hadn't wanted to discuss sensitive issues during my commute. I was always careful to keep White House issues private.

He answered on the first ring. "What's up?"

"You still on duty?"

"Always," he said. "You've seen the news?"

"I did. Anything else I need to know that they didn't show on TV?"

"I'll bring everyone up to speed tomorrow," he said. There was an awkward pause before he asked, "Something on your mind?"

"This may be nothing . . ."

He groaned. "Why, Ollie?"

That got my back up. "Why what?"

"You want to report some unusual observation to me. Or share a suspicion. Or give me advice on how to manage the Secret Service. Am I right?"

Tom had never appreciated my efforts,

despite the fact that most times my intervention helped. I don't know why I expected anything different tonight. "You know what? It's late. Forget I called."

About to hang up, I heard him say, "Hang on, hang on."

If I harbored any unhappiness about breaking off our relationship, this brief interchange banished that regret forever. Tom had never fully trusted my instincts, nor did he appreciate my attempts to help. He saw me as meddling and uncooperative. Although I understood his position as head of the PPD, I also knew that there were agents in the White House who "got" me. Again I thought about Gav: He and I had gotten under each other's skin when we first met, but after working together we'd developed a mutual respect. And that was what had been sorely lacking in my relationship with Tom.

I didn't say anything. I just waited.

He blew out a breath before asking, "What's on your mind?"

I bit my lip, wishing I could come back with some sharp retort. I'd called him for a reason and whether he appreciated it or not, I believed this was something he needed to know.

"It's about Zeller and Bost."

"Okay," he said warily.

"Are they both fully up to date on all that has transpired?"

"We're not on a secure line," he said. "We can't talk about all that has transpired."

"I know that," I said with more than a little snap. "That's why I'm not being specific, okay? I'm just asking if they're fully in the loop or not."

"Why?"

"They corralled me today. Two of them and me in a small room. They barred the door and then suggested that your orders were not in the . . . Family's . . . best interests. I couldn't tell if they were trying to do an end-run around you, or if they were testing to see if I was a security leak."

"They did what?"

Oh, now he was interested. "I just wanted you to be aware."

Tom swore under his breath. "Are you sure, Ollie? Is it possible you just misunderstood their intentions?"

I bit the insides of my cheeks to keep from arguing back. "I called simply to forewarn you just in case you might have trouble with Zeller and Bost." That wasn't exactly true, I'd also planned to tell him about the man in the bar this evening. But right now all I wanted was to get off the phone. "And I've accomplished that. Good night, Tom." With that, I hung up.

CHAPTER 9

As promised, Tom called another meeting first thing the next morning. This time, in addition to Paul, Sargeant, and Gardez — who had left Nourie in the kitchen to supervise Bucky and Cyan — Tom had also included Bost and Zeller. Neither made eye contact with me.

"We are here to bring everyone up to date on the condition of our people at Lyman Hall Hospital as well as discuss the situation with the tainted chicken wings. I have asked agents Bost and Zeller to join us today because they are the agents primarily in charge of the president's children. Both have been fully briefed on our plans to keep the arsenic information quiet at this time." He looked at me and then at his watch. "And since both of them will be leaving shortly to escort the children to school, let me begin. Please hold all questions until the end."

I glanced over again at Bost and Zeller, attempting to read them. Had Tom told them I'd ratted them out for trying to waylay me yesterday? But both watched their boss with impassive looks on their faces. Now there was a skill I needed to master. Right now I'm sure my concerns were broadcast all over my features. I tamped down my curiosity and turned my attention back to Tom.

He explained — without going into elaborate detail — how the hostages had been freed and the part Sandy Sechrest had played in their release. "We've received intelligence that the group that took control of Lyman Hall was, to use a sports term, their second-string." He held up both hands. "Don't ask how we found this out. We are tracking down several issues that have recently come up that we cannot comment on at the moment. I can tell you this: We believe that if the Hyden children had been stricken and taken to the hospital, the faction in charge would not have surrendered so easily."

I wanted to ask so many questions, but held my tongue.

"From what we gather," Tom continued, "the group holding the hostages had to change their game plan mid-play. This siege

116

turned out to be only a trial run. We believe that when the leaders of this group discovered that the ploy to poison the children failed, they decided to go ahead anyway, substituting their first-stringers with those who are in custody right now." He shook his head. "We haven't yet determined how they found out that the wings were not served to the kids. Someone obviously talked. We need to find that leak. And we need to plug it."

I shuddered.

He went on. "As you know, this hostage situation was controlled by the leaders of a radical faction of Armustan. They demanded the release of the faction's ultimate ruler and convicted terrorist, Farbod. We are fortunate that they gave up when President Hyden refused to negotiate." He took a deep breath. "I can't say what might have happened had the kids been involved." He stopped to look intently at each of us. "Both for the kids' protection and for the security of our country, we must never let down our guard. Which is why I need every single person to be on alert at every moment. Even when you're off duty you must be careful to watch what you say, and where you say it." At this he glared at me. I stared back, feeling a flush burn up my neck and cheeks.

Did he not know me well enough to understand I would never compromise security?

Tom looked at his watch again. "One final thing before I release you. One of our butlers claimed he might have seen someone carrying the chicken wing box to the kitchen. I'm not sharing the butler's name, and I warn you that he can't remember who it was — except that it was a male and a new person — but said he remembers it only because he thought it odd that the White House would order chicken wings on Inauguration Day. We will be following up." Tom looked at Gardez. "Please brief Nourie." To Paul and Sargeant, he said, "If you need to share any of this information with staff members, you will clear it through me first." To me, he said, "You need to keep Bucky and Cyan up to date on the importance of keeping the kids secure, but do not let anyone know about the arsenic yet. Is that understood?"

Why hadn't he asked anyone else if their orders were understood? "Yes," I said, "of course."

For the first time since the Hydens had come to the White House, breakfast went off without a hitch. Oatmeal, waffles, and eggs were completed perfectly and on time.

We sent them up to the residence along with a supply of juices, fruit, and two nutritious yet fun school lunches in plenty of time for the kids to enjoy and pack before the family got pulled in ten different directions. "You never know, though," I said to Bucky and Cyan as soon as the butlers wheeled the trays away, "things can still go wrong."

"It's not like you to be such a pessimist," Bucky said. "What's up?"

"I'm not pessimistic, just realistic. Ever since the Hydens came to live here, not one single thing has gone according to plan. Yes, I expect things will turn around. But I'm not counting on it yet."

Gardez and Nourie didn't comment, but both looked as though they agreed with me.

Bucky raised his eyebrows and turned to consult the computer about preparations for lunch. "Well, I think we're in good shape," he said over his shoulder. "From here on it should be smooth sailing."

Cyan looked hopeful. "I think we've turned a corner, too. It's just the newness that makes everybody jittery. As soon as the butlers come back down and tell us breakfast went well, we'll all feel a lot better."

"I hope you're right." I couldn't shake my uneasiness. Sargeant's prediction based on word from his "good authority" had me rattled more than I cared to admit. I started cleaning up the center countertop, mentally working out the timing for today's lunch. The First Lady had scheduled a meeting with her staff; we would provide salads and soup and Marcel was preparing a light dessert. The president had already informed us that he would take lunch in the White House Mess in the West Wing, so we were off the hook where he was concerned.

A half hour later, just as Bucky and Cyan had predicted, the butlers returned, having dropped off the morning's accumulation of plates and trays with our dishwashers. "Perfect," Jackson said as he walked in. "The kids are getting into their routines and everything went like clockwork."

Relief washed over me. Even more than I would have expected. "That's great," I said. Cyan and Bucky looked the same way I felt. Even our two taste-testing guards seemed more cheerful than usual. "It's about time we enjoyed a little success again."

Just then, Paul walked in with a serious expression on his face. "Ollie, can I talk with you for a moment?"

As I followed him out into the hallway, I heard Bucky say, "Well that didn't last very long."

I almost whispered "Please, not the China

120

Room," aloud, but it was clear that Paul had another destination in mind. He made a sharp left turn into the North Hall and continued past the next hallway, taking me by utter surprise when he opened the door directly across.

"Here?" I asked as Paul flipped on the lights and pulled the door closed behind us. Situated under the North Portico, this one-lane bowling alley wouldn't be my first choice for conversation, but I had to admit, it was private. With three giant pins painted along one wall, the place looked like it had been lifted straight out of the 1960s. The utilitarian shoe and ball racks did nothing to dispel that impression. The bowling-pin motif was repeated on the back wall, right where we stood. "I don't understand."

"With so many people in the White House today because of the hostage situation and its aftermath, I needed to find somewhere to talk with you where no one would over-hear. This is about as private as it gets."

"What's wrong?"

"Nothing is wrong, Ollie," Paul said with such pain in his expression that I knew he was lying. "I just want to give you fair warn-ing."

My stomach dropped to my shoes pre-cisely as Peter Sargeant's prediction jumped to my brain.

Expecting to hear that I was being officially reprimanded for Cyan's actions, I steeled myself. "Don't beat around the bush," I said. "Just tell me."

Paul's hair had always been a distinctive salt and pepper, but for the first time I noticed that the white had seriously overtaken the dark. Much like the way presidents age quickly in office, Paul was showing signs of the stress he dealt with every single day. He licked his lips, taking precious seconds to answer me. Whatever he was about to say was not easy for him.

"An official announcement is about to be released . . ."

Could my throat get any drier? I swallowed and it hurt. "About the kitchen?"

He nodded.

I wished he would just get on with it. "Please, Paul. I'm sweating here."

"The president and Mrs. Hyden are bringing on a new chef."

My knees went soft. "I'm being let go?"

"No," he said quickly. "This person will be joining your staff."

I was shaking my head before I could form all the questions running through my brain. "Then why do you look so upset? Is this new chef supposed to take Bucky's position? Is he or she replacing Cyan? Is that it? Is Cyan being fired?"

"The new chef is a 'he,' " Paul said. "His name is Virgil Ballantine."

"So he's *already* been hired."

"Virgil will be brought on as the Hyden family's personal chef." Paul's hands came up. "He will manage the family meals himself. But technically he will report to you."

I had no words. My staff and I would no longer prepare meals for the First Family? Sargeant was right: I was on my way out. "What do we do while he's taking care of the Hydens?" I asked. "Are Bucky, Cyan, and I supposed to sit around and twiddle our thumbs?"

"Please don't read anything into this. I spoke with Mrs. Hyden directly and asked her point-blank if she intended for Virgil Ballantine to replace you and she said she had no such plans."

"Of course she said that," I said, my voice rising, "what else can she say? She's smart. She'll bring this Virgil fellow on and then once the hullabaloo of the inauguration dies down, she'll quietly hand me my walking papers."

"Ollie, calm down. Mrs. Hyden has no reason to let you go. You're overreacting."

I wasn't and he knew it. "Look at it from her perspective. Not only did we have that utterly disastrous breakfast, but the Secret Service seems all too willing to throw me under the bus. Until someone tells Mrs. Hyden that the chicken wings delivered here for her kids were poisoned, all she knows is that I denied the kids a favorite treat. Can you blame her for planning to get rid of me?"

"She's not planning to get rid of you."

"Can you promise me that?"

Paul's eyes clouded. "The announcement is going out Monday. I'll leave it to you to inform your staff."

I worked hard to compose myself, to focus on the facts. "Who is this guy anyway? Do I at least get to see his resume?"

"I'll see that a copy is sent to you directly."

I stared at the painted bowling pins and let my gaze wander down to the picture of the White House at the far end of the alley. What an inauspicious place to receive such devastating news. A long moment of silence hung between us as I brooded over the new information, feeling wounded and suddenly vulnerable. I didn't want to return to the kitchen yet. I didn't want to move until I knew what my next course of action should be. But I knew Paul had a thousand other

124

things he ought to be doing. "I'm sorry for getting upset," I said, "and I appreciate you taking the time to tell me yourself."

"It's the least I could do," he said, his face taking on a bit of brightness. "And I truly believe you have nothing to worry about. As soon as the First Family gets to know you, you'll be just as valued as you were with the Campbells. The Hydens are simply accustomed to having a personal chef."

And what was I? Chopped tuna? "Thanks," I said and moved to take one of the seats along the back wall. "If it's okay with you, I'm going to sit here for a little bit before I go back to the kitchen."

"Of course." Paul patted my shoulder. "Just remember one thing. Nobody could ever replace you, Ollie."

Although I appreciated his compliment, one thought kept running through my mind: Did the Hydens know that?

CHAPTER 10

By Saturday morning, I was determined not to let this news about the personal chef deter me from running my kitchen the best way I knew how. I still hadn't broken the news to my team, and though I rationalized my reasons, I knew it was because saying it aloud would make it more real. I wasn't ready for that. Cyan had the day off to be with her mother, but she and I had made plans to meet later for dinner. I had a feeling she might need a friend today to listen. I know I did.

My mind was on breakfast, but my eyes were on the salsa mixture in front of me. I'd come up with a new recipe for huevos rancheros, but wasn't quite sure it was up to presidential standards. If this didn't fly, we had a backup meal planned, and Bucky was already hard at work across the kitchen. I was beginning to believe I'd gone too heavy on the onions for a morning meal, and reached up to grab a tasting spoon to test that theory.

My hand came up empty. "Aargh!"

Bucky turned to me. "Are we out?"

"Again," I said.

We were running out of basics right and left. The absence of our stricken laundry ladies and butlers was creating a ripple effect through all departments. Several butlers were now pulling double shifts, and a few of the dishwashers were pitching in with laundry duties. That meant plates and silverware moved more slowly through the process than we were accustomed to, and we were obliged to dip into our vast store of duplicates to keep the kitchen running smoothly. Tasting spoons and other flatware were becoming a big problem. Because we had two extra tasters hanging around, we were flying through utensils like butter. I was constantly sending runners to the dishwashing area to replenish our stock.

We had no runners in the area at the moment so I decided to make my way to the dishwashing area myself. "I'll get what you need," Gardez said. He turned to Nourie. "Can you hold the place down while I'm gone?"

Nourie laughed and waved him away. Over the past few days, the two agents had begun to relax just a little. They let us know that they, and the two agents assigned to Marcel's area, had been taking a lot of ribbing about how lucky they were to snag this detail. Cyan and I had discovered that neither of the two handsome guards assigned to us was married, and from what we could tell, only Gardez had a girlfriend.

Right now I turned to Nourie, who was eyeing the salsa from afar. "Do you two ever get a day off?"

"Sure we do," he said. "But until all these new protocols get established, Agent Mac-Kenzie wants to keep us at our posts for as long as possible without interruption. He will probably assign our relief in the next couple of days."

"Makes sense, I guess."

"Hey," he said casually — a bit too casually, "your assistant Cyan has been working here for quite a few years, hasn't she?"

"She has. That girl will have an amazing career. Mark my words: She's a genius."

"Yeah," he said with awe in his voice. "I tried some of that sauce she put together yesterday. Wow."

What was that they said about the path to a man's heart? "She's pretty incredible," I said. At that point I half-expected him to ask if Cyan was seeing anyone, but Gardez returned with a supply of spatulas and tasting spoons. He'd brought dishtowels, too.

"Thought I'd pick these up while I was near the laundry," he said.

"Good thinking." I turned to Nourie to finish our conversation, but he'd gone back to his unobtrusive corner and acted as though he hadn't said a word while his partner had been gone.

Later, as we cleaned up after lunch, I thought about what this new Virgil Ballantine might be like and how his presence would change the tenor of this kitchen. Next week might very well be the last week I prepared regular meals for the First Family.

"I don't smell anything," Bucky said.

I looked up to find him staring at me. "Excuse me?"

"Never play poker, kid. You're either smelling something rotten or you've been dealt a bad hand. And since there's nothing going rancid in here" — he opened his arms to encompass the entire kitchen — "I have to assume you've got troubles."

I heaved a great sigh and Bucky, surprisingly, looked concerned. "What's going on?" he asked.

"Virgil Ballantine."

Bucky shook his head. "Who?"

I'd been hoping to talk with Bucky and Cyan privately and individually, away from the constant scrutiny of our omnipresent guards, but there never seemed to be a moment when one of them wasn't around. The two men were pleasant enough, but bringing on a new chef who would be solely responsible for the family meals was a very big deal, and something I would have preferred to discuss one on one with my staff. I would see Cyan tonight, but Bucky and I were stuck with babysitters. "We're getting a new chef."

Bucky squinted at me. "You hired someone?"

The two guards didn't seem to much care about our conversation. I hoped it would stay that way as I moved closer to Bucky and lowered my voice. "The Hydens are bringing their personal family chef to Washington."

Rendered speechless as he so seldom was, Bucky's mouth gaped. He started to say something, then turned away, his shoulders jerking as though he was in the midst of a silent argument with himself. Knowing Bucky as well as I did, I waited. In a minute he was back again. He kept his voice down. "Is this what Paul pulled you out for yesterday?"

"Yeah. The new guy is Virgil Ballantine. Paul sent me his resume yesterday. Ballantine's worked at a handful of really great establishments. Pretty impressive."

Bucky glared. "What aren't you telling me?"

"He's been the Hydens' personal family chef for the past three years."

Bucky's shoulders slumped. "So this isn't a 'Let's try him out for a while' endeavor. This is a 'Let's bring our guy to Washington' move."

"Pretty much," I agreed.

"You worried?"

"Of course I am."

"But you're the first woman in the job of executive chef here. Don't you think it would be political suicide for them to get rid of you?"

"I'd hardly think it would make a difference at this point. President Hyden is here for the next four years. Wouldn't this be the perfect time to bring a new person on board and replace me as soon as the media storm dies down? Think about it: If the First Lady cut me loose three and a half years from now, the backlash might make a difference. But if they get rid of me a few months from now, nobody's even going to remember by the time the next elections come around."

131

"True," Bucky said. Hardly a cheerful reply. "And with all the trouble you've gotten into over the past few years — I mean, I know the papers are always playing up your exploits — the Hydens have all the ammunition they need if someone criticizes their decision to let you go."

"Thanks Buck," I said. "I'm feeling so much better now."

He waved away my sarcasm. "I'm just saying what you've already figured out for yourself."

He was right, darn it.

"Maybe it's good that Mrs. Hyden doesn't know that the chicken wings were given to the laundry staff," I said. "This way, she doesn't know about my involvement. She's probably heard plenty of stories about things that happened during the Campbell presidency. Maybe if I keep a low profile this time, I'll have a better chance at keeping my job."

"You? Keep a low profile?" Bucky barked a laugh. "Not in this lifetime."

"Your support is overwhelming."

He fixed me with a look. "I know you don't want to talk about *why* you and Tom broke up, but I have my suspicions. You've got to be true to your nature, Ollie, and you usually are. But don't for a minute underestimate the challenges you're stuck with because of it."

That was one of the longest sentiments Bucky had ever expressed to me. Again, he was right and I told him so. "Thanks, Buck," I said. "Now, let's plan to make dinner so incredible and delicious that they tell this Chef Ballantine his services are no longer needed."

I caught Gardez and Nourie exchanging a look that told me they'd heard the entire conversation. Nourie lifted his chin and said, "The new guy doesn't stand a chance."

While Bucky prepared a marinade for tonight's beef entrée, I peeled potatoes for a new side dish we planned to introduce. Deep in our respective tasks, we didn't pay attention to the noise in the hallway and only looked up when Mrs. Hyden and the children walked in.

Mrs. Hyden was tall, with shoulder-length dark hair, a trim build, and a quick smile. "Good afternoon," she said.

Bucky and I both stopped what we were doing and wiped our hands on our aprons. Gardez and Nourie straightened and greeted her with silent nods.

"Good afternoon, Mrs. Hyden," I said. "And hello again, Abigail, Josh."

The two kids said hello, then looked to

their mother. Mrs. Hyden spoke. "The children wanted to come down to visit each department to express our gratitude at making us feel at home. We are all still adjusting to this new environment, but we realize how much is being done behind the scenes to see to our comfort."

"What about me?" Josh asked.

Mrs. Hyden directed a fond gaze toward the boy, then explained, "Josh hopes to be a chef someday, too, don't you?"

He nodded vigorously.

I brought my face down to his level. "I'm sure Chef Virgil will have lots to share with you, but don't forget that you and your sister are always welcome down here in the main kitchen, okay?"

"Really?"

Mrs. Hyden started to protest. "Won't they be in the way?"

"No, not at all," I said. "Unless it's an hour before a major state dinner where we're serving a hundred guests, we can always make time for kids in the kitchen. They can help us come up with treats for school, or Abigail and Josh can invite friends for a pizza-making party." To the two of them, I said, "Whatever you need, we're here for you."

Abigail seemed less impressed than Josh

did, but both children were significantly happier with us than they had been on inauguration night. As though he read my mind, however, Josh decided to bring up the subject. "Whatever happened to the Rene's Wings that I found the other night? Did you eat them?"

I felt a subtle shift in the room's mood. As we'd been talking, Bucky had come to stand beside me, and now he and I exchanged a look. "No, of course not." Thinking about creating a teachable moment, I added, "No one in the White House should ever eat anything from outside, unless we know exactly where it came from."

Mrs. Hyden tilted her head. "I know the matter is moot because wherever the chicken wings are now, we certainly wouldn't want to consume them, would we? But Josh brings up a point I'm not quite clear on. If the box of Rene's Wings was a gift to the children — from what I understand, it had their names on it — then why on earth did you refuse to serve them? Had I been consulted before a decision was made, perhaps we could have worked this disagreement out?"

Her expression was pleasant, but her resolve was steel. She delivered a very clear message: Her children were not to be denied by the hired help.

It galled me to no end to be unable to tell her about the arsenic poisoning. I tried to defend my actions the best way I knew: by telling the truth, short of full disclosure. "I'm so sorry about this misunderstanding. I'm sure once I explain, everything will become clear. Here at the White House . . ."

"I'm aware of protocols. And the reasoning behind your decision to dispose of the children's treat has been explained to me," she began, clearly dismissive. Speaking slowly, she held up one finger. "But I also think it's just possible that you might have imagined conspiracies where there are none."

Forbidden to disclose what I knew, I bit the insides of my cheeks. My face flushed red. I couldn't see it, but I felt the blood zoom hot and straight up from my twisting gut. I had one more ace in the hole. "It isn't just me," I said. "The Secret Service believes we followed the proper course."

Mrs. Hyden's dark eyes flashed. "Are you saying it wasn't your decision to withhold the treat?"

"No, of course not." I squared my shoulders. "I made the decision, and . . ." My stomach fluttered like a wild thing. "I would make the same decision again, given the circumstances."

She humored me with a smile. "It was lovely to be able to talk with you and clear this matter up. Come on, kids," she said, putting her arms out to herd the children back out of the kitchen. Turning to me and Bucky she added, "Thank you both for your time."

As soon as she was gone, I put my head down.

Bucky grumbled under his breath, but went back to work. A couple seconds later he asked, "Is your resume up to date?"

CHAPTER 11

I met Cyan for dinner at one of the more upscale restaurants in D.C. There were certainly plenty to choose from. It wasn't a sense of entitlement after several bad days that tempted us to drop a big chunk of change — it was professional curiosity. A new chef had been hired at the Buckwalk just over a year ago and we hadn't had a chance to check him out yet. He didn't know we were coming, and that's exactly the way we wanted it.

When I arrived, Cyan was already there. I was shown to a small table for two in the center of a quiet dining room. Cyan was just being served a glass of red wine. The stale décor hadn't been updated since the mid-'70s, and although it suffered from lack of design, the restaurant never suffered from a lack of patrons. Despite its tired furnishings, nearly every table in the restaurant was occupied, and I knew that within an hour there would be a waiting line out the door.

All conversations here were hushed. Restaurant-goers seemed much more interested in the food than they did in people-watching. This wasn't L.A. or New York. The luminaries who graced our establishments were generally big-shot politicians, not A-list movie stars. Not unless there was a major bill coming up in Congress that enjoyed celebrity support. Or a movie being filmed locally. I'd seen Arnold Schwarzenegger walking the National Mall once, but I had no idea if his agenda had been political or entertainment-related.

"Hey," I said as I took the seat across from her. The maître d' snapped my napkin out then placed it gently on my lap before handing me a large leather-bound menu.

"What's wrong?" Cyan asked.

"That obvious?"

Our diminutive waiter had a ring of white hair and a tiny mustache. Upon his arrival, he bowed. I asked him for a glass of cabernet sauvignon. "Not white wine?" Cyan asked.

"Not today," I said. "I need something bolder."

"Talk to me."

I did. I broke the news about Virgil Ballantine, and she took it exactly the way I expected she would. "Are you kidding me?" she asked. "Why not just shove us out the door right now? Who do they think they're fooling by keeping us on?"

"Paul promises we won't be affected."

Her look told me she believed that about as much as I did. "I'm so sorry," she said, "this is all my fault."

"How do you figure?"

"They're blaming the whole kitchen for making the staff sick. It's my fault. If I would have listened to you —"

"Actually, it's just the opposite. You're forgetting that Mrs. Hyden doesn't know that the chicken wings were given to the laundry women. She's clearly angry with me for not letting the kids have them." I told her about my interaction with the First Lady earlier today.

"Tom still won't tell her what really happened? Seriously?"

"Seriously."

"That's just dumb."

"He says he has his reasons."

Cyan cocked an eyebrow. "Still defending him?"

My wine arrived and I was spared responding. I asked Cyan how her experience moving her mother into a nursing home went, and she told me. There wasn't much I hadn't expected, but I did notice that Cyan seemed ever so slightly less tense. Given the predicament of the kitchen, that was saying something. "Feeling good about the decision you made for your mom?" I asked.

"Surprisingly, I am." She drained her glass just as the waiter returned.

"Another?" he asked.

"Please," she said.

He gave a solemn nod and told us he would return shortly to tell us the specials of the day.

"Whatever it is, I'm ordering it," I said, closing my menu. "Chef specials are always the way to go."

"What if it's tuna?"

I shuddered. "Okay, not that. I might be capable of *creating* a great tuna entrée, but I'm not particularly fond of eating one."

"Same with me and Brussels sprouts. Remember when Bucky came up with that recipe for President Campbell?"

She was interrupted by our waiter placing a fresh glass of wine in front of her. He gave us a peculiar, though not unfriendly once-over, then proceeded to announce the day's specials.

Fortunately for both of us, nothing du jour contained either tuna or Brussels sprouts. We ordered appetizers of *vol-au-vent des champignons* and tomato-gorgonzola soup. Our waiter nodded again, said he would get them started, and offered to delay taking our entrée orders to give us time to talk and enjoy. We took him up on it.

"When does this new guy start?" Cyan asked.

"No idea. But I'm sure it will be soon. After my run-in with Mrs. Hyden this morning, I'm sure she can't wait to bring him on board and kick me out. To be honest, Cyan," I said, "I have to believe you and Bucky will be safe."

"Not if Tom has his way. I know he wants me out."

No need for me to confirm her fears. Instead, I said, "I figure Mrs. Hyden will probably give me a couple of months to find a new position and if I don't, she'll ask for my resignation."

"Do you really think so?"

The truth was I didn't know. "It could be that we're all just getting off to a bad start. I'm not planning to actively look just yet. If they do ask for my resignation, I'll give it, but I'll also ask for the opportunity to stay on until I find something else."

"Wow, Ollie. You've really given it a lot of thought."

"I have to. I keep picturing Sargeant glee-

142

fully delivering the bad news." I took a deep drink of my cabernet. "Wouldn't that be a bite?"

"We might both be back on the market," she said. "But at least you won't have the shame of poisoning colleagues on your record."

We sat quietly for a minute, each of us deep in our own musings.

Cyan broke the silence. "Which is exactly why you and I need to stop believing the White House kitchen is our life."

"We don't do that."

She gave me a look. "Of course we do. I didn't follow Rafe. Why? Because it would mean leaving the White House. You broke up with Tom. Why? Because he can't handle the fact that you've put your life on the line — literally — for the White House."

"Cyan —"

"I had hopes this time, Ollie. With a new administration coming in — I had hopes that maybe your involvement in things beyond the kitchen would cease. But it hasn't. Who found the tainted chicken wings? You. And because of a stupid mistake on my part, I'm involved now, too. This has to stop."

Our appetizers arrived and we thanked the waiter who chose, wisely, not to press for our entrée orders.

Before Cyan could start portioning the mushroom pastry, I whispered. "But I don't ask to get involved."

Her eyes were bright blue again — she'd been favoring her blue contacts a lot lately — when she looked up at me. "Does it matter? What does matter is that you throw yourself completely into protecting the White House. That's admirable, Ollie. Really it is. But look at the price you pay. You have no social life, nobody to go home to. Not even a cat."

I was about to protest that I had Mrs. Wentworth next door, but that would have sounded pitiful. My neighbor kept an eye on me, but it wasn't as though the elderly woman and I "hung out" together.

Cyan must have read something on my face because she continued, impassioned, "You and I are too young to just give up on fun. There's a whole life out there we're missing because we're so dedicated to our work."

"But it's more than that," I said, "these are our careers, and this is the White House kitchen. You don't get any higher than this."

"There's nothing wrong with being dedicated," Cyan said. "I can't imagine you being anything else. But tomorrow they could let us both go, and then where would we be?"

I didn't have an answer to that.

She went in for the kill. "Don't you think it's about time you started dating again?"

I gave a wry laugh.

"What's so funny?"

"I don't have time."

"Because you spend too much time at work."

"I don't have any prospects."

"Because you never get out."

"Cyan," I said, my voice a warning, "I'm not interested in dating right now. I want to concentrate on being the best chef I can be."

"You're already that and more," she said. "Why not go out with one of our new Secret Service cuties?"

This time I laughed genuinely. "I'm leaving them for you," I said. "Honestly, neither one is my type, although I agree they're both very attractive."

"You need to find someone."

"I'm fine just the way things are right now."

She persisted, "You're too closed off. I'll bet if a handsome man — like the one we saw at the bar the other night — asked you out, you'd find a million excuses why you couldn't."

"You're right," I said, picking up my knife and fork. "And if you don't serve this wonderful-looking appetizer, I will."

We ate in companionable silence, both enjoying the gorgeous combination of flavors in both the mushroom sauce and the creamy-smooth tomato soup, with the gorgonzola's underlying buttery bite serving as the perfect accent. "Mmm, wonderful," I said. "Think we can re-create these for an upcoming menu?"

"Always thinking about work, aren't you?"

I took another spoonful of soup. "With appetizers like this, how can I think about anything else?"

At that moment, our waiter returned. "My compliments to the chef," I said.

He gave us that peculiar once-over again, thanked me, and asked if we were ready to order. I chose the filet medallion trio entrée with horseradish, blue cheese, and mushroom crusts because I wanted to see how the chef here handled them and look for ways we might be able to borrow to improve our version at the White House. Cyan ordered pork loin with figs.

"How would you like your medallions?" the waiter asked.

"Medium-rare."

"Very good," he said. He looked ready to say something more, but evidently changed his mind, grabbed our empty bowls, and left.

"What was that all about?" I asked.

Cyan wiped her mouth with her napkin. "Maybe he has the hots for you."

"He's got to be at least seventy."

She smiled. "Think about what a catch you'd be. He could brag to all his friends at his AARP meetings."

I laughed. "You do realize that AARP starts at age fifty, don't you?"

"Oh yeah? That's still pretty young these days." She raised an eyebrow. "That reminds me. How old was that agent who taught us about explosives . . . that guy who liked you so much? Gav?"

I nearly spit out my wine. "Where did that come from?"

She affected an innocent look. "I'm just trying to be helpful. You need to start noticing men noticing you."

"Gav did not 'notice' me," I said, bringing my napkin to my mouth. "And he's probably just over forty."

She didn't have a chance to say anything else because at that moment our waiter returned. Instead of bringing our entrées — which would have been much too quick —

147

he was accompanied by a tall, wide-set gentleman wearing typical kitchen gear.

"Ladies," our waiter began, "I couldn't help but overhear some of your conversation." He smiled. "It is our honor to have you, Ms. Paras," he nodded to me, "and one of your assistants as our guests tonight. May I present our head chef, Reggie Stewart."

Chef Reggie beamed and stepped forward. "Ah, Ms. Paras, Ms. Paras," he said, "I'm honored to have you visit my restaurant." Reggie's face widened when he smiled. Carrying about forty pounds more than his tall frame was built for, he was nonetheless a good-looking man. In his mid- to late-thirties, he had a full head of black hair, covered by a hairnet. One renegade curl escaped to twist over the center of his forehead, giving him a jaunty look.

As our waiter unobtrusively removed himself from our little group, I attempted to stand to greet the head chef properly.

"No, no," Reggie said, his face twisting into concern, "please stay seated." He offered his hand and we shook. I introduced Cyan.

"Yes, yes," he said, and I wondered if he always repeated his first word. "This is such a happy event. Don told me what you ordered — excellent choices, both — and I will be very eager to talk with you after dinner to find out what you thought of your meals."

I couldn't blame him. We always wanted to know how our creations were received and we rarely got as much feedback as we hoped for. I wished, however, that Reggie had waited to be introduced until after we'd finished eating. Now I felt a responsibility to analyze everything for Reggie's benefit and that would most certainly change the spirit of tonight's excursion. "Of course," I said politely.

"That's wonderful," he said with genuine warmth. "What's it like, Ms. Paras?" he asked. "I mean, how difficult is it to cook for arguably the most powerful man on the planet? Is he a picky eater? Well, I guess you wouldn't know for sure yet. It's only been a few days. Not even a week yet."

Reggie talked so fast I could barely keep up. I never, under any circumstances, shared information about the eating preferences of the president or those of his family. No one on staff at the White House ever shared any information unless approved for release. But I didn't really believe Reggie here was looking for a scoop. He just seemed excited.

"It's great," I said blandly. "I'm sure you can imagine."

"Yes, yes," he said. "I'm sure you can't wait to get to work every day."

I caught Cyan's grin across the table. "That's true. I do love my work."

"Of course you do," he said. Don sidled up and told him there was a question in the kitchen, and he apologized before running off. "I will be back," he said. "After dinner."

Cyan was still grinning. "I think he likes you."

"He likes my job," I said, wishing we still had more of the mushroom appetizer so I could offer it to Cyan and shut her up. "People are always fascinated. It's like working for royalty."

"Mm-hm."

Our food arrived and I was impressed, especially by the horseradish crust on one of the medallions and by the broccoli side dish. The truffle oil and Asiago cheese combined for a wonderful flavor. Cyan tried some, too. "Ooh. Very good," she said.

"We'll have to remember to tell Reggie how much we liked this."

"Should we take notes so we don't forget?" Cyan forked another bite of her pork loin, and smiled.

As promised, the moment dinner was done, Reggie returned. Instead of standing this time, however, he pulled a chair up and joined us. This put his bulky frame smack in the center of a walkway between tables. "How was everything?" he asked.

Cyan and I effused our delight and Reggie beamed. "Really?" he asked, after we'd described how impressed we were with some of his choices. "You really enjoyed it?"

He directed almost his entire conversation to me and chatted a great deal about preparations and kitchen protocols. Again he asked if we'd *honestly* enjoyed dinner. "Yes," I said for the third time. "Very, very much."

"You have no idea what this means to me."

I was beginning to get an idea. He had been sitting with us for more than fifteen minutes and while the crowd had died down, I imagined his assistant chefs would prefer to have their boss back in the kitchen rather than sitting out here chatting with the guests. The waiters, still busy bringing coffee and drinks to patrons, were bumping into one another because one of their routes was blocked.

"As much as I love talking shop," I said, wiping my mouth with my napkin and placing it on the table, "we really must be going. Do you think we can ask Don for our check?"

"Tonight is on the house," Reggie boomed. "This is my pleasure."

"Well, thank you," I said flabbergasted. "You really don't have to —"

"It is my great delight to have you both as my guests."

Cyan and I stood, shook hands with Reggie, and thanked him again. As soon as he departed, she and I left a tip, then walked to the front of the restaurant. We were surprised to find Reggie waiting. He asked if we were returning to the White House now or going home. "Home," I said.

"You probably keep much earlier hours than I do," he said, continuing the conversation a lot longer than I'd expected.

"Yes, I imagine that's true. You're generally here late, aren't you?"

"Very."

Cyan had donned her coat and now leaned forward to grab my arm. "Hey, I really need to get going. See you bright and early tomorrow, Ollie. Nice meeting you, Reggie." And before I could answer, she was gone.

"She must be an able assistant."

"Yes," I said, "and a good friend."

Reggie didn't seem to be ready to head back to the kitchen, so I pulled my own jacket on, and thanked him yet again for a wonderful dinner.

He cleared his throat. "I would be happy to cook for you again some time."

"Oh, I don't really eat out all that often," I said. "I just wanted to see what you were doing here. I've heard such rave reviews." I was quick to add, "And they're all very well deserved."

"Perhaps you and I could check out another local chef one of these days. I hear that Jacob Flannery at the Morgenthal Hotel is supposed to be magnificent."

"I've heard that, too."

"When is your next day off?"

Taken aback, I couldn't think fast enough to do anything but answer honestly. "Ah . . . Monday."

"I hope you don't consider me presumptuous, but I would very much like to take you to dinner there."

Speechless, and intent on declining, I was so concerned about hurting his feelings that I began by thanking him for his lovely offer.

"Wonderful," he said, taking my meaning entirely wrong. "May I pick you up at your home?"

"No," I answered quickly. Bad enough I'd just agreed to a date when I didn't mean to, I wasn't about to share personal information — like where I lived. How did I get myself into these things? Being polite was a curse sometimes. Right now he looked so excited that I couldn't bear the thought of declining. Not after I'd already — accidentally — accepted. "I'll meet you," I said.

He seemed even more excited than he had when he first arrived at our table. "This is wonderful. I'm going out with the finest female chef in the nation. This is certainly my lucky day."

When I left the restaurant, I was surprised to find Cyan shivering outside, waiting for me. "Took you long enough. So, when are you two going out?"

CHAPTER 12

Sunday morning, I turned on the television to catch the early news before I headed in to work. There's something quietly weird about watching third-rate political pundits discuss global events at 4:00 in the morning. I kept the volume low and went about preparing for my day, listening as the three men and one woman, seated in soft chairs around a studio coffee table, dispensed advice for our new president.

"Think about the ramifications," one of the men said. "Negotiating with terrorists this early in President Hyden's term would have established a dangerous trend."

A second man said, "We dodged a bullet this time. We got lucky. But what would we be saying right now if one of the hostages had died?"

"But no one did," the lone woman said, "thanks to Congresswoman Sechrest's efforts. If she hadn't —"

155

"We're looking at a conspiracy here." This third man, a young, bearded fellow wearing a striped shirt and an eager expression, leaned forward. "We never found out why there were so many White House staff members at the hospital that day, did we?" he asked. "Don't you all find that curious?"

The first man waved him back. "One of the White House laundry machines leaked. Fumes from the concentrated cleanser affected several individuals in the area."

"And you believe that?" the young man asked. "You buy into their misinformation that easily?"

The woman interrupted his tirade. "I think the bigger question is what we have to fear going forward. Those radical Armustans aren't going away just because their people failed in their attack. They are still insisting on the immediate release of Farbod from that Wisconsin prison. We need to consider that. We need to determine where this army will strike next and we need to be prepared going forward."

Her face flushed as her voice rose. "One of the men was released on a technicality. A technicality! But is anyone watching him?" She signaled offstage and a black-and-white photo of a man appeared on-screen. Thirty-something and ordinary looking, the man was white with dark hair and average features. I probably wouldn't recognize him if I bumped into him on the street. From behind his photo, the woman's voice warned: "This is Devon Clarr. Everyone in the viewing public needs to memorize his face. Clarr was released — on a technicality — and is walking free. I'm convinced — as Congresswoman Sechrest is convinced — that we have not seen the last of this man. We need to be on alert. Keep your eyes open for suspicious activity. And if you see him —"

The young man interrupted, "Whatever happened to innocent until proven guilty?"

I shut the TV off, but the woman's argument lingered. The idea of this radical faction striking again scared me. Whatever they were planning, all indications suggested it was coming soon. Strike before President Hyden gained traction in the new job. Strike close to home. I believed it was coming, and I had to figure that the men and women in charge of protecting our country from attacks believed so as well. I sighed, knowing there was little I could do.

Taking a look outside my patio doors, I stared at the dark morning sky and wondered if Mrs. Hyden had already decided to let me go, or if she was giving me a chance to prove myself. Mornings always felt full of promise. Hope swelled in my heart. Maybe I *had* been overreacting. Maybe she really just wanted to bring this Virgil Ballantine on board because he'd been a valued member of her staff in the past. Maybe he wouldn't start work at the White House for another three months. By then I would have had the chance to impress the Hydens. And I knew I could do that.

With a cheerier outlook than I'd had last night, I headed to the White House.

For the first time since the inauguration, the kitchen was humming without distraction. My good mood from early this morning spilled over and everything was going exactly as planned. Nourie had delivered very good news: All White House staff members who had been taken hostage at the hospital were now healthy enough to be sent home.

Cyan's voice trembled. "They're really okay?"

"They seem to have suffered no ill effects from being held hostage. They are all in good spirits and eager to get out of there." Changing the subject, Nourie turned to me. "What are we taste-testing next?"

"Haven't you eaten enough?" I asked. He

and Gardez had sampled every one of the items we'd sent up for the family to share for Sunday brunch. I was delighted to have provided a stellar menu for the First Family as they spent this precious time together. We all knew it wouldn't last. When one is the president of the United States, there really are no days off. It seemed there were few days off for our Secret Service guards as well. "I would have thought you'd be tired of our cooking by now."

Nourie glanced at Cyan. "I never get tired of this duty."

"I'm glad to hear it," Cyan said, smiling. "At first I thought having the two of you around would be a pain in our butts, but now it's like you've always been a part of the kitchen."

I wouldn't have gone that far, but then again, I wasn't flirting.

The two of them chitchatted about everything and nothing as we got our work done, and I enjoyed hearing their playful banter. As for myself, I was content to have done a good job, and more determined than ever to prove to the Hydens that we didn't need to bring on a new "personal" family chef.

"What a great day," I said to Cyan after Sunday brunch was served and we cleaned up. "It even seems as though the stainless-steel countertops are shining brighter this morning."

She laughed. "I would guess your good mood is either because it's Bucky's day off or because you have a date planned for tomorrow night."

Her reminder brought me back down to earth. "Reggie," I said, dropping my shoulders. "I forgot about that."

"You *forgot* that one of D.C.'s premier chefs is taking you out to dinner?" She feigned shock. "Ollie, you really are beyond hope."

Gardez chimed in, "What's this? Ollie has a date?"

"Want us to screen him for you?" Nourie asked. "We've got connections."

I laughed. "No, I think I'll be okay. And it's just a professional collaboration," I said. "He and I are checking out another chef's work."

"Uh-huh," Cyan said, singsong.

"Sure." Nourie gave an exaggerated wink. "You're just checking out the competition. Nice try."

I laughed and it felt good to do so.

Until Sargeant strode in. "What do you know about dietary guidelines for citizens of Armustan?" he asked.

"Good morning, Peter," I said, refusing to

allow him to ruin my mood. "As it happens, we know a great deal about Armustan. President Campbell entertained their chancellor several years ago. Just after I started working here as a Service by Agreement chef."

He wrinkled his nose. "That was before my time."

"Why are you asking about Armustan? After recent activities, I would think they would be the *last* dignitaries invited to the White House."

"Hmph," he said with a little head-waggle. "It's a good thing no one consults you on matters of international affairs then, isn't it? I am putting together an information sheet on Armustan and will require your assistance."

Cyan spoke up. "It wouldn't hurt to ask instead of order, you know."

Sargeant leveled an angry glare. "I'd be careful if I were you, young lady."

He looked ready to launch into a lecture, so I asked, "What will you need from me, Peter? I have a number of files and it would help if I knew what you wanted me to pull up."

He frowned at my interruption. "I'll let you know," he said. "But count on it soon."

When he left, I sighed. "I really don't get

it. What makes him so valuable?"

Cyan shrugged. "Don't let him spoil your good mood."

"I won't."

Just as I said that, Valerie Peacock knocked on the wall, and walked in. "Good morning," she said, smiling brightly. "Mrs. Hyden asked me to tell you how much the family enjoyed breakfast this morning. She said it was truly one of the finest meals they've ever had."

Cyan and I exchanged a happy glance.

"I'm here to discuss some big plans for your kitchen," Valerie continued, "events that are coming up very soon. President Hyden will be announcing his intention to open talks with Armustan and has invited Ambassador Kourosh to be his guest here at the White House for an official dinner."

Darned if Sargeant hadn't been right. "I'm surprised," I said.

"It's a controversial move, of course. But as you know, this administration wants to focus on building friendships with other nations. Even those with whom we have traditionally disagreed."

Armustan's wild-card rebels had taken our people hostage. I'd call that a lot more than a disagreement. But then again, I wasn't the leader of the free world. President Hyden and his advisors certainly had more experience in international affairs than I did.

I moved to the computer to access the calendar. "Do we have a date for this official dinner?"

She opened a folder to consult her notes, but I'm sure she had no doubt of the date. "February fourth."

"Wow," Cyan said, echoing my reaction. "Less than two weeks."

"Tensions have escalated with this . . . incident, and the president wants to move forward as quickly as possible to establish boundaries with these people," Valerie said.

We'd produced amazing dinners on far less notice than this. I wasn't worried. Still at the computer, I asked, "How many guests?"

"Approximately seventy-five."

I nodded, then asked her a few more pertinent questions about the event while I scribbled notes. "That's not too bad," I said. "We can have a menu to you very soon. Can we schedule a tasting for Mrs. Hyden this week?"

Valerie consulted her folder once again. "Let's see," she said as she flipped through pages. "It looks like Wednesday . . . no, sorry. Friday will work."

"Friday," I repeated, again making notes.

"Lunchtime?"

"Mmm, no." She jotted as she answered me. "I think this would be a lot of fun for the kids to take part in. How about we make it for later on Friday, after the kids get home from school?"

The kids' presence would change the tone of a tasting, for sure. But I was determined to roll with the punches. "Four o'clock?" I asked. "Five?"

Turning pages as she concentrated, she shook her head. "The First Lady has commitments taking her until six-thirty. Let's shoot for seven o'clock Friday evening, shall we?"

"Sure." I wrote it in.

That done, Valerie looked up, bright-eyed once again. "I have to say that I'm impressed with how accommodating everyone is here at the White House. You didn't even blink an eye at the short notice for the upcoming dinner."

"Ollie's the best," Cyan said. "She could probably pull off the dinner single-handedly and still impress all the guests."

Still beaming, Valerie turned to me. "That's wonderful to know. But I have some additional good news that ought to help make things easier for you all. Virgil Ballantine has decided not to take any personal time and will be here first thing tomorrow morning."

Like I'd taken a kick to the stomach, I flinched. "Already?"

"We are delighted to have him join us so quickly. The First Lady was afraid it might be several weeks before he was available, but he said he's eager to get started."

"That's great," I lied.

"And since he will be taking over the responsibility of the First Family's regular meals, that should free you and your staff up to work on the upcoming dinner. As well as others, of course. This administration will be entertaining quite a bit more often than the prior one did."

"That's great," I said again. Lying again.

"We will be holding a press conference at ten A.M. tomorrow to introduce Chef Ballantine and explain his new role at the White House. The First Lady would like you to be there as she makes the announcement. You won't be required to say anything, so don't worry about that. She just wants you there in the background so that the nation sees your support."

"Of course," I said.

As soon as she was gone, Cyan silently gripped my arm.

"In the background," I said. "Tomorrow I

get to come in on my day off to stand in the background while the new chef gets presented to the world."

"It'll be okay, Ollie," Cyan said.

But we both knew better.

Chapter 13

Cyan rushed in Monday morning, about ten minutes late. "Is the new guy here yet?"

In the middle of mixing batter for waffles, I didn't look up. "Nope. Paul left me a note. I guess Chef Ballantine isn't scheduled to arrive until just before the press conference." I gave an exaggerated look around the room. "And our babysitter guards are gone."

"That's weird. I wonder where they are." Peeling off her coat and donning an apron, Cyan frowned. "So no chance for us to meet the new guy before it's all official, huh?"

"That's what it sounds like to me."

Cyan grabbed a bowl of navel oranges and set herself up across from me to peel and section them. "You aren't supposed to be working today. Where's Bucky?"

I gestured upward with my chin. "He's talking with Marcel in the pastry kitchen," I said. "Since I'm here anyway, I might as well pitch in."

"Why are you here so early, anyway? The press conference isn't until ten."

"Are you kidding? I couldn't sleep."

Cyan gave me a sad look. "It's hard to think of a person we don't know taking over our kitchen, isn't it?"

Wiping my hands on my apron, I heaved a sigh. "My stomach is in knots."

"You'll be fine at the press conference."

"Yeah," I said. "In the *background*."

Bucky returned and we finished preparing breakfast. "What do we do now?" he asked when two butlers appeared to take the meal up to the residence. "Gardez and Nourie appear to be AWOL."

I placed a quick call to the Secret Service office and was connected to a female agent. I started to explain the situation, but it was immediately clear that she knew our agent guards were missing. "Didn't anyone contact you?" she asked.

"No," I said, "but that doesn't matter right now. We just need direction. All our meals were being taste-tested before they were served to the First Family. Breakfast is ready to be served. How should we proceed?"

There was a puzzled pause on her side of the line. "You don't have to worry about serving the First Family this morning," she finally said. "Breakfast has been prepared and is being served in the residence as we speak."

"What?" The exclamation came out before I had a chance to curb my reaction. "Wait, wait — what?"

"Agents Gardez and Nourie escorted the new chef to the residence early this morning," she said apologetically. "I was under the impression you'd been informed he was starting today."

As much as I felt like lashing out, I knew this wasn't her fault. Anger bubbled up so quickly, I had to stop myself from shooting the messenger. That would not only be unprofessional, it was just plain wrong. "I didn't know he'd be in this early," I said weakly. "Thanks for the update. I appreciate it."

I hung up, grateful that at least we'd been spared the embarrassment of serving breakfast to people who had already eaten. I turned to Bucky and Cyan, who watched me uneasily. "I hope you two are hungry," I said.

At 9:50, one of Valerie's assistants appeared in the kitchen. "We're ready for you, Ms. Paras," she said, hurrying me with a wave of her hand. "Don't forget your chef's hat."

169

No danger of that happening. The toque gave me a little height and I was going to need every inch I could get if I hoped to stand toe to toe with this new guy. Although I'd Googled him — repeatedly — there were no clear photos available of him online. There had been a few group shots where his face was very small, and a couple of side-view action shots of him preparing food, but nothing that gave me any indication of what he really looked like.

"Ms. Paras?" the assistant said again, her tone strained. "We need to get upstairs."

I had removed my stained apron and pulled on a dress tunic. "Yes, let's go," I said, positioning my toque on my head. With a final glance to Bucky and Cyan, who stared back morosely, I followed the assistant upstairs.

Today's press conference was to be held in the Blue Room, and my escort and I took a roundabout way past the gathered crowd of reporters through the State Dining Room and the Red Room to get there. The first floor buzzed with muted conversations, camera operators testing equipment, and Secret Service personnel directing visitors as White House assistants tried to herd groups into the Blue Room in an orderly manner.

Wearing a vibrant red dress and a concerned expression, the First Lady stood in the doorway to the Green Room. She nodded repeatedly to the aides prepping her. I tried not to look anxious, but couldn't withhold my gaze from racing around the room, looking for the mysterious new chef who had commandeered this morning's breakfast.

"This way, Ms. Paras." The assistant, whose name I didn't know, gestured me toward the back of the Blue Room and asked me to stand near the windows. The view to the south was beautiful, even on this cold January day. I tried calming myself by recalling the amazing experiences I'd had over the years here, but the memories felt strangely bittersweet — as though I sensed I might not ever experience such things again.

The assistant left me there and I dragged my attention back to the busy collection of reporters who jostled one another, wrote notes, and chatted among themselves while waiting for their audience with Mrs. Hyden. I glanced at my watch. Just a couple of minutes before the conference was to begin and I still hadn't caught sight of my new nemesis.

And then, there he was.

Milling about in the Green Room, he came into view just beyond Mrs. Hyden. I wondered if there was some conspiracy against my getting to see what he looked like, because just like with the Google shots online, I couldn't get a clear look at him. There were lots of aides in the Green Room and even though he now had his back to me, I could tell by his body language and the aides' rapt expressions that Chef Virgil Ballantine was having an easy and enjoyable conversation with them. Mrs. Hyden drew away from her small group to tap Chef Virgil on the shoulder and speak close to his ear.

Whatever she said, he found funny because they both laughed. And when he finally turned to face me I nearly gasped.

He was the "fan" who had bought us drinks when Cyan and I had visited Fizz.

At that very moment, he caught my stare and waved a small hello. Instinctively, I waved back. I'm afraid my mouth was open.

"It's time," someone said.

Bright lights flashed on as Mrs. Hyden and Virgil Ballantine stepped into the Blue Room to introduce the new White House chef to the world.

I removed my toque and gave Cyan and

Bucky a brief breakdown of the meeting upstairs. "It wasn't so bad," I lied when they asked me how it went. "I mean, even though both Mrs. Hyden and the new guy kept their backs to me for the entire press conference, it was nice not to be the center of attention for a change."

"I don't believe you for a minute," Bucky said. "This job has always meant everything to you. You live to work here."

I tried to cut him off. "I wouldn't exactly say that —"

"Well, I would, and I'm saying it because it's true and somebody needs to set you straight. This place is more than just a job to you, Ollie. And even though all of us feel privileged to work here, for you it's much more. Everybody knows it."

"We all —"

"I know what you're going to say, but think about it. How many other White House chefs have ever put their lives on the line the way you have?"

Bucky's accolades — if that's what they were — were embarrassing me. "So what are you telling me?" I asked. "That I'm fooling myself by believing I have a future here now that the new guy is on board?"

"Yeah. Pretty much that's exactly what I'm saying."

A few more of these gut-punch revelations and I might start getting used to them.

Cyan interrupted, clearly trying to defuse the situation. "Are you sure it was the same guy from Fizz?"

"Absolutely," I said. "I would have said something to him, but they shuttled me back down here just as soon as the official announcement was done."

Cyan asked, "Where is he now?"

I picked up a new apron and thought about putting it on. "Still upstairs. Taking questions from the crowd on his own." I stared at the fabric in my hand. "The assistant who walked me back told me that he's not returning to the kitchen today. Chef Virgil has a full day of interviews scheduled with various food magazines."

The looks on their faces reflected the acute disappointment I was feeling. "This is really happening, and there's nothing we can do about it but start fresh with him tomorrow morning," I said. "How are you two holding up?"

"Fine, great," Bucky said. Cyan agreed.

"Well then, how's this for a plan?" I asked. "Today's my day off and if you both are up to handling the day by yourselves, I'm going to take advantage of the time I have."

"Great idea, Ollie," Cyan said.

I put the apron back where I'd found it and tried to smile at my staff. "It's all going to work out. Maybe not the way we expect, but things always work out for the best eventually, right?"

Neither of them answered, but as I left, Cyan said, "Have a good time on your date tonight."

Oh yeah. That again.

I played Minesweeper on my computer until my eyes started to cross. Although a copy of my resume was open directly behind it, I couldn't summon enough resolve to actually work on it. I did change a couple of small things: I included my start and end dates as a Service by Agreement chef, but the time between when the White House hired me full-time until now was a gaping hole in my record. The idea of distilling my experiences in the White House kitchen to a few mere sentences seemed wrong. Rather than face a problem and tackle it head on the way I usually did, I'd opened up the game of Minesweeper instead. So far, I'd lost far more games than I'd won.

This family-chef challenge was taking more out of me than I would have expected. Although I had the resolve to face this new twist, it seemed as though I suffered a full-body slam at every turn. It was neither like me to give up, nor to procrastinate, but Sargeant's insidious predictions of my demise kept drumming in my head reminding me my days were numbered.

"This is stupid," I said aloud, and clicked out of the game.

After a moment's thought, I clicked out of my resume document as well. I needed to get outside. I needed to clear my head. I needed to find my mojo again.

As predicted, the day was drizzly and cold so I grabbed my heaviest jacket before I left. Just outside my door, I stopped to make sure it was locked.

"How are you, Ollie?" Mrs. Wentworth asked.

My hand jumped to my throat. "I'm doing just fine, how about you?"

"Sorry to startle you, honey," she said. "What do you think about that new chef your boss just hired?"

"I haven't actually had a conversation with him yet."

"He's kind of good-looking." She waved her cane toward my door. "And you don't have a boyfriend."

"I'm sure he's not my type."

"Now, how can you say that when you haven't even talked with him yet?" she chastised. Squinting, she peered at me for an extended moment. "Something bothering you?"

"No, not at all," I lied. "Just really busy."

"Hmm," she said, clearly not believing me. "I know there's things you can't tell me, but if there's anything troubling you, you feel free to come by for a chat. You hear?"

I nodded. "I will."

"Good girl." She cocked her head toward the elevators. "Now get outside in the fresh air. You look like you could use some."

I started out south toward 23rd Street. I wasn't hungry, but there were several home-grown restaurants that way, and I decided to visit one. I always felt better when I had a destination in mind, and a cup of hot coffee might be just the thing to perk me up.

With my collar close to my face against the sharp wind and the snap in the air keeping my steps brisk, I decided that I'd wallowed enough and it was time to either cook or give up my pots. "And we all know that's not gonna happen," I muttered to myself.

A woman dressed in expensive running clothes, jogging with a black lab, stopped as though startled. "Did you say something?"

I peeked my face up out of my collar

enough to answer. "Just talking to myself. Sorry."

She laughed. "We all do it." Resuming her trot as the lab pulled at the leash, she added, "Hope you find your answers."

Answers were exactly what I needed, and wasn't getting any. I slowed at the curb as a car turned left in front of me, and picked up my pace as soon as the walkway cleared. Although it stung, the cold felt fresh and invigorating. D.C. winters were much milder than the ones I remembered from my childhood in Chicago. If I ever moved back, I wondered if I'd be able to handle them again.

Taking a new job could give me the opportunity to move closer to my mom and nana. They were getting on in years, and I didn't get to see them nearly as often as I liked. They'd visited me out here exactly once, and although they had both come to appreciate our nation's capital — and my mom had even acquired a gentleman caller — I could tell they couldn't wait to get home. They felt safe and comfortable there, while I felt safe and comfortable here.

I stopped at the intersection, halted by a sudden realization. This was my life we were talking about. I wasn't just facing a job loss. I was facing the loss of an existence that had become almost as important to me as breathing. Bucky had nailed it this morning, though I hadn't wanted to admit it at the time.

Walking west, at a slower pace now, I put it all together. Instead of updating my resume and preparing for the worst, I needed to hold on to what I had with both fists. I'd always fought for what I wanted and I couldn't figure out why I was suddenly switching gears when it mattered most. Fortune favors the bold, so they say, and that's how I'd lived my life thus far.

Bolstered, I realized I *was* prepared to fight for what I wanted — and what I wanted most of all was to continue serving as White House executive chef until I retired.

I stopped in front of Uncle Pavel's Java Hut. This realization called for something stronger than an ordinary cup of coffee.

I pulled open the door and stepped up to the counter. The dark-haired young man asked, "What can I get you?"

"Café mocha, large. Extra hot, and don't be stingy with the whipped cream."

"Coming right up."

As I licked whipped cream from the top of the steaming beverage and stared out the window at the pedestrians with their heads tucked against the wind, I let myself relax. I was good at what I did. No. I *excelled* at what I did. This new fellow, Virgil, who barely made a mark on Google, would have no idea how to run the White House. He might be a good chef, even a great one. According to Paul, however, he would report to me. A chef like that would require a significant learning curve before he'd be able to take over the executive position.

I took a long sip of my chocolaty drink and convinced myself I'd been worried for nothing.

CHAPTER 14

A car wasn't a necessity in Washington, D. C., but there were times having one sure came in handy. Like right now, as I headed out for my date with Reggie. Rather than take the Metro and risk his offering to escort me to my station after dinner, I drove. I knew I'd pay dearly for valet parking, but there was no better way I could think of to make a quick and graceful exit if the opportunity presented itself.

I pulled up to the curb at the Morgenthal Hotel exactly five minutes early. The doorman accepted my keys and handed me a claim check. Before I could take three steps toward the automatic entry, a brown-uniformed valet had jumped into my little vehicle and zoomed off. I hoped they would be just as prompt when I was ready to leave.

Silently chastising myself, I entered the slow-moving revolving doors, determined to stop expecting the worst from the evening. I hadn't been out with anyone since Tom, and nervous jitters were to be expected. This could be fun, after all. Reggie was an accomplished chef — an award-winning one at that — and if nothing else, I knew we could have fun talking shop.

He was waiting for me just inside — holding a wool coat over his arm and a small bouquet of flowers in his hand. Wearing black pants, a black button-down shirt with an open collar, and a gray sport coat, he was leaning against a giant marble pillar that soared to the massive hotel's gilt ceiling. He smiled when he saw me and pushed away from the pillar to say hello.

"May I take your coat?" he asked.

Give him points for gentlemanliness. I unbuttoned my long down coat with the faux fur collar and allowed him to help me out of it.

"Wow, look at you," he said.

Because the Morgenthal was a classy establishment, I'd worn a black dress and black heels and, in a nod to comfort, had also tacked on a gray sweater against the ever-present restaurant chill. My outfit matched Reggie's ensemble almost exactly, and passersby might believe we'd intentionally coordinated our outfits.

"Isn't this cute?" he said as he moved a

bit closer.

His body language led me to believe he planned to greet me with a kiss on the cheek, which I neatly sidestepped as I reclaimed my coat and accepted the proffered flowers. "You really shouldn't have," I said, taking a polite whiff to express my appreciation for the profusion of blooms. "They're very beautiful. Thank you."

"Do you like roses? I've never met a woman who didn't like roses."

"Yes," I said, "very much. These are a lovely shade of pink. But really, you didn't need to go to any trouble."

He grinned. "I didn't really. As I was walking here, I saw them in the window of the drugstore down the street and thought they would set just the right tone."

I didn't know precisely what tone he was hoping to set, but decided it was better not to ask.

"I saw you pull up," Reggie continued. "You have a car? Where do you live?"

"Not too far." I gestured vaguely. "What about you?"

"I have an apartment nearby," he said. "I walk to work."

"That's pretty impressive." And it was. Here in the heart of D.C., apartments weren't cheap. I was well-paid, but a chef of

Reggie's caliber could make considerably more, especially if he taught classes or ran seminars for would-be chefs and foodie aficionados.

"Shall we?" he asked, gesturing across the expansive lobby. "Our table awaits."

My heels clicked on the high-gloss marble floor as we made our way to the elevators. The hotel's namesake restaurant was on the top floor and we shared the short ride up with another couple who stood so close together and smiled so often at each other that it was clearly not their first date.

We disembarked together, but let the other couple approach the maître d' first. Eschewing small talk, I used the brief wait to check out the surroundings. The entire outside wall of the restaurant was made up of floor-to-ceiling windows with gorgeous views of the Capitol, Washington Monument, and the National Mall.

The maître d' consulted his notes, smiled at Reggie, and escorted us to a table in the center of the dining room. "I requested a window view," Reggie said.

The maître d' glanced around. "I'm so sorry," he said. "There was no mention of that on your reservation. I just seated the couple before you at the last available window table."

"But I made a request specifically," Reggie said. "Did you catch my name?"

"Your name? I . . . it . . ."

"Stewart," Reggie said. "My name is Reggie Stewart."

Confusion twisted the maître d's features. "I'm sorry, sir . . ."

Clearly miffed, Reggie took a deep breath. "If my name doesn't mean anything to you, then maybe my date's does."

Instinctively I grabbed Reggie's forearm to prevent him from making a scene. He misinterpreted my gesture and placed his hand over mine, clasping so that I couldn't pull away without making a scene of my own. "This is Olivia Paras, the executive chef at the White House," he said loud enough for everyone to hear. "I can't believe you can't find a window seat for her."

Was it my imagination or did half the diners suddenly reach for their cell phones? I imagined a sudden rush to take my picture and tweet the headline: *White House diva executive chef demands special privileges at posh D.C. restaurant.*

"Please, Reggie," I said, trying to discreetly tug my hand back. "This is fine. I don't care to sit by the windows anyway. The food will taste just as good here." I smiled at the suddenly panicked maître d'.

"This is great. Thank you. We'll be fine."

Reggie, still holding tight said, "But I made a special request. This is a special night."

The maître d's eyes lit up. "Oh, a *special* night?" As though suddenly divested of an enormous weight, he said, "We do have a preferred table upstairs that we hold for very special patrons."

If either of them said the word *special* one more time, I was liable to grab a nearby dish and crack them over the head. Reggie first. "Really," I said, finally tugging my hand free and stepping away from the two of them. "This is fine. I like this table."

But Reggie had already begun to follow the maître d' toward a small, unobtrusive staircase I hadn't noticed earlier.

I hesitated before following. Had fifty people not begun to take notice of our antics in the center of this posh dining room, I might have used the opportunity to tell Reggie exactly where he could put his "special" table. To do so now, however, would be to bring more attention to an already uncomfortable situation. I reluctantly followed, reaching into my coat pocket to finger my valet claim check, and counting the minutes until I was back behind the wheel of my car.

If I had harbored any hope of checking out chef Jacob Flannery's cuisine without being noticed, those expectations were most certainly dashed. Working hard to make nice, now that he knew we were "important" guests, the maître d' nearly fell over himself in an effort to ensure we felt welcome. With great flourish, he sat us at a lone table in a tiny carved-out plateau just above the restaurant's main level.

I wriggled in my chair, more anxious than ever to get out of there. Leaving at this point was not an option unless I wanted to endure a media storm about my erratic behavior. For the most part I was able to shop, dine, and pretty much act like a normal person in public places without notice. Even with everything I'd been involved in at the White House, my face was not that well known — which was just the way I liked it. But the moment Reggie had proclaimed my status to everyone within hearing distance, all bets were off and my best manners were on.

I stared out the window next to me and sighed, wishing I was home in my flannel pajamas reading a book or watching TV. Anywhere but here.

"Beautiful, isn't it?" Reggie asked, misinterpreting me yet again.

The moment we were left to ourselves at

this lonely table, I tried to take control. "Reggie," I said, "I would really have preferred we sit at the first place he put us."

He grinned, completely ignoring me. "I wanted nothing but the best for you tonight."

I tried again, a little less gently this time. "The best would have been to *not* make a scene." Leaning forward and gesturing with my hands, I lowered my voice even though there was no one within range to hear me. "I don't like people knowing I work at the White House. There's too much that can go wrong."

He grasped my right hand. "I'll protect you."

I yanked my hand away. "That's not what I mean. I have to protect my image."

He sat back, decidedly amused. "I get you now." Nodding sagely, he continued. "I can be a diva because I'm a famous chef. You can't be a diva because it's the White House that's famous. Not you."

Not exactly how I'd put it, but whatever worked. "Something like that," I said.

"I gotcha." He leaned his head forward, looked both ways, spy-like, and whispered, "I'll be more careful."

"Thanks," I said, not meaning it at all. Fortunately for me, the waiter appeared just then to take our drink orders. I told him I would be fine with water, which disappointed Reggie to no end.

"Wouldn't you like to do a pairing?" he asked with wide, hopeful eyes. "I've heard marvelous things about this restaurant's sommelier."

The sooner dinner was done, the happier I'd be. "I'm driving, sorry."

Reggie ordered a bottle of red. I didn't know exactly what vintage he'd chosen because he simply pointed at the wine list and smiled when the waiter said, "Very good, sir."

After the customary uncorking, smelling, and tasting, Reggie pronounced his choice perfect and the waiter filled his glass. He poised the bottle over my empty one and I demurred once again. "No, thank you."

"You mean you're going to make me finish this great bottle all by myself?"

I smiled with my hand still over my glass. "I will never make you do anything."

We finally placed our dinner orders and conversation resumed a more normal path. I listened as Reggie recited story after story — every one sharing the same theme: Poor Reggie had been wronged again and again. He never got credit for being the fantastically amazing guy he was.

He started to repeat himself. "Did I tell you about the guest who returned his meal to the kitchen five times before accepting it?"

"Yes, you did," I said. Because I couldn't take another minute of his constant self-praise, I asked, "So what was wrong with the food, anyway?"

"Nothing was wrong with the food." Reggie gave his wineglass an indignant swirl. "In fact, the fifth time he sent the plate back, all I did was stick it in the microwave and zap it until it was ridiculously hot and hard as a brick. I topped it with a couple of carrot shreds and an extra sprig of parsley and, voila! The customer suddenly found it perfect."

"Lucky for you."

"No luck," he said. "Talent. I know people. This guy was just going for the power play. Trying to prove to his tablemates that he knew food better than I did." Reggie drained his glass and then refilled it. "I showed him."

The waiter reappeared with our food and I picked up my knife and fork just as soon as my plate touched the table, intending to dig right in and hoping to encourage Reggie to do the same. He watched me for a moment. "Don't you want to examine the dish before we taste it?" Frowning, he lifted one edge of his plate and tilted it from side to side. "What do you think of his color palette?"

"Gorgeous," I said. "Stunning." I sliced off a sizeable serving of scallop and popped it into my mouth, immediately making a "Yum" face so that he would understand why I couldn't wait to gobble the food all up.

"Don't you think your plate is far too yellow?" He pointed. "Look at the china pattern. Don't you think the chef should consider color presentation when he's creating his meals?"

I swallowed and gestured toward Reggie's plate with my fork. "Yours looks fabulous, too. Better enjoy it while it's hot."

Again he tilted his plate from side to side. As the juices from his medium-rare Morgenthal Signature steak rolled back and forth, I sensed he was making a decision. "This hasn't been properly charred," he finally said. Glancing around, he tried summoning our waiter. Of course, being the only table on our level made that a little tricky.

"You're sending it back?" I asked between mouthfuls.

"Of course," he said clearly distressed.

"Can't you see that this is all wrong? I can't accept this. Not in good conscience."

Please, please, please just eat, I silently begged. The sooner he finished, the sooner this painful evening would be over.

He stood, grabbing the linen napkin from his lap and waving it in the air in an attempt to catch our waiter's attention. I kept my eyes averted, pretending to be somewhere else. Reggie sat solidly and proclaimed, "He's on his way now. About time, too."

Much to my disappointment, Reggie did return his meal for proper charring. As the plate was whisked away, amid much apologizing, I placed my utensils back on the table.

"Go ahead and eat before it gets cold," Reggie said with the first real look of concern he'd displayed all evening. "No sense in waiting."

Torn between politeness and not wanting to waste food, I started in again. Without a meal to occupy his attention, Reggie started talking again. "What can you tell me about that hostage situation at the hospital?" he asked.

With my mouth full of scallop, I couldn't do much more than shake my head. I raised my napkin to my mouth until I was finished with that bite. "Not much more than what you've seen on TV or read about," I said. "The men who arranged the siege have been incarcerated — all but one of them. If it weren't for Sandy Sechrest's intervention, I'm sure things could have gone much differently."

He narrowed his eyes. "I bet you know more than you're telling. Come on, you can't tell me that you don't hear secrets in the White House."

I smiled, and forked another bite from my plate. "They wouldn't be secret anymore if I told you, would they?"

He leaned forward with a strange glint in his eye. "What would you say if I were to tell you that I know a White House secret? A big one."

My fork hovered between the plate and my mouth. "I'd think you were bluffing."

He laughed and leaned back. "I like you. You're so funny."

I glanced back in the direction the waiter had gone. Where was Reggie's dinner?

"But I do have inside information," he said, his tone practically begging me to ask what it was.

Instead, I sliced off another large piece of scallop and popped it in. Couldn't talk with my mouth full. Whatever he had to tell me about the White House was not worth the effort.

"This information," he continued, not letting the subject die, "is part of the reason why I wanted to ask you to dinner tonight. I thought you ought to know, and I thought it would be best if you heard it from me."

He wasn't going to stop until I expressed interest. "Well then, please," I said without any enthusiasm whatsoever, "don't keep me in suspense another minute."

With a self-satisfied smile, he leaned back, glanced from side to side, and then leaned forward again. At that moment, the waiter returned with a heavily charred, giant steak, which he placed before Reggie. "Our compliments, sir," the waiter said. "For your inconvenience, we have provided a more generous cut and prepared it according to your preferences."

Reggie stared down at the sizzling plate with obvious satisfaction. "That's more like it."

Looking relieved, our waiter asked if there was anything else we needed and left.

"Ah," Reggie said, slicing a big chunk of steak. "Perfection." He winked at me. "See, this is how they understand who's boss."

I wanted to ask how his reasoning jibed with his earlier diatribe about the unpleasant patron who had sent food back to the kitchen. Tempted as I was to ask what made *this* situation different, I figured I probably already knew the answer: Reggie — whether in the role of chef or diner — couldn't ever possibly be wrong.

Shoving food into his cheek, he grinned. Despite the fact that he wasn't a bad-looking fellow, this was not a pretty sight. "I'm telling you, it's a good thing you're sitting down for this tidbit," he said, clearly pleased with himself. "You ready?"

I placed my utensils on my plate, signaling I was finished eating. "Believe me, I'm ready."

Reggie had dark eyes, and in the split second before he opened his mouth, I caught a flash of cruelty in them. Whatever he was about to say gave him pleasure, and I could tell he expected I wasn't going to like it.

"You know that new chef they announced today?"

"Virgil Ballantine, yes."

Reggie sliced another piece and chewed, stringing out the suspense. "How much do you like your job?"

"Why?"

Smiling now, sensing he had me engaged, he gave a self-deprecating shrug. "Virgil and

I go way back," he said. "We went to culinary school together, but I got the better job when we graduated and I've been moving up the ladder ever since." With a so-so motion of his head, he went on. "Virgil gets some good write-ups, for sure. He's no slouch. But he just doesn't have the personality I do."

Thank God for that.

"Virgil's more into skill and creativity than he is the business of being a chef." As though that were a terrible proclamation, Reggie said, "We used to think we might start a place together. But when we both got out of school, I knew it wouldn't be right. I decided against working together, even though Virgil really wanted to give it a go. I knew it wasn't going to work."

I wondered what the real reason was behind their preempted business plans.

Reggie added, "He's gunning for your job now. Told me about it last week when he was in town. I think he's seen how successful I've been by cooperating with the media, and now he wants the life I have." Pointing at me, gun-style, he pretended to shoot. "He's aiming for you."

I just sat there, wanting more than ever to rush out of this place and never return.

With a nasty grin, he splayed his hands

over his dish in a "What do you have to say about that?" gesture.

"If this guy is your friend, then why forewarn me?"

He resumed eating, staring down at the plate as he sliced off another hunk of meat. "You and I are very much alike."

"We're nothing alike."

He stopped chewing and looked up. "Sure we are."

The waiter made it to the top of the steps, warily gauging our progress. "I'd like this wrapped, please," I said. So consumed was I with the prospect of escape, I'd barely noticed any flavors in the expensive scallop dinner I'd eaten. At least there was enough on my plate to take home.

He whisked my plate away and asked if I would like coffee.

"No, thank you."

"I'm not even halfway done," Reggie said petulantly when the waiter departed with my dish. "I can't believe you had him take yours while I was still eating."

"I just couldn't stand it any longer," I said.

He nodded, appeased. "I get you. Yeah, the sauce was starting to congeal. Very unappetizing."

He had no idea.

When the waiter came back with my

leftovers in a fancy bag, Reggie pushed his plate forward. "This was all right. Nothing to write home about." He winked and pointed at me. "Tell your chef she said that."

"But I didn't."

Reggie waved a finger over his plate. "I'll take mine to go, too. Gotta leave room for dessert."

The waiter gave a little bow, then asked, "Shall I put these in the same bag?"

I gave a sharp jerk. "No!"

After what seemed like forever, Reggie received his own take-home bag and the waiter inquired about dessert. "No, no," I said quickly, having anticipated this moment. "I really need to get home. Early start tomorrow."

"What do you have going?" Reggie asked.

"So much I can't even begin to list it all. It gets like that before state dinners, and we've got one coming up soon."

"Virgil was always especially good at managing large affairs," Reggie said thoughtfully. "That was one skill he really excelled at."

Oh, joy of joys. Now the one thing I thought I could hang my hat on — the one thing I had been certain would prove I could cook circles around Virgil Ballantine — was being whisked out from under me as quickly as my plate had.

Downstairs in the Morgenthal lobby, Reggie offered to get my car from the valet so I wouldn't have to go out in the cold. "I'm fine," I said. "I like this weather."

God save me from all the lies I'd been telling lately.

He walked me outside and insisted on waiting with me until my car was retrieved. "I really enjoyed our dinner," he said. "Maybe I'll let you return the favor. You can take *me* out next time. It doesn't have to be this nice. I figure I make more money than you do."

Appalled, I was struck speechless once again.

"What are you doing Friday?" he asked. "I've got the night off."

Right then, my car arrived. "Sorry," I said, running around the back before Reggie could move in for the kiss. I tipped the valet and waved him away, even though he clearly wanted to close my door for me. Over the roof of my car I said, "I'm running a tasting Friday night. First one with the new lady of the house. It'll take hours."

He frowned, then raised his hand to wave as I dropped into my seat and slammed the door. "I'll call you," he shouted.

I put the car into drive and pulled away. "Yeah, but I won't answer."

CHAPTER 15

I drove home in a silent huff, furious with myself for agreeing to the disastrous date in the first place. I'd known better. I should have trusted my gut. But I'd hedged this time. I knew exactly why I'd agreed to go out with Reggie even though I hadn't wanted to: I was afraid of hurting his feelings. Shaking my head as I drove, I wondered how many people in this world were stuck in uncomfortable situations at this very moment just because they'd attempted to spare someone else's feelings. I realized that instead of making me feel worse, the thought actually made me smile. I wasn't alone. Lots of people would have done what I did.

Just as I made it through the front door of my apartment building and said hello to James at the desk, my cell phone rang. "No," I said aloud, knowing without a doubt that this was Reggie calling to tell me what a nice time he'd had and how much he wanted to do it again.

James looked up. "That the White House calling you back in to work?"

I pulled up the little device and checked the display. "No," I said. "I don't recognize the number." I also noticed I had one missed call.

Waving good night to James, I made my way toward the elevators. "Hello?"

"Ollie?" Not Reggie. My whole body relaxed.

"Yes."

The caller was silent.

"Who is this?" I asked.

"Are your deductive skills so rusty that you can't figure it out?" The voice mocked me and then I heard, "*Tsk.* I was sure you'd have me at hello."

I felt a rush of pleasure. "Gav?"

There was a smile in his voice when he answered, "That's my girl."

"How are you? Where are you?" I asked. I hadn't heard from Special Agent in Charge Leonard Gavin for some time. Although he and I kept in occasional contact, we'd only run into each other once or twice over the past few years.

"I'm in town," he said, keeping it intentionally vague, as I knew he would. "Official stuff, what else? I thought I'd give you a call and see why you haven't solved the recent crisis yet."

I laughed. "According to the TV reports, everything's solved. Haven't you heard?"

Again the *tsk*. "My sources tell me there's more going on in the background. So deep even Momma Bear doesn't know."

"Well, aren't you plugged in?"

"Just doing my job, ma'am."

I stood in the quiet elevator bank, hearing my voice echo. "I'm going into an elevator right now. If we lose signal, can I call you right back?"

"I only have a minute here anyway," he said. "I just wanted to see if you were free Friday night. I thought we could get coffee and catch up."

"I'd love that," I said, then stopped myself when I remembered. "Oh, but I can't. I'm doing a tasting Friday night. And you know what that means."

"Yeah." He sighed. "But it was worth a try."

Impulsively I asked, "What about Saturday?"

"Can't do Saturday. I might be gone by then. Lots of stuff happening. I can tell you some of it, but not on the phone."

"Now I'm really tempted."

"You weren't before?"

"Of course I was." I laughed, then immediately sobered. "I'm sorry the timing isn't going to work out." I hoped he could hear the disappointment in my voice. "Let me know if things change."

"Things *are* changing, Ollie. That's part of what I wanted to talk with you about." Someone in the background called to him. "Gotta go," he said. "I'll be in touch."

He hung up before I could say anything further.

It didn't sound as though I'd be hearing from him again anytime soon. But as I rode up the elevator to my floor, I made sure to program his number into my phone for future reference.

The next morning, Cyan came rushing in, her face still red from the outside chill. "How was your date?" she asked as she unzipped her jacket. "I wanted to call you last night, but I didn't know if it went" — she waggled her eyebrows — "extra late."

"Don't even go there," I said, putting up my hands. "Any more evenings like that one and I'll be begging Tom to take me back."

She looked at me with sympathy. "That bad?"

I didn't have a chance to answer when,

speak of the devil, Tom walked in. His manner was far too casual for comfort. He made an effort to consult with Gardez and Nourie, and say hello to my staff. Something was up. After an extended schmooze, he turned to me. "Got a minute, Ollie?"

"You're in early," I said, checking my watch as I followed him out of the room. "What's up?"

"I know you're going to be busy with that new chef today, so I wanted to catch you privately before the day got away from both of us."

We stood in the center hallway just outside the kitchen. At this time of the morning, the place was relatively quiet. "You can't talk in front of Bucky and Cyan?" I asked.

"There's been a development," he said. "I'll be speaking with a few members of the staff, including Paul, a little later today to bring everyone up to date. You were in the meeting when we discussed one of the butlers possibly having seen one of my agents carry in the chicken wing box."

"Right."

"I can't get into details, but we've discovered who that agent was."

I gasped. "Who was it?"

"Not now. Not here. But I can assure you he has been removed from duty and is being questioned."

This was big news. "You really believe one of your agents —"

He held up a hand. "This is not for discussion. But I needed you to know."

"Why? What do you need from me?"

"You may be called in. Corroboration, if possible. What I need you to do is to go over every moment of Inauguration Day in your mind and try to think if there was any detail, no matter how small it might seem, that you left out."

I was about to assure him that I'd already done that, but I could tell Tom wasn't in a particularly chatty mood. "I have a lot of follow-up today," he said, dismissing me. "And I'm sure you do, too."

"Does this mean your department is being investigated?"

"What do you think?"

Pieces clicked in my brain. "Gav," I said. "Gav is in charge of this investigation."

Tom's face twitched. Looking ready to explode, he stepped closer, "I'd like to know how you happen to have that information about Special Agent in Charge Gavin."

"He called me last night."

"To tell you about his assignment?"

"Of course not." I jammed my fists into my hips. "He wanted to go for coffee Friday night," I said. "He didn't say what brought him to town, just that he was here. It doesn't take a rocket scientist to put two and two together, you know."

Tom pulled back. "He asked you out?"

"Not like that," I said. "We were just going to catch up."

His frown relaxed. "*Were?* So you're not going?"

"Can't," I said. "Mrs. Hyden's first tasting is scheduled for Friday night."

"Good."

Part of me was dying to ask if he was jealous, but I knew if I did, he'd only clam up further. We were slowly but steadily working to find a comfortable common ground. Joking about our prior relationship could jeopardize the rocky alliance we'd forged.

"Am I dismissed?"

Tom nodded and began to turn away.

"Oh hey, one more thing," I said to his departing back.

He lifted an eyebrow.

I closed the distance between us and lowered my voice. "There's nothing *forbidding* me from talking with Special Agent Gavin, is there?"

The hard expression was back. "I thought you weren't planning to see him."

I waved to encompass the area. "If he's

investigating this, he's going to be around."

Tom got a strange look on his face. "He's working out of a remote location."

I shrugged. "But Agent Gavin is completely apprised on the whole situation?"

Visibly exasperated, Tom answered, "Yes," pivoted, and strode away.

"Thanks for the update," I said.

He just kept walking.

Paul called to us from the doorway almost immediately after I returned to the kitchen, "Good morning, everyone. I'd like to introduce you to our new chef." He smiled at me. "Ollie, I believe you've already met Virgil Ballantine."

I stepped forward, hand extended. "It's a pleasure to get a chance to actually speak with you," I said. "We didn't even have the chance to say hello during the media event."

"No, we didn't," Virgil said. His handshake was firm, his age probably a shade younger than I had originally pegged him when he'd nodded hello at Fizz. I put him in his late thirties.

He raised dark eyebrows and smiled, exposing deep dimples. "I'm so glad to finally get this chance to experience the real White House kitchen," he said. "So far I've only worked upstairs in the residence. This," he pointed downward, "is where the magic happens. I'm honored to be here."

Give him points for making a good first impression. "We are very happy to have you join us," I said, momentarily confused. I had been under the impression that this Virgil Ballantine would be working almost exclusively upstairs, and only here with us as required. Then I remembered. "Especially with our upcoming state dinner next week."

Virgil's head tilted. He turned to Paul. "Did I miss a memo?"

"Some staff members are new here," Paul began. I knew he was talking about Mrs. Hyden's social secretary, Valerie. "We're all still trying to work out the most efficient way to get information out to all key personnel. I'm sure it was just an oversight."

Recovering from this bit of news, Virgil said, "Well, that just means we get to work that much faster, doesn't it? Who are we entertaining?"

I told him. "And," I added, "I understand you have a great deal of experience with these sorts of events."

Virgil's eyebrows came together. Someone really ought to tell him they needed trimming. "Who would have told you that?"

Might as well get everything out in the open. "I had a chance to talk with one of your friends recently." Too bad I hadn't had a chance to bring Cyan completely up to date on last night's fiasco. Pointing to her, I said, "Cyan and I had dinner at the Buckwalk a few nights ago."

"Ah," Virgil said, understanding now, his expression less than pleased. "Reggie."

"He was very excited to meet Ollie," Cyan said. She looked ready to tell him that Reggie and I had gone out on a date, but after reading the warning look on my face, she must have thought better of it. "He seemed very nice."

"How was the food?" Virgil asked, artfully steering the subject away from discussion of his friend. I recognized the tactic; I used it myself all the time. "That's why you went there, right?"

"Pretty excellent," Cyan said.

Paul stepped back, and clapped his hands together. "It seems you are all set here. I won't keep you from your work."

Virgil turned to him expectantly. When Paul turned to leave, Virgil stopped him. "I'm sorry," he said, "but don't you have more to share with the staff?"

Taken aback, Paul sent me a quizzical glance. "I don't think so," he said. "Ollie has had a copy of your curriculum vitae since we found out you were joining the team. Knowing her, she's gone over it closely and I'm sure you're going to be very happy here." Paul, as always, was extremely polite and attuned to those around him. I could tell he was sensing the same thing I was: Virgil was still unsatisfied. Obviously unsure of what that was, Paul said, "I know I join the entire staff in welcoming you to the White House."

We waited through a long, awkward silence.

Virgil nodded. "Thank you. Of course. Thank you very much." He coughed. "I find myself in an uncomfortable situation here." Smiling, though his eyes were anything but cheery, Virgil turned to all of us. "I am very pleased to take over here, and I'm very, very delighted to discover that you are all so experienced in all White House protocols. That's exactly where I'm lacking, but of course most eager to learn."

A sickening feeling began to crawl up my insides.

He continued, "I feel so strange here." With a laugh meant to cover his nervousness he opened his hands. "I expected my appointment as head chef to be mentioned during the introduction. I find myself in the uncomfortable —"

It was at that moment I felt my heart drop

to the floor. I swore I could hear it go *splat.*

"Wait a minute," Paul interrupted. "This is not my understanding. Ollie is the executive chef here. That hasn't changed."

"But . . ." Virgil's eyes widened in alarm, "when I was hired, I was told that I would be in charge of all the family's meals."

"Yes," Paul said. "Their *personal* meals. The running of the main kitchen remains in Ollie's capable hands."

Like magic my heart leapt back to its proper place. It might have even swelled a little.

"But," Virgil said, turning to me. "No disrespect intended, I was promised total control of the kitchen."

"Of the residence kitchen," Paul said firmly. "I have a copy of your employment agreement and there is no mention whatsoever of you taking over the executive chef position."

"But when . . ." Virgil stopped himself.

"Perhaps we had better discuss this in my office," Paul said wearily, leading a flabbergasted Virgil out. At the doorway, Paul turned and gave me a smile that I think was meant to give me confidence. But my insides had turned to Jell-O.

The moment they were out of earshot, Bucky and Cyan were at my side. "What was that all about?" Bucky asked.

The two of them peppered me with questions I had no answers for. "I don't know," I said. "It seems there's more bad news or more trouble every time I turn around." I couldn't explain why, at that moment, the old joke, "Well, then . . . quit turning around!" came to mind.

"Can Paul really prevent Virgil from taking over your job if the First Lady insists?" Bucky asked, echoing my very thoughts.

"I don't think so. Whatever the First Lady wants, she's going to get. I don't know what to do here."

"Don't panic," Cyan said. "That's what you always tell me when things go wrong."

"I'm not," I said, then amended, "Okay, that's a lie."

Cyan's eyes were purple today, but the concern in them was clear. "Maybe you should take today off. We can handle things here."

I barked a laugh, which came out so rudely that I quickly apologized. "I know you mean well, but that's the last thing I should do. With a state dinner scheduled for next week, I can't possibly leave today."

Cyan opened her mouth to argue, but I cut her off. "Not to mention that I need to be here when Virgil and Paul return." I had no doubt they would. Probably soon, too. "A show of strength. No matter what the outcome, I need to face it, head on."

They murmured agreement, but I could tell their hearts weren't in it. Cyan gripped my arm. "The job isn't everything. Remember that. You have to look out for yourself. Decide what's right for you."

Even Gardez and Nourie looked away. I was getting pretty tired of having so many dramatic moments play out in front of an audience.

Trying to find a bright side — of which there really was none — I reasoned that if Chef Ballantine did indeed snag the top job, these two Secret Service babysitters might be assigned elsewhere. The problem was, maybe I would be assigned elsewhere, too.

I pulled away. All this sympathy was making me feel trapped. "The right move for me is to throw myself into making this reception a success," I said, jamming my index finger onto the countertop for emphasis. "That's it. I am still the executive chef here, even if it's just for the next five minutes. It's my responsibility to make sure we create the best state dinner ever."

CHAPTER 16

An hour passed, minute by agonizing minute. I glanced at the clock — again — wondering what was taking Paul so long to get things squared away with Virgil. Had the issue been cut-and-dried, they would have been back in five minutes. This was taking a long time. Much too long for it to be good news.

The Chesapeake crab agnolottis I hoped to serve the First Lady at Friday's tasting, and ultimately at the state dinner, were giving me fits. I blamed my lack of concentration for the pasta's overstickiness. Although I'd kneaded the mound of dough for the full fifteen minutes before rolling it out, it just didn't feel right.

The dough was supposed to be smooth, golden, and elastic. Even stretchy. But it sat there like a pale, rebellious lump, daring me to make it succeed.

"You sure you measured right?" Cyan asked.

"I thought I did." Sighing, I looked at the pile on the countertop. "Maybe I forgot the last cup of flour," I said.

"That might be it."

"Quit looking at me with such pain on your face," I said.

"I'm sorry." She gave a surreptitious glance toward the clock. "What's taking so long?"

"I wish I knew." Then the light dawned. "He's probably preparing lunch. That's got to be it. I mean, we can't let the president and his wife go hungry while staffing issues are sorted out, can we?"

"I'm sure you're right," Cyan said, and went off to prepare the basil oil, which we would drizzle over these agnolottis, if I ever got that far with this mess. Rather than start from scratch, I added flour to my recalcitrant mixture, and within minutes it started to behave.

Having consoled myself with the belief that Virgil was busy upstairs with foodstuffs and that his talk with Paul was undoubtedly settled, I finally started to lose myself in my work. We had prepared the crab filling ahead of time, so once the agnolotti dough was in shape, I set to the laborious, but normally fun, process of assembling them. If these came out the way I expected them to, the First Lady would be thrilled to serve them to our state dinner guests.

So absorbed was I in my task that I actually forgot to keep tabs on the clock, and indeed let my mind wander. I wondered what Mrs. Hyden's reaction to the tasting would be. I remembered the first one I had conducted on my own, just a few short years ago for Mrs. Campbell. Peter Sargeant had been new on the job, but that hadn't prevented him from commandeering much of the event. Bucky, who had come up with a fabulous Brussels sprouts recipe, had been crushed when our sensitivity director had removed it from the list with derogatory statements about the little green sprouts.

We had since served Bucky's delightful dish at other events — to much success and many compliments — and my first order of business after taking over as executive chef was to keep Peter Sargeant from participating in any tastings going forward.

I smiled. There hadn't been a lot of changes here in the kitchen since Henry, the former executive chef, left, but I was pleased with our progress, and proud of all the wonderful food we'd prepared for the First Family and their guests over the years.

With few exceptions, every dinner had been a major success.

"What are you thinking about?" Cyan asked, breaking into my reverie. "Last night's date?"

"Yeah, right." I rolled my eyes.

"You didn't get a chance to tell me about it," she said. "I can't believe it was as bad as you're making it sound."

I kept my voice down. "I don't think I can even describe how terrible it was, Cyan. The man is so stuck on himself I'm surprised we didn't need to pull up extra chairs to accommodate his ego."

She giggled. "Maybe he was just trying to impress you."

I dampened my fingers again before running them along the edge of a filled pasta square and placing another square atop it. "Oh, he impressed me, all right." I pressed the edges together. "And he's good friends with our executive chef wannabe."

"I was going to ask you about that."

"Trouble," I said. "That's all we seem to run into lately."

Cyan's gaze jerked up, over my head. "Well, here it comes again," she said.

I turned, expecting a gloating visit from Sargeant. I was surprised, instead, to see Virgil Ballantine, alone. "Can I speak with you for a moment, Ollie?" he asked. His face was a solemn mask. Those bushy eyebrows were pulled together tightly, obscuring his eyes.

"Sure." I wiped my hands and Cyan said she'd take over for me. I started to gesture toward the refrigerated area, but he shook his head.

"Would you mind if we went out here?" He tilted his head toward the hall. "This will just take a couple minutes."

My stomach threatened to expel whatever I'd eaten so far today, and my face felt hot and tight. But I said, "Sure," again, and followed him out.

Just as we stepped into the hall, Valerie Peacock hurried over. She had been speaking with another staffer at the east end, but stopped when she saw me. With a clipboard pressed to the chest of her tweed jacket, she ran on her toes, as though to keep the heels of her black sling-backs from clacking against the floor. "Great," she said, "I'm so glad to catch you both. I have some updates on the state dinner."

I glanced to Virgil, but his expression was inscrutable. Valerie's manner as she handed us printed updates gave nothing away. I was sure she not only knew which one of us was the head of the kitchen, I was absolutely certain she'd recently been consulted on that very matter. All business, Valerie asked us several questions about the menu. "I like the menu, very interesting," she said.

"Thank you," I said. "We like to feature American food at every opportunity. I have ingredients being brought in for the tasting and if all goes well, I . . . er, that is . . . *we* will be placing orders for the dinner next week."

She nodded. "Of course."

She had several more questions about procedure that Virgil wasn't able to answer, and after about ten minutes, headed back toward the East Wing to consult with the calligraphy department.

The moment she left, Virgil started toward the China Room. I pointed slightly farther ahead. "Let's use the Vermeil Room instead."

Nodding agreeably, he let me enter first. Often called the Gold Room, and featuring a collection of vermeil — gold-plated silver — the space also featured famous paintings of many First Ladies. I wondered, idly, if Mrs. Hyden's portrait would ever hang here alongside those of Jackie Kennedy, Pat Nixon, Eleanor Roosevelt, Nancy Reagan, and others. I was sure it would. The walls were soft yellow, the fireplace similar, if not identical to the one on the China Room's adjacent wall. I ran my fingers along the mantel and tried to encourage the quiet cheer of the room to bolster my spirits. I had no idea what Virgil Ballantine was about to say. I was just glad we weren't in the kitchen.

Leaving the door open, he joined me at the fireplace. "I think we may have gotten off to a bad start," he said.

I opened my mouth to answer before I knew exactly what I planned to say — a habit I hoped to break one of these days — but was spared by the arrival of an older woman who knocked at the door and walked in. Although we hadn't yet met, I knew her immediately as Grandma Marty, Mrs. Hyden's mother. "Excuse me," she said with a wide smile. "Am I interrupting?"

"Not at all," Virgil and I said in unison.

I was about to ask if I could help her in any way, but she was clearly making a beeline for Virgil. "How are you, dear?" she asked, reaching both hands out to clasp his. With only a flash of crow's-feet next to her eyes, and tiny, shallow lines around her mouth, Grandma Marty looked a lot younger in person than she really was. She carried a few extra pounds around her middle, and she'd let her short, tight hair go gray, but I would never have tagged her as the mother of a woman over forty.

"I'm doing very well," Virgil said.

Grandma Marty released Virgil and turned to me. "I'm the children's grandmother," she said politely. "And who are you?"

My throat caught. Was I still the executive chef or wasn't I? "Olivia Paras," I said, "but I much prefer that you call me Ollie."

Still smiling, she gave me a head-to-toe once-over. "Well, I can tell you work in the kitchen. And what a lovely name, Olivia. It suits you."

"Thank you."

"Virgil, dear," she said, returning to her original conversation. "I'm planning to have a few of my old friends come to visit next week. Do you think you can pull something together for a bunch of old ladies?"

"What did you have in mind?"

She waved her hands in front of her face. "Oh, you always work such magic. And you know what I like. Just surprise us."

He nodded.

She winked at him. "Good, I knew you wouldn't mind." She started toward the door. "It was very nice to meet you, Olivia. Don't let Virgil work you too hard." This time she winked at me. "From all reports he cracks the whip over his employees, but they love him for it."

I could feel my temples throb. Every inch of me wanted to scream. I couldn't just hand my livelihood over to a man who had never run — never even *worked* — in the White House before. This wasn't fair. Instead, as she walked out of the room, I tried to quell the buzzing in my brain, the rush of heat from my chest to my face, and the sheer panic that was making my fingers twitch. I swallowed around sandpaper in my throat.

"She's such a nice lady," Virgil said.

Was he completely oblivious to my angst? In one wild and angry moment, I wished he *would* take over the kitchen. Right now. Today. Let him run this house and the upcoming state dinner. Let's see how well he would do, coming in cold like this.

I blew out a breath, and, at the very moment I let that thought take hold, I also realized he would do just fine without me. He would still have Bucky and Cyan. They were professionals who excelled at their jobs. Even if all Virgil did was sit in a corner and drool, Bucky and Cyan would make the man look good.

I swallowed again. It still hurt. There wasn't much I could do at this point except make a graceful exit. "Well, good luck," I said.

"I forgot to ask her which day next week."

"Excuse me?"

Virgil made a face at the doorway. "I'm sure Valerie will know. But I was so pre-occupied with our conversation," he used his index finger to make a you-and-me gesture, "that I wasn't concentrating on what Grandma Marty was saying. But I do know what she likes, and I'll come up with a good menu. She's always so easy to please."

"That's great," I said blandly. There were a thousand questions running through my brain. I wanted to know if I was still employed. Since Paul wasn't here to deliver this bad news, I assumed I still had a job at least. I wondered what my new title would be. I wondered what the media would have to say about this shake-up. I could almost hear the reporters' glee. There had been too many instances where my name appeared in the paper when it had nothing to do with food, and I worried that they would take advantage of an opportunity to sell more papers.

I realized Virgil was waiting for me to speak. But I couldn't imagine what else there was to say. Holding my hands up, I asked, "Well?"

"I'm very sorry," he said.

I knew what was coming and I steeled myself to hear the actual words.

"When I came here to the White House, I knew that I had been hired as the family's main chef . . ."

All I could think was: *Cut to the chase, already!*

But he droned on about how much the Hyden family meant to him and why this position was the culmination of all he'd worked for. Yadda, yadda, yadda.

"Or so I thought," he said.

My silent critiquing came to a screeching halt. "What do you mean?"

"I'm trying to apologize."

"For what?"

He looked away, then back to me, then away again. "I came to this job under the assumption that I was taking over control of the kitchen — all the kitchens. I was wrong." The faraway look on his face told me that if he'd known better, he might not have been so eager to relocate to D.C. "I am not the executive chef, nor has there ever been any intention to appoint me as such. I misunderstood." He frowned. "I really blew that one." Meeting my eyes he continued, "Not that I would have turned this position down.

I want to be here. This really is an important step for me. It's just that I . . . misunderstood what the circumstances would be."

He was obviously uncomfortable, but all I felt was a rush of excitement. "You're not taking my job?"

"I can only imagine how much of a pompous ass you think I am," he said, shaking his head.

I didn't think he was looking for me to comment, so I kept silent.

Pointing toward me with both hands, he kept going, as though talking to himself. "I mean, come on. You're the first female in the job. It would be political suicide to replace you with a man right out of the box." He was quick to add, "No offense. I'm sure you're fine at what you do."

So he was saying he was the better chef after all. I said nothing.

As though finally hearing himself, he held up his hands again. "What I mean is, I believed I was getting your job. I even think I deserve it. But I'm not getting it. And I'm sorry for any problems my misunderstanding caused."

A peculiar apology if I'd ever heard one. But I was so happy I didn't care. "How do things stand now?" I asked. "Are you working upstairs alone, or are you in the main kitchen with us?"

His eyes clouded. "Main kitchen. With you." After a beat, he added, "I . . . I report to you."

"That's good to know."

"I hope there won't be any hard feelings," he said. "It really was a misunderstanding."

So euphoric was I, at not only *not* getting sacked but also discovering I was still the chick in charge, that I held out my hand to shake his, trying to tamp down my obvious glee. "No hard feelings," I said. Heck, I would be working with this man going forward and there was no gain in holding a grudge. "None at all. I'm just glad we got everything settled early."

"Yeah," he said.

Cyan and Bucky looked up in alarm when we returned. They must have read the relief and happiness on my face because, in tandem, their expressions softened.

I was about to bring Virgil over to my two staffers and to explain the reporting structure going forward, but from behind me, Virgil spoke. "I'm sure you're all wondering what we were talking about out there."

Surprised, I turned. Virgil held his hands out, inviting not only Bucky and Cyan to listen, but our two Secret Service attendants as well.

227

With a voice too loud for the relatively small space, he continued. "And you all have a right to know. I intend to clear the air immediately. Olivia here" — his expression didn't make me feel particularly warmed — "remains your executive chef. And although I will be working here, with all of you, I will be responsible for the day-to-day meal preparation for the First Family. That is not to say that you won't be called upon to step in on my days off. Nor does it preclude my helping out from time to time when situations require my assistance."

I stood speechless for half a second. Even though he was stating that I was in charge, his method of delivery managed to usurp my position nonetheless. Time for me to take control.

"Thank you, Virgil," I said, cutting him off from whatever he was about to say next. "I'm sure you know how much your help will be appreciated, especially as we prepare for the state dinner next week." Clapping my hands together the way Paul always did whenever he wanted us to focus, I concluded with, "Right now we need to focus less on our reporting structure and get moving on plans for the tasting. So, let's get started."

I felt the mood in the room shift. The drama was over and we were back to work. I had done that. Feeling empowered once again, I turned to Bucky. "How are things going?" He brought me up to date on the agnolottis I'd started. We would make a fresh batch for Friday's tasting, but we needed to test, sample, and adjust to ensure they were just right before we even offered them to the First Lady as an option.

The White House kitchen is not huge, so carving out a spot for Virgil to work presented a challenge. The upside, of course, was that we were free to use the rest of the space for state dinner preparations, and could focus on that project without having to stop every few hours to make breakfast, lunch, and dinner.

Much later, while I was back at the computer, inputting expense numbers, Cyan sidled up. "I miss working on the family's meals," she whispered.

I shot a quick look around the kitchen, but Virgil was across the room. No way he could hear us. "Me, too," I said. "Take a look at the stuff he's preparing for them." I pointed at the screen.

"Holy moley," Cyan said. "The man has expensive tastes."

"I hope he cleared all this with Mrs. Hyden," I said. "I'm going to have to have a talk with him. Virgil probably doesn't realize that the First Family is responsible for their own food expenses. This is pricey stuff." In addition to the normal items we might have expected him to order, such as fresh fish, cuts of meat, and organic vegetables, Virgil had requested a hefty supply of caviar, truffle oil, and a vintage of wine that even I recognized as expensive.

Cyan noticed it, too. "Is he planning to use that for *cooking?*"

I nodded, indicating the recipe he'd ascribed it to. We had always created excellent meals at the White House, but we'd done so within reason. Most families had certain favorite dishes but rarely were these favorites the sort of meals Virgil had planned. While we might go all out and bring in unusual and expensive items for a state dinner, food served to the First Family was generally simpler fare. All the families so far had preferred it that way.

I turned to speak with him, "Virgil," I began.

Just then, the room exploded with activity. Abigail and Josh came in, their faces pink from being outside. Agents Bost and Zeller crowded in behind, their eyes rapt on their young charges.

"Virgil!" Josh ran up to my new assistant chef with an expression of pure excitement on his face. "Do you really mean it? My mom said you're going to let me work here with you."

Virgil grinned, but I could tell it hurt him to do so. "Well, Josh, I'm not so sure anymore. Things have changed a little bit."

The boy's expression fell. "What do you mean?"

"This morning, when I spoke with your mom about you helping out in the kitchen, I thought you could learn a few things down here with the staff while I took care of the family food."

My ears perked up. Not that I hadn't already been paying close attention.

"It turns out that I'm going to be down here, and Ms. Paras is in charge." He held a hand out toward me and shook his head regretfully. "I thought the staff here might be able to teach you a few things while I was busy upstairs, but it turns out I'm not the boss."

Josh's jaw dropped. "You're not?"

"Sorry, kiddo."

"Hang on," I said. "Josh, don't you remember? You're welcome here in my kitchen any time at all." I'd accidentally said "my kitchen" but it felt good coming out of my mouth.

"Yeah," he said, almost whining, "but Virgil was going to teach me. I want to learn how to make stuff like he does."

"I understand," I said. "But, just like I told your mom . . . unless there's a big dinner coming up that keeps us too busy, I would like it a lot if you came down here. We would all be very happy to teach you some cool chef tricks."

Josh's eyebrows came together as he squinted at me. "Are you just saying that?"

"Nope. Trust me. We're here for you, okay?"

With a skeptical look that might have made me laugh if he hadn't been so serious, he said, "Okay. I want to learn *real* stuff, though. Not just how to peel a potato."

He was so cute, so earnest, that I wanted to reach over and ruffle his hair. "You got it, Josh. And if there's anything in particular you want to work on, just let us know and we'll plan ahead."

Mollified, he nodded.

Bost was quick to add, "You are only allowed in here when I'm with you, remember."

Josh made a face. "But what if you're not around? Can't I ask another agent to come with me?"

Clearly displeased by the question, Bost answered without answering. "Let's not involve other agents at this point. I am assigned to you, and the only time I am off duty is when you are in the residence. I will talk with the staff and ensure that I am always consulted before you come down here."

The poor kid didn't know how to parse that information and obviously decided it was better to keep quiet than ask for clarification. Bost struck me as a no-nonsense agent, but with his recent questions about Tom's competence and this uncompromising answer to the First Son's question, I was starting to wonder if he was the best choice to guard his small charge.

Abigail had turned to Zeller and was speaking in low tones. When Zeller nodded, the First Daughter turned to Virgil. "My school has two days off next week. I'm having a sleepover with my friends at Camp David. Do you take care of the food up there, or does somebody else do that?" She shrugged as though it meant nothing to her. "I just want to, you know, plan out what we're going to have."

Virgil opened his mouth to answer, but he

clearly had no idea what to say. He turned to me.

"Camp David has its own kitchen staff," I said. "Will you be staying in Aspen Lodge?"

Abigail looked to Zeller, who nodded.

"If there's anything you want them to prepare for you and your guests," I continued, "all you have to do is let us know. I would be happy to coordinate menu plans with you."

Virgil cleared his throat. "Ms. Paras means that *I* would be happy to do that. In fact, if I'm not needed here that day, I would enjoy a trip to Camp David to take care of you and your guests." He looked to me expectantly. "Is that all right with you, Chef?"

Nothing like putting me on the spot. "What days next week?" I asked.

Abigail glanced back and forth between the two of us. "We were going to spend Tuesday and Wednesday night there."

The very same time we would be in the final crunch for the state dinner. There was no way Virgil should be away from the kitchen at that time, but I didn't want to have this discussion in front of Abigail. I smiled. "We'll get back to you really soon on that."

Unappeased, she said, "Okay."

Virgil held his hands up in a "too hot to

234

touch" movement. "Whatever the boss says, Abby. I guess your question will have to wait."

Stifling my annoyance, I shifted gears. "We're really looking forward to our first official tasting with your mom this Friday. You and your brother are coming, right?"

"I guess."

Clearly disappointed with me — yet again — Abigail turned to Zeller. "I'm going to start my homework now," she said. "Can I just go upstairs by myself?"

Zeller was stone-faced. "I'll walk you up there."

Annoyed, Abigail turned away and headed out the door. Zeller followed. Josh gave me another of his suspicious looks. "You really mean it, right?"

"I do," I said.

As soon as he and Bost were gone, I breathed a sigh of relief. Why were all my interactions with the kids so tense? I couldn't understand it.

Just as I started back to work, Virgil interjected, "I won't have time to coach Josh, you understand."

I pointed upstairs. "But you told the First Lady . . ."

"I said that the kitchen would help him, I didn't mean me specifically."

I stopped myself from snapping. "And you promised this when you believed you were being named executive chef."

He had good sense enough to affect a sheepish look. "I just thought . . ."

"That we would handle the kids while you took care of the important things," I said, finishing his thought for him.

He tried to correct me. "The kids are important, too."

"Oh, I know that," I said. "I'm just surprised to hear that you do."

"You heard the agent assigned to Josh. He isn't even supposed to be down here without permission."

Why did I sense that Virgil was relieved not to have to deal with a young boy's kitchen curiosity? "Agent Bost is new here," I said. "He's trying to prove himself and that's fine. In a month or two, when everything settles, I believe we'll be seeing a lot of little Josh down here. And that's a good thing."

Virgil headed back to his station, muttering under his breath.

"I didn't catch that," I said.

He turned to me. "I just said that kids don't belong in the kitchen."

CHAPTER 17

Cyan had asked me to meet her after work again and we'd settled on a little diner just a few blocks southeast of the White House. We'd both eaten there before and knew we could count on basic comfort food done right. She'd left before me, claiming to have a few errands to run. Virgil had taken off for the day shortly thereafter, leaving me and Bucky to finish up. When I finally was able to leave, I exited the Southeast Gate and headed to Pennsylvania Avenue going east. The weather was brisk and I hunched my shoulders against the cold. Flipping open my phone, I dialed one of my favorite numbers.

"Ollie! Wonderful to hear from you," Henry said. It was just as wonderful for me to hear his voice. Henry had been executive chef at the White House for years before I'd even begun working there, and had recommended me to succeed him. I owed him a

237

lot already, but that never stopped me from calling him for additional advice.

"I don't know if you're going to be so happy to hear from me once you realize I'm calling to complain."

Immediately solicitous, Henry asked, "What's wrong?"

I told him about our new upstart, Virgil, and how he'd believed he would be named executive chef over me. "I've got a bad feeling about this guy, Henry," I said. "And I guess I'm just looking for words of wisdom."

He laughed. "Then you called the wrong number. I only looked good because I had you and Bucky and Cyan there behind me."

"Oh, come on, Henry. Don't be modest. I know better. You're already starting to formulate ideas for me, aren't you?"

He laughed. "Maybe some. But I'm on my way out the door right now."

"Going out with Mercedes?"

"As a matter of fact, I am. But you know I always have time for you. And I would like the opportunity to continue this discussion."

"How about Saturday night?" I asked. I named a time, and a place we were both familiar with.

"Hmm," he said. "That's date night, isn't it? Shouldn't you be out with some lucky young man?"

"Not this weekend."

"Or any weekend lately, I'd wager. Okay. It's a date. I'll finagle a couple of things and we'll be set. Can we make it closer to six o'clock?"

"Don't change plans on my account."

"Ollie," he said with such warmth in his voice it made my throat hurt, "don't you understand? I make time for you because I want to."

Cheered, I said, "Then it's a date. I'm looking forward to it."

"As am I." He laughed. "No canceling now. If our new president asks you to work late, you're just going to have to tell him no."

"You got it. See you then."

Walking into Sylvester's Diner was like walking into a hot wall of bliss. Sizzling scents of onions, burgers, and mac and cheese met me as I unzipped and peeled off my jacket, looking for Cyan. At the table nearest me, a man was about to dig into an open-face turkey sandwich with steaming gravy over everything, including the fries. It wasn't pretty, but I bet it was good.

Cyan was in a fat turquoise booth in the far corner, waving to get my attention. I saw her, all right. And I saw Agent Nourie sitting right beside her, looking happier than agents normally do.

Dodging the pink-uniformed waitresses and tray-laden busboys, I made my way to the back of the diner. "Hey," I greeted them, not knowing what else to say, "this is a surprise."

"Is it?" Cyan wrinkled her nose and eyed me suspiciously. "I thought you had us all figured out."

"Nope." I took a seat. Any and all conversations I had planned to have with Cyan about Virgil went out the window. "Nice to see you, Agent Nourie," I said.

"Call me Matt." He jostled Cyan's shoulder. "We're off duty."

In all the time I'd dated Tom, he'd never smiled and claimed to be "off duty." According to Tom, he was on call all the time, even when he wasn't. I didn't know if I was annoyed that Nourie could relax, or if I found his attitude refreshing. Either way, it was clear Cyan was happy. I smiled at Nourie, thinking that Cyan was coping well without Rafe after all. "Sounds good, Matt."

"Hey, how about that chef Virgil?" he said. "I get the impression he's not too happy with his position as second banana."

"Well," I said slowly, "technically Bucky is the first assistant. I think we'll just have to

240

wait until everybody settles in. I'm sure in no time it will be like we've worked together forever."

"Very diplomatic," he said.

"Thanks."

We placed our orders with a twentysome-thing waitress named Bippy, and the moment she departed Cyan said, "Matt has been filling me in a little on Bost."

I sat back and glanced around. So many conversations were going on in this high-ceilinged, busy restaurant that the likelihood of anyone overhearing us was virtually nil. Still, it seemed wrong to discuss any White House topics in public. Nourie apparently agreed because he tapped Cyan on the shoulder and held a finger over his lips.

"Nobody knows who Bost is," she said, clearly annoyed by my reaction and his admonishment. "I could be talking about my cat."

"That may be true," Nourie said, "but it's still not worth the risk."

"Okay, fine. I'll bring you up to speed later, Ollie." Cyan turned to Nourie. "If that's okay with you."

He nodded. "I never share anything that's classified." With a gentle glance at me, he added, "I'm sure that's not new news to you after your time with Tom."

Taken aback, I realized that apparently Cyan had no compunction about sharing information with him about me. "Right," I said. "Speaking of Tom — are you bringing this relationship out in the open, or keeping it quiet?"

Cyan was the one who answered. "We're keeping quiet for now. Just until the new admini . . . er . . . the new people are settled." With a look around the loud restaurant meant to allay my fears of being overheard, she said, "But in time we plan to come out. Don't we, Matt?"

He looked like he wanted to pat her hand, but settled for a beneficent smile instead. Oh I could see where these two were headed. They both had that starry-eyed look that said they believed they'd found their soul mates. Having known each other for just over a week, I had my doubts. I worried about Nourie being the "rebound guy." Cyan needed to feel wanted and appreciated right now, and Matt just happened to be in the right place at the right time. Maybe everything would work out and they'd have a long, happy relationship. Maybe.

As we talked — keeping to safe subjects like favorite movies and books — I felt my mind wander back to my early days of dating Tom. He was so strong-minded, so confident, so decisive. All the attributes that had combined to make him a great Secret Service agent had twisted when it came to being a boyfriend. Rather than see me for who I was — rather than accept my quirks and try to understand my need to be useful — he'd tried to force me to become what he envisioned a girlfriend should be. And the cracks in our relationship had started when he tried to make me behave according to his rules.

To be honest, I understood it. Tom had a job to do and he did it well. Just as I had a job and I strove to do my best. The problems came when my role inadvertently expanded — on occasion — to include the protection of the White House and its inhabitants. Clearly his territory. No matter that I was good at helping out; he didn't want me involved. I didn't blame him, but I wasn't willing to change who I was to match his ideal. And so we parted ways. But that didn't mean it didn't hurt.

As though reading my mind, Cyan said, "I'll bet you have a theory about who left the you-know-what in our kitchen?"

Startled out of my reverie, I shook my head. "I don't."

"Come on, Ollie," she said. "You always

243

have some weird instinct that gets you into the middle of everything."

"I don't," I said again. With a pointed look at Nourie, I added, "I'm sure you've heard about my run-ins."

He nodded. "Part of our briefing."

"Except for our initial involvement," I said, "and what Tom has been sharing with me, I'm keeping out of this one completely."

Cyan gave me a skeptical look.

"The last thing I need is to cause any trouble with the new family," I said. "Believe me, I'm keeping my nose as clean as possible this time. I have no capital with them and recent fiascos are causing me enough grief already. My hands are tied."

Cyan smiled and jostled Nourie's shoulder. "That's what she says now. Just wait. She'll get into the middle of this."

"Our team has everything covered," he said, smiling at me. "I think you're safe this time."

Although I maintained a cheery attitude and upbeat demeanor throughout dinner, I couldn't wait to get away from them. All I wanted was to be by myself.

I rode the Metro home, alone, staring at the world outside rushing by. Dinner with Cyan and Nourie made me think of Gav. I'd missed my chance to see him this weekend, and for some reason that made me very sad.

"Did you see this?" Cyan asked when I got in Wednesday morning.

"What are you doing here so early?" I asked her.

She didn't answer my question. Not that I couldn't have figured it out. Agent Nourie was at his post, overseeing Virgil's breakfast preparations. With Virgil in the kitchen these days taking care of the regular meals, there was no reason for the rest of us to get in every day at 5 A.M. I still held the overall responsibility for the kitchen so I made it my business to be here, but Cyan didn't need to. Of course, where new love was concerned, what did a few hours of sleep matter? I glanced around the kitchen. Where *was* Virgil?

"Come see this," she said. "Congress-woman Sechrest is making a statement."

"Right now?" I asked, "What did I miss?"

Cyan shook her head as she raised the volume.

Recorded in the Brady Press Briefing Room, Sandy Sechrest held on to the sides of the lectern with both hands. Concern tightened her forehead, and she spoke halt-ingly. "The president has asked me to update you. He will make a personal statement later, but he is currently in talks with a representative from Armustan and cannot be pulled away."

This was odd.

"As you all know, Lyman Hall Hospital was taken by force a week ago. The terrorists responsible were arrested, and the hostages were freed without further casualties. What we have learned from our contact from Armustan, however, is that this faction will not be deterred. Although the faction claims to be working on behalf of Armustan, they are not supported by the country's government. Their goal is to have the known terrorist, Farbod, freed from the prison in my jurisdiction in Wisconsin. The rebel faction struck here in Washington, D.C., but we have intercepted intelligence that suggests other strikes across the nation are being planned. We need the American people to remain vigilant and report any suspicious activity."

Questions from the reporters — the room was surprisingly full for this early in the morning — were all over the place. One member of the press stood up and said, "If this is just one faction, aren't you and the president overreacting?"

Her answer chilled me to the bone.

"No," she said very quietly, then added, "The people we are talking about are ruthless. They will stop at nothing to achieve their objective — the freedom of their leader, Farbod. We cannot relax our efforts. Not for one moment. Not until every single one of them is incarcerated."

"And you believe this small group can wreak havoc on the entire country?"

She nodded. "Not all at once. But we have intercepted enough to know that they are capable of striking at our very heart. They are ruthless and they are smart. We cannot let our guard down. We must get the word out. Every American needs to be our eyes and ears. We need to report every suspicious activity, no matter how small . . ."

As Congresswoman Sechrest continued, the press conference muted and a reporter broke in to sum up. "There you have the latest, recorded at the White House earlier this morning. As requested by the president, we will rebroadcast Congresswoman Sechrest's comments throughout the day." She turned to face a different camera. "Reactions from around the country are mixed. Many individuals are confused by Sechrest's warnings — people claim they don't understand exactly what to look out for. Authorities are concerned about widespread panic, and police departments are already reporting an influx of calls, most of which have turned out to be unfounded."

The shot cut to a police sergeant in front of a row of palm trees. He removed his hat to wipe his forehead. "This is nuts," he said. "We're running around here trying to follow up. It's a field day for the small-time players because our department is stretched too thin. You ask me, this is all a hoax. They just want to make American cops look like idiots, chasing shadows." He turned to answer the crackling of his radio. "Sorry," he told the reporter. "Gotta go."

Cyan turned the sound down. "Congresswoman Sechrest was in negotiations with the president and leaders from Armustan till early this morning."

"Nobody told us." I panicked. "Did somebody make sure they got fed?"

"I guess they didn't need to tell us. Virgil was here and took care of everything."

That was good, although the belated update set me off-kilter. I should have been here, ensuring things went smoothly. There was always plenty of food in our kitchen and the one upstairs for butlers to arrange meals, but I hated to have the president in any type of negotiations without the best possible fare to provide calm comfort when

248

it might be needed. "Where is Virgil now?"

She pointed up. "Sleeping."

"What?" I took a look around the kitchen. "What about breakfast?"

"He started, but handed it off to me when I got in. Said he was up all night."

I was glad the kitchen had been covered, but upset that I hadn't been consulted. Still, I couldn't complain as long as the president was happy. "How did everything go? Did Virgil tell you?"

"Said it went very smoothly. No problems."

"Good," I said, and meant it.

Cyan and I finished the breakfast Virgil had begun. Although I had to give the guy credit for creativity, I thought it was too much. I would not have paired prunes with pumpkin yogurt and then topped it with walnuts and cut-up figs. Fiber was important, but I thought he'd overdone it. From what I had gathered, the president preferred light breakfasts of toast or croissant and coffee. He was more of a lunch man. But the yogurt went up along with an unusual fish quiche. I was very interested in how these items would be received. Virgil had cooked for this family before. He obviously knew something I didn't.

Maybe it was good he was on staff after

all. I was always open to learning new things, and I suspected Virgil had a great deal to teach — if he was willing to do so. Time would tell.

As soon as a bleary-eyed Virgil returned to the kitchen, Bucky, Cyan, and I dove into preparations for the tasting on Friday and the subsequent dinner the following week. There were some basics the First Lady would not need to taste, and Marcel in the pastry kitchen would prepare the dessert options to offer along with our fare on Friday night.

"You're actually making all this food just to taste-test?" Virgil asked midafternoon. "How many people will be testing?"

"Usually just a few, but we're adding the kids this time around," I said. "And Mrs. Hyden has also invited Valerie and a couple of other staff members to offer their opinions."

He nodded, but didn't seem terribly impressed.

"How did breakfast go?" I asked. "We sent up everything just as you arranged, but I haven't heard back from the butlers. I was particularly interested in that yogurt."

"That's one of my new creations."

"I tried it," I said, "before it went up."

"What?" His face reddened. "Didn't you

trust me?"

Surprised by his reaction, I got a little defensive myself. "We always taste-test." I pointed to the containers of spoons we kept everywhere in the kitchen. "It's part of the job."

"Not when it's food I prepare," he said.

"Not to split hairs, Virgil, but we did the preparing."

"You were second-guessing me."

"I was doing nothing of the sort. And anyway, if you haven't already figured it out, everything that leaves this kitchen for the Hyden family table gets taste-tested." I pointed to Nourie and then to Gardez. "By them."

"What is wrong with you people?" He held up both hands and backed away. "Wait, don't tell me. This isn't my kitchen. I don't make the rules." Pursing his lips he made a face. "I'll just head back to my corner now, thank you very much."

This was a twist I hadn't anticipated. "Virgil —" I began.

"No, no. You go ahead. Work on your precious state dinner while I take care of the *president of the United States* and his family." With his hands still up he said, "I'm just a nobody here." Under his breath he added, "As though feeding the leader of the

251

free world was of no consequence."

"Virgil," I said, this time sharply. "May I see you a moment?" I pointed. "Out there."

He followed me into the hallway, which was surprisingly deserted. He looked as though he wanted to speak first, but I cut him off.

"I do not tolerate that sort of outburst in my kitchen."

At the words *my kitchen,* he raised his eyebrows. Let him.

"If we are to work together, then we have to respect each other."

Again, he looked as though he was ready to jump in. Again, I cut him off.

"I don't care what you may really believe, but in this kitchen, just like in this residence, you check your politics and your personal opinions at the door."

He didn't seem to comprehend, so I spelled it out for him. "I don't care what you think of me, but in this kitchen, in this house, you better learn to fake it."

He took a step back, as though surprised by my reaction.

Just then, the elevator next to us landed, and the doors opened. Mrs. Hyden emerged. I pasted on a pleasant expression and hoped Virgil would do the same. "Good morning," the First Lady said. "Just the two people I wanted to see. How is everything in the kitchen?"

"Wonderful," I said.

She nodded, as though she'd expected me to say just that. "I know that we're all going to work best together if we maintain an atmosphere of openness."

My heart sank. What now?

She smiled, but I could tell it was more to set us at ease than as a precursor of happy news. "I would like to talk about breakfast this morning." Her eyebrows came together as though she was trying to put a puzzle together. "You didn't prepare it, Virgil, did you?"

"No," he said, gesturing to me. "Ollie and Cyan . . ."

"That's what I suspected." Again the bad-news smile. "Ollie," she said kindly, "I know you're trying very hard to impress us and discover our tastes through experimentation, but this morning's menu was" — her nose wrinkled — "a bit too unusual." She turned to Virgil. "I know you were up all night with my husband, and that's why Ollie and . . . and her assistants . . . took over this morning. Maybe it would be best if you coached them going forward." When she smiled at Virgil, it was with real warmth. "After all, you have a much better handle on our preferences."

I looked to Virgil, expecting him to volunteer that it had been *his* menu we'd prepared, but he remained maddeningly silent. Of course. Why should he admit that he'd been the one to come up with superprunes and fish quiche? His expression was unreadable and for the first time, I wondered if he'd set us up.

As though to smooth out her reproach, Mrs. Hyden turned to me again. "But from what I hear, you are the master when it comes to preparing lavish state dinners. I'm very much looking forward to our tasting on Friday."

"So am I." At that moment, I vowed to create the most impressive state dinner ever produced. If I could accomplish that without Virgil's assistance, all the better. Maybe he should go to Camp David with Abigail after all.

"I didn't mean to interrupt," she said. Giving a three-fingered wave, she strode toward the Palm Room, en route to the West Wing.

"You threw me under the bus," I said the moment she was gone. "I won't forget it."

I pivoted and returned to the kitchen without giving him a chance to reply.

CHAPTER 18

Thursday afternoon, Josh arrived in the kitchen after school, practically skipping. "I'm here," he said. "I want to help."

"Hey, Josh," Nourie said, tousling the boy's head. Despite the fact that no further direct threats to the White House had materialized, both Secret Service taste-tester agents remained at their posts. According to Tom, if all went well, they would be released from the kitchen and returned to regular duty right after the state dinner. The two men hadn't been any real problem, but I would be happy to have them gone. Big boys took up valuable work space.

Gardez asked, "Where's Bost?"

The large, angry agent appeared in the doorway. "Right here."

Josh nudged Virgil's elbow. "I'm here," he said again. "What can I do?"

"Josh," Virgil said, the weariness in his voice so apparent that Josh's shoulders dropped, "this isn't a real good time."

"But I thought I could do something to maybe help out." Josh looked over to Bost, who held his hands up as though to indicate he had no say in this matter. "I've been watching all the cooking shows, and I learned a lot already."

Bucky, Cyan, and I kept working, but our attention was on the little drama playing out in front of us. Josh, with his soulful brown eyes, stared up at Virgil with a mixture of admiration and fear.

Virgil was in the middle of dinner preparations. As much as I would have liked to know exactly what he was creating, I'd been so consumed with my own work for the tasting tomorrow, that I'd mostly ignored him. Was it bad of me to hope he was coming up with another prune-yogurt or fish quiche dish?

The kitchen was silent as we all waited for Virgil's response. "Listen, Josh," he said without looking at the boy, "this is a real working kitchen. It's dangerous in here." Flicking a glance up to Bost, he added, "I think it's irresponsible of your bodyguard to let you run around like this."

Josh shook his head. "I'm not running around. I want to do real cooking."

"You're only eight."

"I'm nine."

"That's still too young."

Josh pointed at me. "But Ollie said —"

Sensing that Virgil was ready to dismiss the boy, I interrupted. "Hey, Josh, maybe you can help me instead."

Next to me, Bucky rolled his eyes. I ignored him.

Josh's mouth twisted with uncertainty. "But . . ."

"Here." Thinking fast, I pulled out dough I had set to rise. "Do you know how to knead?"

Josh's eyes lit up. "I do." He named one of his favorite Food Network heroes and painstakingly explained the steps he remembered about making bread. He was so intense in his recitation that I couldn't find it in my heart to tell him I already knew.

"That's great," I said when he finished. And it was — he'd remembered every step of the process.

I thought I heard a grumble from Bucky, but I ignored that, too.

I pulled my stool up close to a clear space on the center countertop. "Why don't we get you set up over here? Go wash your hands first. Really, really get them clean, okay?"

Bost looked bored. Or maybe annoyed.

Hard to tell on a face that was carved from stone. Virgil took great pains to keep from interacting with either of us, as though he was afraid of being pulled in to cooperate. Bucky's eyes rolled so far back into his head — again — that I thought they might stick there.

Josh took his spot on the stool and cheerfully began kneading the dough. He treated the pale mound more like Play-Doh than food, but I didn't really mind. Even if he dropped it on the floor, it wouldn't matter. I had more dough mounds stored in back, just waiting to be punched down. "You tell me when you think that's done, okay Josh?" I asked.

He said, "I sure will!" with such joyful confidence that I felt my breath catch. What a cutie. Kids had never been part of my future plans. To be honest, I'd never really gotten to know any very well, and I'd never felt any maternal urges. But this kid was a real charmer.

Cyan came over to whisper in my ear, "You're a better woman than I."

Bost put an end to Josh's kitchen exploits after about an hour. In that time, Josh had kneaded three piles of dough, refilled our tasting spoons, and helped me make a hummus snack by squeezing a lemon and blending it with chickpeas, tahini, and garlic.

"It's time for homework," Bost told him. "Your mother's schedule."

Josh reluctantly surrendered his spot. "Okay."

"Before you go," I said, "let's get the bread from the oven and see how it turned out."

Josh and I donned mitts and removed a fat, gorgeous, nicely browned loaf from the rack. "You did a great job," I said.

Josh beamed.

"I'm going to send this upstairs with you so you have a snack while you do your homework. But you'll have to let this cool," I said. Turning to the hummus mixture that I'd stored in a bowl, I gave him directions for digging out the center of the cooled bread. "Put the hummus in there and you can dip the bread pieces in. What do you think?"

"This is great," he said.

Bost had to help him carry everything, but within moments they were out the door and I smiled after them, knowing I'd made Josh feel good. Something, at least, had gone right.

Virgil was next to me in a heartbeat. "Did you forget that the family's food is my responsibility?"

"Nope. Didn't forget," I said, and before

he could complain further, I turned away.

"You shouldn't have sent those items upstairs," he said to my back.

I ignored him.

A little while later, Virgil disappeared. Cyan wanted to ask him about a recent order he'd placed but he was nowhere to be found. "Maybe he went to the washroom?" I suggested.

"For half an hour?" Cyan asked.

Had he been gone that long? I hadn't noticed. Maybe I hadn't wanted to.

"I hate to say this," I said, "but I think I need to talk with Paul. Virgil may technically report to me, but he's obviously unhappy with that arrangement. As much as I don't want to admit it, we might be better off if he handled food from the residence kitchen. The sooner he's out of our hair, the better."

Cyan wiped her hands on her apron and started to speak, but Bucky stopped her with a look. He addressed the two Secret Service agents. "No offense, guys," he said to them, "but we should probably not be discussing sensitive kitchen issues in front of you."

Nourie and Gardez exchanged a glance. Gardez smiled and made a key-turning movement in front of his lips. "I'm not go-ing to say anything."

Nourie had his eyes on Cyan. "Nobody's business but your own."

Bucky didn't seem satisfied; he came close to me. "I think you *should* talk with Paul. Something just isn't right with that guy. The longer we wait to fix it, the sorrier we're go-ing to be."

"My thoughts exactly," I said. "Can you two handle everything until I get back?"

"You know it," Cyan said.

I washed my hands at the sink, and dried them well. I didn't often just drop in at Paul's office and I didn't even know if he would be there right now, but this wasn't a matter I cared to handle over the phone.

I took the steps up to the first floor and was just outside Paul's office when I heard a familiar voice.

"She's harassing me," I heard Virgil say.

He had his back to me as he complained to Paul.

Paul spied me from over Virgil's shoulder. He held up a hand in greeting, which I knew was more for Virgil's benefit than for mine. Virgil ignored it and kept complain-ing. "It's bad enough I have to report to her, but now she's grabbing my responsibili-ties. She sent food upstairs with the Hyden's son . . ."

"Josh," I said, interrupting.

He spun, his face contorted in anger.

I was incredibly composed. Virgil's anger and fury only fueled my inner calm. "The Hyden's son's name is Josh," I said. "It wouldn't hurt to call him that."

Paul moved to step between us, almost as though he expected us to come to blows. "I understand there's a difference of opinion on where each of your responsibilities begin and end . . ."

"I'll say," Virgil interjected. "She's out to get me. I tried to talk with her and get us started on the right foot, but she resents my being here." He cast a derisive look my way. "Not that I blame you for that. I would feel threatened, too, if a chef of my caliber suddenly appeared on staff. No hard feelings."

"No hard feelings?" I said incredulously. I bit back my next retort. It wouldn't do to lose my temper in front of Paul. Not at all.

At that moment, my cell phone vibrated in my pocket. I chose to ignore it.

Paul had his hands up. "We're all adjusting," he said. "It would be foolish to expect everything to run smoothly right away. Let's all just step back and try to see what the best course of action is." He took a step back in emphasis, but didn't give either of us a chance to respond before saying, "What we should do is schedule a meeting. Just the three of us, where we sort out grievances and establish ground rules." Turning to me, he said, "I know you're swamped with preparations for the state dinner, Ollie. Why don't you come up with options that are good for you . . ." he turned to face Virgil, "and then you and I will coordinate. How does that sound?"

Virgil's voice rose. "Ridiculous, that's how it sounds. Are you planning to take more of my responsibilities away? I don't know why I even agreed to come here in the first place."

I turned at the sound of heels against tile. Valerie had come up the same steps I'd used. Clutching a portfolio, she hesitantly approached. "Am I interrupting?"

Paul smiled. "What can I do for you?"

She pointed to Virgil as she joined us. "I need him. Photographers are here from *Masterly Male* magazine for the feature they're doing on our new chef." She gave a sheepish grin. "Can I steal him away from you for a little bit?"

Virgil's face underwent a total transformation. Pulling his shoulders back, he smiled broadly and checked his watch. "They're right on time. Thank you, Valerie." To Paul, he said, "Don't underestimate what I can do for this place."

Paul and I watched him go. As soon as they were gone, I asked. "What did I do to deserve him?"

"You managed to turn Bucky around," he said. "Maybe whatever worked on him will work on Virgil Ballantine, too."

I shook my head, talking half to myself. "Bucky comes from better stock. He might be moody but he was here with Henry and he understands how things work. Virgil is a diva. He's in this for himself, and has his own agenda." I looked at Paul. "I worry what will happen if he succeeds."

"Succeeds?"

"In pushing me out of here."

"He's not —" Paul must have seen my face because he stopped arguing. Instead, he said, "Give him time."

"I don't have time. The First Lady already isn't terribly fond of me." I mentioned both the disastrous first breakfast and the one this morning where Cyan and I followed Virgil's instructions to the letter. "She hated it. And he led her to believe the menu was my idea."

"You didn't correct him?"

"How could I?" I asked. "We were talking to the First Lady. I didn't want us to come off as two squabbling children. But that's exactly what we are."

"I'll try to set up the meeting I mentioned."

I thanked him for his concern. "And I've got plans to talk with Henry Saturday. It will be nice to get his take on all this. I feel like I'm in over my head."

"Don't underestimate yourself. Henry left the kitchen in very good hands."

"Thanks, Paul."

I checked my cell phone as I walked down the stairs. One missed text. I opened the phone and clicked to read a message from Gav. *Saturday has opened up. You free around five? Coffee? Dinner?*

I was about to text back that I'd love to meet him, when I remembered my plans with Henry. Instantly disappointed — despite the fact that up until this very moment I'd been looking forward to seeing my former mentor — I knew I couldn't cancel. Henry had made it clear he'd arranged his evening to fit my schedule, and it wouldn't be fair to change things on him now. Reluctantly I texted back that I had plans. Before hitting "send," I added, "with Henry." Gav knew our former executive chef. For some reason, I didn't want Gav to think I might be out on a date.

Back in the kitchen, Cyan and Bucky wanted the scoop from my visit with Paul. Maybe I was just too tired to go over it again — maybe I just felt as though I needed to stop allowing Virgil to be such a driving force in this kitchen — but I waved them away and told them things were being handled. We had far too much to worry about to allow Virgil's negativity to slow us down.

An hour later, Bucky looked at the clock. "He's *still* with the photographers?" Pointing to the vegetables Virgil had left unchopped when he'd stormed out in a huff, Bucky added, "Dinner is not finished. According to his schedule" — he pointed to notes Virgil set out on the counter — "he's serving in forty-five minutes and he has an item here that requires almost that long to bake. He's got a lot of work ahead of him and he's not here. You and I both know he's not going to make it."

I blew out a breath. Save his hide by finishing up dinner and serving it for him, or let his preparations sit and make the First Family wait for their meal?

I muttered an expletive, and asked again — rhetorically — what we'd done to deserve him. Finally I said, "I can't do it."

Bucky and Cyan were both fully aware

that Virgil had blamed us for the unpleasant breakfast. Bucky's face brightened. "You mean you refuse to save his —"

"I can't let the First Family go hungry," I said with finality. "Not from my kitchen. We'll finish what he started and get it served on time."

Deflated, Bucky narrowed his eyes. "Be careful, Ollie. If you don't start protecting yourself, Virgil's going to get his way and this *will* be his kitchen."

"We have to do what's right," I said. And although my heart wasn't in it, I consulted Virgil's list and reminded myself that it was important to always take the high road.

I'd just picked up a knife when our temperamental chef came around the doorway. "Out of my way," he said. "I have a masterpiece to create and no time for foolishness." Stopping when he saw me, he gave me and the vegetables a once-over. "What are you doing?"

"Making sure you don't miss your deadline."

He made a shooing motion with his hands. "What do you take me for?" he asked. "I'm a professional. Everything is under control."

"Great," I said, happy to step away. "More power to you."

"Oh and by the way," Virgil said as he

chopped carrots almost as fast as one of our assistant chefs, Agda, had, "I have plans to meet Reggie this weekend." He gave me a pointed look. "I'm sure we'll have a lot to talk about."

"Stop."

He looked up.

I pointed to the carrots. "Stop," I said. *"Now."*

He stopped chopping.

I held a finger up and spoke in a low voice. But not so quietly that the rest of the kitchen would be unable to hear. I could tell they were listening. The very air vibrated with anticipation.

"Breathe one word about the White House," I said, advancing on him, "just one word — about the First Family, the staff, the kitchen, or even me — and I'll make sure your head will roll." I felt the blood rush to my face. "I promise."

CHAPTER 19

In the late morning on taste-testing day, Mrs. Hyden called down to the kitchen and requested a meeting. With me.

We hadn't seen Virgil all day. The butlers told us that he'd been in ridiculously early to prepare breakfast and that the First Lady's light lunch was being "handled." Whatever that meant. I hated being out of the loop. Today's tasting would take the place of dinner, and Virgil had left us a cryptic note mentioning he would be tied up and would not be back in the kitchen until Saturday at the earliest.

Mrs. Hyden requested my presence upstairs in the residence. I didn't get up there very often, even though we maintained a garden greenhouse on the third floor. Being January, we didn't have a lot to harvest up there. I couldn't remember the last time I'd been in the East Sitting Hall, where the First Lady waited for me.

I stood in the large archway, waiting to be summoned in to the soft yellow room. Sunlight streamed in through the massive fanlight window behind the sofa where Mrs. Hyden and Valerie sat, consulting with several women, none of whom I recognized. The room was bright and welcoming, with a crystal chandelier, white woodwork, pale carpeting, and potted ferns. From what I could gather, the women were discussing furnishings — what was available to be moved in from the warehouse in Maryland, and what should be moved out. When Valerie saw me standing there, she held up a finger indicating I should wait, and whispered to her boss.

Mrs. Hyden looked up, smiled, and asked the women surrounding her if they could give her just a few minutes. Gathering up their notes and supplies, they quickly departed, leaving Mrs. Hyden and Valerie on the sofa together.

"Have a seat, Ollie," Valerie said, indicating a yellow-gold wing chair with a leaf motif.

I sat, realizing as I did so that my knees had gone wobbly. "Thank you."

Mrs. Hyden turned to her assistant and held out her hand. "Do you have the list?" she asked.

Valerie pulled it out and handed it over. "Right here."

Mrs. Hyden studied the paper for a short moment, but it was clear she was already familiar with its contents. "I've been presented with a bill," she began.

I knew what was coming.

"Have you seen this?" she asked, holding the sheet out in front of me.

"Not the bill," I said. "But I have seen the list of items that were submitted to create the bill."

Mrs. Hyden studied me as I spoke. I couldn't tell if she was angry or just curious. I waited.

"How do you explain these exorbitant prices?" She smiled, but as before, the expression was meant to disarm. "I don't think my family has ever incurred grocery bills of this magnitude in a year, let alone a week."

"I understand." I took a breath. "And I can explain."

She crossed her hands over her knees, still holding the food bill. "Please."

"Every executive chef — for as long as I've been aware — has had this conversation with the new First Lady. I sent you a note with the list I prepared, but I think it's best we discuss this in person as well."

One of her perfect eyebrows arched.

I held my hand out. "If I may?"

She gave me the bill. "This is pretty high," I admitted. "But there are several elements at work here. The first week of a new administration is always expensive. We're stocking all the shelf-stable items you requested, and we're preparing as many favorites as possible to help you and your family feel more at home."

I was losing her. I could tell by the look in her eyes. She pointed. "But that bill is ridiculous."

I nodded. "It's unfortunate that we have to be so careful about the food we bring into the White House. We have to take extreme precaution with every single item. There can be no slip ups. That means we often buy at a premium. The Secret Service does most of our acquisition. I try to keep to a budget — a budget you and I can work on together, going forward — but the reality is that everything that comes into the White House is the best of the best."

She blinked in the way that people do when they don't quite agree, but are too polite to call you out directly. "I understand that," she said, "but that doesn't explain these extravagances. We provided lists of our preferences, favorites, likes and dislikes. I don't recall specifying a regular diet of caviar or truffles." Pointing a long, manicured finger toward the sheet in my hand, she asked, "And is that expensive bottle of wine allocated for cooking?"

Blood pounded in my ears as I did the only thing I could — and said the only thing I could say — given the circumstances. "Virgil Ballantine has free reign over the family meals. These are his purchases."

She took that news with quiet calm, but I could see that she hadn't anticipated my answer. "But isn't he required to clear his purchases through you?"

"No, ma'am. I was told — specifically — that I had no say whatsoever with regard to his preparation of family meals."

She gave me that skeptical smile again. "But that's not entirely true, is it? You and your assistant prepared that unusual breakfast even though Virgil was here that day."

"He wasn't available because of the long overnight hours with Congresswoman Sechrest and the president," I said, "but the menu was all Virgil's." I couldn't believe how good it felt to finally tell her that. I wanted to be entirely clear, so I added, "He came up with the menu. We simply followed the directions he left."

"Hmm," she said, with a glance to Valerie.

273

Back to me, she asked, "What did you think of that breakfast menu?"

I couldn't tell her what I really believed. To do so would be unprofessional and reflect badly on me. I searched for the best word I could come up with that would neither be a false compliment nor the full truth. "Ambitious."

She held her hand out and I returned the bill to her. "What about this state dinner next week? How much will that cost?"

"Today's tasting, the state dinner, and all expenses associated with it are not part of your personal costs," I said. "Whenever we have an event like that, we code our purchases differently. You can be certain your family will not be charged for any of it."

"This is all very new to me," she said, and in her tone I caught what might have been an apology.

"I understand. As I said, every First Lady has this conversation with the executive chef at some point. It's part of the start-up curve."

For the first time since she had met me, she smiled warmly. "I suppose we're all learning together, aren't we?"

Bucky hurried over the moment I returned to the kitchen. "Did she tell you where Virgil is?" he asked.

Cyan came up behind him and I noticed that Gardez and Nourie were paying close attention to our conversation.

"No," I said slowly. "His whereabouts didn't come up. We talked about food expenses."

"Well, guess where our new chef buddy is right now."

"No idea." Clearly, I was the only person in the room not in the know.

"Playing golf." Bucky crossed his arms. "With the president."

The first thing that popped into my mind also popped out of my mouth. "But it's January."

"The president was invited to golf with some bigwig in Florida."

"And he took Virgil with him?" The room went utterly silent. Bucky nodded solemnly.

My reaction would normally have been, "Are you kidding me?" But they were most definitely not. Digesting the news, I nodded. Finally, I asked, "Why?"

Bucky gave me a look of utter disgust. "Supposedly he's a real good golfer."

"I mean, why —"

"I know," Bucky interrupted. "I don't understand it either."

Everyone in the room seemed to be waiting for my reaction. "Okay," I said. "It is what it is. If they want a family friend on staff — someone who conjures up weird meals but looks good in plaid shorts — so be it." I looked at all of them, noting their guarded expressions. "We are here at the pleasure of the First Family and we will serve them as we have served all the administrations that have come before. We can't allow ourselves to be distracted."

I waited, but no one moved. "That's it," I said. "We have food to prepare and time is getting tight."

Before we knew it, the time for the tasting had arrived. Bucky and I took the narrow circular staircase up from the kitchen level to the butler's pantry on the first floor. Cyan remained downstairs to send our samples up in the dumbwaiter as needed. At the top step, I let go of the handrail and wiped my palms down the sides of my apron.

Behind me, Bucky asked, "Nervous?"

"Yeah, you could say that."

"Marcel is making what again?" he asked.

We'd passed him on our way up, but we were all so intent on our jobs this evening that we hadn't even exchanged a word. "Mixed berry cobbler is his pièce de résistance," I said, "It features one of his masterful crusts. If they don't care for that — and I can't imagine how they won't — I believe he has a homemade ice cream he plans to offer. But he's hoping the berry dessert knocks their socks off."

"Just as you're hoping this menu will wow them."

"Yeah." I swallowed around what felt like a wide cactus in my throat.

Bucky set up on the far end of the west counter. "I'll work here. That will allow you better access to the dumbwaiter and give you total control over timing."

"Thanks, Buck."

He was silent for a moment. "I'm glad Virgil isn't here today."

I chuckled. "Me, too. Maybe we shouldn't look a gift horse in the mouth, huh? Even if he is playing golf with the president."

The butlers had carefully arranged seating in the family dining room. Mrs. Hyden, flanked by her two kids, sat at the middle of the east side of the table. Valerie and another assistant sat near Abigail, and two other assistants sat near Josh, who fidgeted.

The entire west side of the table was chairless, giving the butlers total freedom to easily serve each small plate and allow me a perfect view of reactions to the offerings.

We started with the agnolottis. After careful tweaking, we believed we'd gotten the proportions exactly right. If Mrs. Hyden's reaction was any indication, we'd been successful. Even the kids liked the crab dish. We served every option we'd prepared one at a time, and finally — like I had a good luck charm over my head — everything went just right.

I took notes as Mrs. Hyden and the group taste-tested. The butlers kept water glasses filled and the kids seemed to enjoy the process as well. Abigail didn't care for the Nantucket sea scallops, but everyone else loved them so they remained on the menu. I held my breath when it came time to tally results. I was surprised and pleased to discover that the adults unanimously approved everything I had planned.

"I like the spinach," Josh said. "Can I have another taste?"

The butlers hurried to accommodate him as Marcel brought out dessert. His French accent always got thicker when he was nervous, so I could tell this event was taking as much a toll on him as it was on me. "Wouldn't you prefer to save some room for . . ." he lifted the silver lid of a covered dish to display his mixed berry cobbler.

Josh pulled his spinach closer.

Mrs. Hyden put her arm around her son.

"He's never had much of a sweet tooth."

Once all the samples were tasted and the menu finalized, I thanked Mrs. Hyden for her time, and then thanked all the guests. "Olivia," Mrs. Hyden said, stopping me from leaving. "A moment?" She turned from side to side. "Kids, you can head upstairs now if you like."

"That was really good," Josh said, squirming out of his chair. "Thanks."

Abigail smiled shyly. "Thank you," she said and hurried off with her brother.

I waited. The five ladies around the table grew quiet. They obviously knew what was coming next. I did not. I stood on the west side of the table, feeling like an accused party facing a jury. To break the silence, I asked, "What can I do for you?"

Mrs. Hyden smiled, but didn't ask me to sit down. "Virgil Ballantine approached me about starting a garden," she said. "It's a wonderful idea he came up with — an official White House garden. The media is all over us to be more green and organic. I support those endeavors, of course. Having a garden on the White House grounds will send a meaningful message to the rest of the country. And it could help with our food bills." At this she laughed, as though all was forgiven. "I wanted to talk with you first because I know that Virgil ultimately reports to you and you have final say on such matters."

She and I both knew better. The First Lady had final say, but I appreciated her gesture. "We already have a garden," I began.

"I don't mean the greenhouse. I mean something more substantial."

"We have a real garden," I said. "In addition to the greenhouse on the third floor. The White House garden has been in existence now for several years." I knew because I'd started it. "We always have quite a bountiful harvest."

"Why haven't I heard about this before?"

I couldn't really answer that, and I said so. "In the coming weeks I would have consulted with you to discuss what you would like planted there —"

She cut me off. "How large is it?"

"About three hundred square feet, I'd say. Give or take."

Valerie jumped in. "That's pretty small. We need to look at expanding, don't you think? Let's design a significant space, maybe three times bigger." She turned to her boss. "If we do this well, we can garner a lot of great media attention. We can donate the excess to local food pantries, maybe have school kids help plant. This could be huge."

All the women started talking at once, throwing out ideas about how to maintain the garden, what media outlets to contact, and a lot of other things. It seemed as though they'd forgotten I was there.

I heard one of the assistants say, "That Virgil Ballantine really comes up with great ideas, doesn't he? I can see why you brought him on."

I wanted to remind them — again — that we already had a garden in place. A good one. And we already did donate excess food to local pantries. But not wanting to appear petty, I again held back. I needed to find a way around that problem of mine. Maybe if I could just get them to see me in the same way they viewed Virgil. I cleared my throat. "I have another idea," I said.

Surprisingly, they quieted to listen.

"What we don't have nearby is a local farmer's market. What if we opened up part of the south grounds, say weekly or monthly, to local producers to sell?"

One of the assistants gave me a skeptical look. "Oh, I don't know about that." She turned to Mrs. Hyden. "Don't you think that would be a security nightmare? Would every farm stand owner have to submit to a background check? What about people who just come to buy a couple of cucumbers? Can you imagine how crazy it would be here if the public was allowed in every week?"

"That's a very . . . ambitious idea, Olivia," Mrs. Hyden said. "We'll think about it. Thank you."

Dismissed, I left the Family Dining Room. The butlers would clean up while Bucky, Cyan, and I took care of the kitchen. Every single menu item I'd recommended had been approved. So why didn't I feel more triumphant?

CHAPTER 20

I had Saturday off, so I ran errands, cleaned my apartment, thought about getting a cat for the thousandth time, and dismissed the idea for the thousandth and first. Subjecting a pet to my oddball hours wouldn't be fair.

But when I dropped my keys in the bowl by the door and carried my groceries in to the kitchen, I couldn't help but think how much nicer it would be to come home to a warm welcome. Even if it were from a four-legged friend.

Just before I left to meet Henry that evening, I thought about calling the White House to check on Bucky and Cyan. I resisted. I didn't usually make a habit of calling in on my days off, and I knew my staff would handle the kitchen expertly. That wasn't what was bothering me. After Mrs. Hyden's group meeting last night that had turned into a virtual lovefest where Virgil was concerned, I felt as though any time away from my position was one more opportunity for him to grab a handhold and crawl his way up.

The restaurant Henry and I had agreed on was about a half hour away, so I set off at 5:15, always preferring to be early rather than late. Those of us in the world of haute cuisine were always nosy about other chefs and I was probably the nosiest of all. I'd chosen a restaurant that was getting very good buzz because it was overseen by a top chef from television. Broken Crown was the establishment's unlikely name, and it featured Mexican food served counter-style. I hoped there wouldn't be a long wait for a table.

Henry was waiting outside when I arrived. "And there she is," he said grandly. "My Olivia."

I reached up to give him a big hug. "Gosh, it's good to see you."

He squeezed back, hard, then held me at arm's length. "You're looking wonderful, as always. How's our kitchen treating you?"

We joined the line to place our orders. Even though I had already told Henry a little over the phone, I started at the beginning. "It's Laurel Anne all over again," I said, referring to the woman I'd vied against for the executive chef position. "But this time his name is Virgil and he clearly has the inside track."

"You thought that about Laurel Anne, too," Henry said.

both knew better than to share specifics where others could be listening in, so I kept things vague as I told him how "The Mrs." had brought one of her favorite people to join our group and how he had set his sights on my job. Henry's expression went from jovial to concerned.

At the counter, I decided on two steak tacos with rice and beans and Henry chose one of their signature burritos. Nothing fancy. Grabbing a couple bottles of water, we paid for our meal and found a nice quiet table in the restaurant's back corner to wait for runners to bring our orders.

"Ah, privacy," Henry said as he sat.

I brought Henry up to date on everything, and by the time our food arrived, he was peppering me with questions. "I've been through several new administrations as executive chef," he said, "but this is your first experience in that role. I confess I've never had to deal with a family bringing on their personal chef." His voice rose. "We always provided every meal for the . . ." Stopping himself just in time he continued in a whisper, "We always handled the family." With a slow shake of his head, he stared at me sorrowfully. "I don't know what to tell you."

We talked for more than an hour about Bucky, Cyan, and his lady friend, Mercedes. My tacos were the best I'd ever tasted, and Henry had good things to say about his burrito as well. He had only one small gripe. "They could be a bit more generous with the avocado."

As our conversation wound down, and I reached to take a last swig from my water bottle, he covered my hand with his. "This situation with the new guy is a challenge, Ollie. But I know you're up to it. Follow your gut. Remember, your instincts haven't steered you wrong yet."

I took immense comfort from the warmth of his hand and the strength of his words. "Thanks, Henry."

We parted in front of the restaurant with promises to make time for each other more often. I left feeling a little better. Nothing had been decided, but knowing that Henry had faith in me gave me a welcome boost.

On my way home, my cell phone buzzed. Gav texted: *Still with Henry?*

I dialed his number and he answered on

the first ring. "How's it going?"

"Great," I said. "What's up with you?"

I could almost hear him shrug. "I'm still in D.C. for a while longer. Done for the day and I find myself flipping channels here in my hotel room. I don't know why I texted you. Maybe just thought . . ."

"Flipping channels, huh?" I looked at my watch. It was a little past 8:00. "Does that mean you have time to meet?"

"Now?"

"Unless it's past your bedtime."

He laughed. "I'm not that old. Yet."

"Did you eat?"

"I grabbed some peanuts and an apple earlier."

"That's not dinner."

"It is when I'm on the road."

Impulsively, I said, "Come over. I'll make you something."

" 'Come over'?" he repeated. Then asked, "How soon?"

He had shadowed me at least once after an attack on my way home, so I knew he knew where I lived. "I'm heading there now," I said, as I mentally inventoried my refrigerator and cupboards. Thank goodness I'd gone shopping earlier. "I should be there in twenty minutes and I'll get started cooking right away. Call me when you get there, and I'll buzz you in."

"I don't want to cause you to work on your day off . . ."

I felt a lightness in my heart I hadn't felt in a while. Not even when I was talking with Henry. "Well, okay," I teased, "if you'd rather just sit in your hotel room eating peanuts, instead of enjoying a homemade dinner . . ."

"You sold me," he said. "I'll be there in twenty."

I made it back to my apartment building by 8:30. As I crossed the parking lot, I spotted a lone figure in the shadows, leaning against a nondescript car. I'd been around enough of them to recognize a government issue when I saw one. "Hey, Gav," I said as he pushed himself up to walk over.

He stepped into the spill of overhead light and I could see he was smiling. I was used to seeing him in a suit and tie, so it took a little adjustment to get used to the blue jeans and sweatshirt. He looked a lot younger than I remembered. How long had it been since we'd spoken in person? A year? Two?

"Aren't you cold?" I asked, pointing to his leather jacket, which he'd left unzipped.

He shrugged. "You get used to it."

"You made good time."

"For a home-cooked meal? You bet," he said, falling into step beside me.

"I thought it was the pleasure of my company."

He chuckled softly, sending puffs of air swirling into the night to disappear in front of him. "After all the grief you put me through?"

I laughed.

We stepped up onto the sidewalk in front of the building at the same time. Without warning, he stopped and turned to me.

I stopped, too. "What?"

"It's good to see you, Ollie," he said, looking as confused by his unexpected pronouncement as I was. "Really good."

Like a fog lifting from my brain, I felt it, too. I smiled up at him. "I know," I said, realization dawning. "I . . . I think I missed you."

He grinned and started walking again. A sudden, pleasant awkwardness had just settled upon us, but I liked it.

James was asleep at the front desk and we tiptoed past him. "That's James," I whispered.

"I know."

I shot him a look. "How much background

checking did you do on me when we first met?"

A smile twitched at his lips. "Enough."

We rode up in companionable silence, and I couldn't get over how different he appeared when not dressed like an agent. "You look good," I said.

He stopped staring at the numbers and turned to me. "So do you."

The elevator dinged loudly and I wasn't terribly surprised to see Mrs. Wentworth's door crack open to spy on my arrival. One very surprised eye stared out at me before she opened the door full wide. "Ollie," she said, stepping out into the hall, effectively blocking our path. "Is everything okay?" Although she addressed me, her scrutiny was on Gav. "You look familiar," she said to him. "Have we met?"

"This is . . ." I had been about to introduce him as Special Agent in Charge Leonard Gavin, but I changed my mind midsentence. "This is a friend of mine. Leonard."

"Nice to meet you, Mrs. Wentworth," he said.

His knowing her name rendered her almost speechless. She narrowed her eyes. "Oh, so you're one of them, are you?" She fixed me with a smile, then returned her attention to Gav. "You take care of this girl, you understand?"

"I promise," he said.

"Have a good night," she called as I pulled out my keys.

As I shut the door behind us, I cringed. "Sorry about that. I bet Mrs. Wentworth is thinking all sorts of wild and crazy things right now."

"I like that she looks out for you," he said, "but one thing . . ."

I threw my keys in the bowl by the door and turned to face him. "What's that?"

"How about next time you introduce me as Gav? I hate the name Leonard."

"You got it," I said, then thought, *next time?*

I took his jacket and hung it up in my tiny front closet. "Well, this is it," I said, leading him into the living room. "Believe it or not, I cleaned today, so I'm less embarrassed than I normally would be." I turn into my kitchen and flipped on the lights. "A lot smaller than the one at the White House, wouldn't you say?"

He followed me in. "I would have thought you'd have a monster kitchen with every newfangled tool out there. This looks so . . . normal."

"Disappointed?"

"Not at all," he said. "I like it. It's comfortable."

"Have a seat."

He did and we talked while I asked him for food preferences. Lucky for me, I'd impulsively left some pork chops in the refrigerator after food shopping, rather than freezing them. As the oven preheated, I prepared them the way my mom used to when I was a kid — with crushed ranch-flavored chips as breading. "These will only take about a half hour to bake," I said. "That okay?"

"I have all night." His cheeks went pink, as though hearing how that came out. "I mean, sure. I'm more concerned about you. I know you get in superearly."

"Not so early these days," I said, and told him about Virgil.

As I worked at the counter, he got up from the table to join me. "Let me help."

Together we prepared a salad and a couple of small side dishes. And we talked about everything going on at the White House. Like Henry had, Gav advised me to trust my gut. "You have good instincts, Ollie. Like I told you, you spot things others miss. Just keep your eyes open and keep doing your job."

His words cheered me more than I cared

to admit. "What about you?" I asked as I placed a salad in front of him. "What's going on in the department?"

"Aren't you going to join me?"

I wasn't hungry, but I didn't want him to feel uncomfortable. "I'll have a little," I said, and fixed myself a smaller plate. Pulling out a bottle of Riesling, I held it up. "Wine?"

"Can't," he said, digging in. "I'm on call 'round the clock. But you go ahead."

I sipped my wine and checked on the pork chops as Gav ate. Putting a few finishing touches on a simpler version of the spinach I planned to serve at the state dinner, I asked him again, "So, what can you tell me about all that's going on?"

By the way he attacked his food, I could tell the poor guy had been really hungry. It did my heart good to see him enjoying the fresh greens, and I looked forward to putting the hot meal in front of him just as soon as the chops came out of the oven.

"Well," he said, "we've heard rumblings."

Guessing — based on what he'd said before and what Tom had told me — I asked, "You think there's a problem with one of the agents?"

Gav's eyes clouded. "How much has Agent MacKenzie told you?"

Agent MacKenzie? So formal?

"Not a great deal. I was there when the tainted chicken wings first showed up."

"And from the reports I've read, you single-handedly saved the children from being poisoned."

I waved him off. "Anyone following protocols would have done the same thing."

"Not from what I heard."

"I just wish the Secret Service would tell the First Lady what really happened. She and I have gotten off to a bad start. She blames me for disappointing her kids. Not that I blame her — she just doesn't know the whole truth. And let me tell you, it's been mostly downhill from there." The timer rang and I opened the oven door. Gav studied me as I stood at the stove. "You don't mind if I fix your plate from here, do you?" I asked.

"This informality is nice," he said. "I could get used to it."

I felt my face grow hot, and it wasn't from the burners. Turning my back, I said, "Good," and slid a chop onto his dish, adding sides of spinach and leftover mashed potatoes I'd warmed up. I placed it in front of him, feeling oddly comfortable with this arrangement. Still full from my tacos, I took a small helping of spinach for myself. Too many more evenings of eating out and I'd have trouble tying my apron strings.

"Why aren't they telling Mrs. Hyden about the arsenic in the chicken wings?" I asked.

Gav had closed his eyes. "This is wonderful," he said around a mouthful. "You're a miracle worker." He opened his eyes again. "I mean it."

I'd originally pegged Gav in his mid- to late-forties, but sitting here — relaxed — wearing a hooded sweatshirt, I revised my guess. Maybe it was the suits that aged him. Maybe the responsibility.

He leaned forward over his plate. "You and I may both believe that Mrs. Hyden has the right to know there was a threat against her children. Of course we think that — because you and I would both want to know if it were *our* kids in danger."

"Do you have kids?"

He shook his head. "Never married. You?"

"No."

Shifting in his seat, he forked more food up. "But MacKenzie is doing this right. The spill of information in this situation must be controlled. Mrs. Hyden is new here. Everybody on the Secret Service staff knows she's unhappy with you for holding back those chicken wings. That tells us something: that she doesn't yet understand — let alone embrace — our security protocols. We can't bring her in on the truth until we know the information won't go any further." Shoving the food into his mouth, he kept talking as he chewed. "Sorry. I know this is rude, but this is so good. And I'm starving."

I laughed. "I don't stand on ceremony here. Enjoy."

"The Secret Service believes she would feel compelled to tell her kids what's going on."

"I hadn't thought of that."

"Yeah," Gav said as he scooped up more potatoes. "Try to put a muzzle on a nine- or a thirteen-year-old. Ain't gonna happen. Once the kids get wind of it, the news is out. We have to be very careful here."

"Even if it means offering me up as the sacrificial lamb."

He swallowed. "Afraid so."

"I guess I understand." I took a long sip of wine. "If it weren't for this Chef Virgil, I might feel more confident. I just get the sense that Mrs. Hyden is looking for the first chance to kick me out on my duff."

Gav sliced off another bite of pork chop. "You have friends in the department. We'll do our best to look out for you."

"I think there are plenty of agents who would like to see me fall on my face."

He chuckled. "You are a handful. I swear, when you first showed up at that bomb briefing, I couldn't figure out why the Campbells kept such a mouthy upstart on staff. And when we had that one-on-one tutorial —"

"You enjoyed making me sweat."

"I did," he said, looking pleased with himself. "But remember, that was still early on. Little did I know . . ."

I waited for him to finish that thought, but he didn't. "Little did he know . . ." what? Popping another piece of chop into his mouth, he told me again how wonderful everything tasted.

"So," I said, "how come?"

He raised his eyebrows, silently asking what I meant.

"How come you never married?"

His eyes sparkled and he smiled. "I could ask the same of you."

"Career."

"Same here," he said, looking down. "Mostly."

Now I raised my eyebrows.

He placed his fork and knife down on either side of his plate, and met my gaze.

Uh-oh, I thought. *He's got a long-time girlfriend and I've been reading all these signals wrong.* I felt my face flush. "Forget I

297

asked," I said.

"No." He took a deep breath and tried to smile, but it didn't work. "We're friends. Good friends. Despite all the trouble we caused each other when we first met. Right?"

I nodded.

"Then you should know this about me." He looked as though he was trying to arrange his face to put me at ease, but it was having the exact opposite effect. "I always figured I would get married, have kids, the whole shebang. I came close, in fact. Twice."

I waited.

"In my twenties I was engaged to Jennifer. But . . ."

This was hard for him, I could see it in his eyes.

The corners of his mouth turned down as he took a long breath. "She was . . . the last victim of the Maryland Murderer."

I'd been in my teens and only vaguely remembered the case. "Were you an agent then?"

"Not yet."

"The Maryland Murderer picked people at random, didn't he? Just like that Washington sniper."

"Very similar." His mouth was still twisted down. "Jennifer was out for a jog on a beautiful Sunday morning. It was her killing that broke the case. The guy got sloppy and they caught him." He tried to smile again. It still didn't work. "I guess that's something. Took me a long time to get over her. Never thought I would." His eyes got a faraway look in them. "Right after that I joined the agency, immersed myself in my job, and tried to pretend I didn't need anyone. But then, about five years later, I met Morgan."

The expression on his face told me what he was going to say next, even before he said it.

"A week after we got engaged she was killed, too. A drunk driver."

I reached across the table to touch the back of his hand. "I'm so sorry."

He entwined his fingers with mine. "Morgan died twelve years ago. Since then, I've put all my efforts into the job. I decided I was a jinx and I never wanted to inflict myself on another person I cared about."

My heart was pounding so loud I was afraid he could hear it. Quietly, I asked, "Do you still feel that way?"

"I don't know," he said. "I'm afraid."

His unexpected vulnerability twisted my heart.

"You are not a jinx," I said.

His eyes clouded again. "Sure about that, are you?"

"You saved my life. More than once."

"You saved your own life."

"Only because you taught me what to look for. And you believed in me."

He gave my hand a quick squeeze and pulled away. Leaning back, he returned to his dinner. The odd, intimate moment we'd shared was gone.

"Where is home for you?" I asked. "I thought you were a D.C. native, but you said you were in a hotel room."

As he ate he explained, "I have an apartment just outside the city, but I was on assignment out of the country for a year, so I sublet to another agent." He shrugged. "The hotel isn't so bad."

"How long are you here for?"

"Until this gets resolved."

"This," I asked, clarifying, "meaning how the chicken wings got into the White House?"

"We know the group responsible overall, but what we can't figure out is who else is in on it. They had to have help. From inside. That's what scares me the most."

"You don't go undercover or anything, do you?" I asked. "I mean, you're in charge, so you're not in any real danger, are you?"

His eyes narrowed ever so slightly. "To anyone else who asked me that, I'd say that information is classified. To you, I'll say that I can't share specifics."

"That worries me," I said.

He wagged a finger — the matter was closed. "Can I have more of that spinach?"

We talked until after midnight. We could have continued far into the morning, but Gav said that he had a meeting at 6:00 and I wanted to get in early, too — despite the fact that Virgil would cover the First Family's breakfast on his own. I handed Gav his jacket and walked him to my door.

"I think Mrs. Wentworth has probably given up for tonight," I said. "So you don't have to be worried about being waylaid on your way to the elevator."

Stepping into the hallway, he made a show of checking her door. "It's closed," he whispered. "I think we're safe."

He thanked me again for dinner. "I had a really nice evening," he said. This would have been the time for a visiting friend to say, "Well, good night. See you soon." But Gav didn't move. We stood inches apart. So close I could feel his warmth.

"I'm glad you called," I said, looking up at him. "I'm glad you came over."

He took a half-step closer and for the

briefest of moments I thought he was going to kiss me. I wanted him to. And I wanted to kiss back.

I reached for him. "I . . . I don't want you to go."

The same pain I'd seen in his eyes earlier flashed there again. "I have to. We both know that."

"You're not a jinx."

He brushed hair off my forehead. "You don't know what it's like."

"Gav . . ."

"Maybe it would be better for both of us if we didn't do this again."

"You don't believe that."

He flexed his jaw and pulled away. "I'm sorry," he said. "I probably shouldn't have come."

I watched until the elevator doors closed behind him, wondering what had just happened here.

CHAPTER 21

I decided not to tell Cyan about Gav's visit. She would want all the juicy details — not that there were any — but I wasn't yet ready to share. I knew it would take some time before I sorted it out myself. Gav had been such a pain in my backside when he first arrived at the White House, but now . . . Now I felt a profound change. I wanted to know him better. A lot better.

Midmorning, when Tom strode into the kitchen, I felt a strange combination of sensations. Guilt over having Gav at my apartment last night; glee because this was a secret I was happy to keep; and, for the first time since Tom and I had broken up, relief. Seeing Tom so soon after my encounter with Gav made me realize I really was okay again.

I felt myself smile. This was good.

"I have news for you," Tom said as soon as we gathered around him. Bucky, Cyan, and I were there, along with Virgil, Gardez, and Nourie. "First things first." He pointed to the two Secret Service agents. "You are both being reassigned."

Before anyone could react, he addressed Gardez. "Please report to Agent Martin at once. He has your orders." To Nourie, he said, "I need you to report to Mrs. Hyden immediately."

I spoke before I could stop myself. "Mrs. Hyden?"

Tom shot me a "Why do you always have to question me?" look. To Nourie, he added, "She's waiting for you."

Both agents took off in a flash.

"You mean we're babysitter free now?" I asked.

"You are. But that doesn't mean that we won't have a presence down here at all. Expect agents to pop in from time to time just to check on things."

"Fair enough," I said. "We'll continue to cooperate and be as open as we can."

Cyan raised her hand to get Tom's attention. "What's up with Agent Nourie?"

Tom snapped, "Why?"

"Just wondering. We kinda got used to him down here."

"That's part of why he's being re-assigned." Flicking a glance at me, he continued talking to Cyan. "Contrary to what you might believe, fraternization between Secret Service agents and White House staff members is discouraged."

Cyan's face went so red I thought she might explode. "I was just asking."

"All personnel changes are effective immediately."

That didn't answer much, but Tom wasn't finished. "I have a few other matters to discuss with all of you." He turned to Virgil. "Would you mind stepping into the hall for a few moments, please? I need to consult with these individuals privately."

Taken aback, Virgil said, "Sure," but he clearly wasn't pleased to be excluded.

As soon as he was gone, Tom lowered his voice. "You all know about the tainted chicken wings." Turning to Bucky and Cyan, he added, "Ollie was ordered not to tell you that arsenic was found on the wings, but you two aren't stupid. I appreciate that you've kept the matter quiet thus far, despite the obvious temptation to share the information with Mrs. Hyden."

Gav's explanation last night about why Mrs. Hyden was being kept in the dark went a long way to keeping me appeased.

The three of us nodded.

"Ollie already knows that we have been

questioning one of our agents in the handling of the tainted food."

Bucky and Cyan exchanged a worried glance. "One of the agents brought the wings in here?" Bucky asked.

Tom grimaced. "Yes and no. We have fully investigated him, and corroborated his story. It appears that the box of chicken wings was brought in during the move — as we suspected — but no one actually saw who might have included them in the moving van with the Hydens' personal belongings. The agent we've been questioning found the box in the Diplomatic Reception Room, where everything had been staged. He thought that the wings ought to be served from the kitchen. So he brought them here."

"He didn't think anything was suspicious?"

"No one would have found it suspicious. There was an extremely efficient and tight chain of custody from the time the Hydens' belongings left their home until the time they arrived here to be unpacked. Whoever added that box is someone with high clearance."

"My God, that means you can't trust anybody," I said.

"What we've done is reassign all agents. Anyone who had direct access to the Hydens' possessions that day has been assigned to positions outside the residence. That is, except for a few key personnel who we hope to God are above suspicion."

"Like you?" I asked.

He nodded.

"So that's why Gardez is gone," I said. "I remember meeting him, and Bost, on Inauguration Day."

"All such agents are being reassigned. Not just them."

"This seems to be coming awfully late," I said. "I mean, if you really suspected anyone on your team, shouldn't these reassignments have come before now?"

Tom bristled. "Hindsight is twenty-twenty, isn't it? If you'd been listening, you'll recall this is all coming on the heels of what we learned from the agent we've been interrogating." Anger flashed in his eyes. "Still the Monday-morning quarterback, aren't you?"

I swallowed my anger. But Tom shook his head. "I apologize. That was uncalled for." Regaining his composure, he went on, "Sorry, I've been under a great deal of stress." He made eye contact with the three of us. "As have we all. My department has come under scrutiny — as it should. But this morning, during a six o'clock briefing" —

Hmm . . . the meeting Gav mentioned?

— "we were ordered to make these personnel changes." Tom chose that moment to stare straight at me. "The agents in charge of this investigation have made it clear that you — the kitchen staff — need to be kept in the loop."

"Really?" Cyan said.

Again Tom stared at me. "The higher-ups believe that since the three of you were involved from the very start, and that the children were spared because of your actions, it is imperative we keep you updated. It is also imperative that you understand that just because the 'babysitters,' as you so fondly termed them, are gone doesn't mean we believe the threat to the White House is over." He frowned. "They believe placing Secret Service agents in the kitchen full time is not a good use of our resources. They have full confidence in the three of you."

I wanted to ask Tom if that meant *he* didn't have confidence in the three of us, but instead I asked, "What about Virgil? Why did you ask him to leave?"

"Virgil is not considered a threat to the First Family's safety, but he is a threat to security. If I told him what I've just told you, he would undoubtedly run straight to Mrs. Hyden with the story. We can't have that. He knows nothing about the connection between the chicken wings and our stricken staff members. Any information he has on the hostage situation last week would have come from the news. It's best if we continue to keep him out of the loop."

We asked a few more questions, and were just about wrapping up when Virgil knocked on the wall behind us. "Can I come back yet? I have work to do."

Tom waved him in. "Just finishing up here." To the group, he said, "Any questions about these changes should be brought to my attention. You know where to find me. I will ask that you do not discuss these matters with anyone other than me, or the agent in charge of the investigation who has been brought in."

"Who's that?" Cyan asked.

I already knew.

"You've met him. Special Agent in Charge Gavin."

Cyan looked at me. "Gav?" she said. "Didn't he call you the other day? Did you know he was coming back?"

I mumbled something incomprehensible, all the while aware that Tom was watching me.

"Thanks, everyone," he said, then turned to me again. "I have one more item to discuss with you alone." He pointed out to the hall. "Do you have a moment?"

I didn't know what to expect. Had Gav mentioned that he and I had gotten together last night? No, Gav was smarter than that. Plus, nothing had happened. And maybe nothing ever would. Butterflies danced in my stomach as I followed Tom out.

Two butlers maneuvered a cart toward the elevator, so Tom walked east, stopping just short of the China Room. Looking up and down the hall, he whispered, "This is just for you, okay? Don't share it with anyone else."

"Of course." I still had no idea of what he was about to say.

"You called me the other day," he began, "about Bost and Zeller."

I nodded.

"You were right about them. They did an end-run around me and took their innuendo straight to your friend Gav. That's another reason why they're being reassigned. Gav is a sharp guy and he's handling it professionally. If they had had solid grievances, they could have gone through channels. Instead it became obvious they were gunning for promotion."

Tom's lips came together tightly. "I just wanted to thank you for giving me the heads-up. I know I wasn't exactly gracious on the phone when you brought it to my attention."

I was about to dismiss his apology and explain that I understood, when we heard footsteps coming down the nearby stairs.

Tom turned, and straightened the moment we saw who it was.

I was about to say, "Gav!" but remembered where I was. "Special Agent in Charge," I said warmly. "It's good to see you again."

Gav took a moment to assess the situation. I caught a quizzical look in his eyes as he nodded hello. "Ms. Paras," he said. To Tom: "Agent MacKenzie, I trust you've brought our kitchen staff up to date."

At that moment, Gav looked at me, and I at him. There was nothing in his eyes to give away what he might be feeling. He was all business. And yet . . .

Tom stepped back shifting his gaze between us. "Yes," he said. "And I was just thanking Ms. Paras here for her assistance on another matter."

"Very well." Face impassive, Gav continued. "I will be unable to run the meeting at fourteen-hundred today. Will you take that

311

over for me?"

Tom looked surprised, but recovered quickly. "Of course," he said. "You were going to address all the personnel changes with the remaining PPD. I thought you wanted to handle that personally."

"If I could be there, I would."

There was alarm in Tom's expression. "Are you —"

Gav held up a hand, stopping Tom mid-sentence. "A situation has come up." Nodding to me again he said, "Very nice to see you again, Ms. Paras," then walked away.

"What's up with that?" I asked, because I couldn't *not* ask. "Is he going into some kind of danger?"

Tom's eyes narrowed. "What do you know?"

"Nothing really," I started to say, but I'm such a bad liar, I stuck mostly to the truth. "He just seemed preoccupied, and abrupt. Didn't you think so, too?"

Tom studied me a moment longer. Finally, he said. "Gav is sharp and he's smart. He'll be fine." He consulted his watch. "Thank you again, Ollie. But now I have to run."

I stared after them both for a long moment, knowing I had no control over either man's destiny, but wishing, at least in Gav's case, that I did. Both were good guys. Both strong and smart and kind. Tom was probably right. Gav would be fine. I stared upward and whispered a little prayer to protect him.

CHAPTER 22

The four of us were hard at work in the kitchen. Bucky, Cyan, and I coordinated with the social secretary's office, the calligraphy office, and Kendra to get the flowers just right for the state dinner. Just three days away, we were in that crazy period where everything that can go wrong usually does, and time slips by twice as fast as it should.

"Virgil seems less . . . painful to be around," Cyan whispered when he stepped out of the kitchen. "What's up with that? You think he's starting to fit in?"

Bucky moved closer. "He didn't pitch a fit all day yesterday," he said, then gave a wry chuckle. "Maybe it's you, Ollie. You weren't here. Let's see how he behaves today."

"He's still adjusting. I'm sure things will get better in time," I said. "I spoke with him about Mrs. Hyden's budget concerns with regard to food."

"When?"

"This morning. I expected him to bite my head off, but he took it rather well." I shrugged. "Maybe now he's starting to understand that he's cooking for a family now, not for important write-ups in newspapers and trade journals."

"It's about time he showed a little respect for what we do around here," Cyan said.

"This has got to be a tough adjustment for him. After all, he came in thinking he'd snagged the top job. I'd be surprised if we didn't see any backlash from him at all. He just needs to settle in. Although he understands his role, I don't think he's happy about it. When I explained Mrs. Hyden's displeasure over the costs of ingredients he'd ordered, he seemed genuinely shocked."

"As soon as the media folk stop covering his every move and 'innovation,' he'll get bored," Bucky said. "Mark my words: A year from now, he'll be executive chef at some posh hotel in New York." Turning to Cyan, and obviously remembering Rafe's flight out of the White House, he said, "Sorry. I didn't mean it like that's a bad thing."

Cyan patted Bucky's arm. "No problem. I'm over him now."

One thing I had to admit: Having Virgil in

315

charge of the family meals had taken a great deal of pressure off of the rest of us during the preparations for the state dinner. I couldn't say that I was happy to have him part of our kitchen, but I'd come to a place where I didn't resent him quite so much.

I suppose I shouldn't have spoken so quickly.

Valerie Peacock swooped into the kitchen. "Good afternoon," she said with a bright smile. "How are plans for Wednesday progressing?" She glanced around the room as though looking for someone.

"Perfectly." I wiped my hands on my apron and approached her. "We've got all the staples on hand, and the fresh meats and produce will arrive late Tuesday or early Wednesday morning."

"Will you be at full staff all week?"

Unusual question. "Bucky has tomorrow off. But Tuesday and Wednesday, we will all be here."

"Where is Virgil?"

"He stepped out," I said.

"He does that," Bucky added. "A lot."

Her smile didn't dim. "How much will Virgil be involved in the state dinner?"

"He's mostly tied up with family meal preparations," I said, "but we will probably

316

need him to pitch in at the last minute."

"You and your staff are the ones actually handling the dinner, right? And you don't foresee any problems?"

"We will be bringing in Service by Agreement chefs — assistants — Wednesday morning. But I'm curious why you're asking."

She smiled a bit too hard. "We might need Virgil for a few hours on Wednesday."

"For what?"

"I'll let you know," she said. "But that's not important now. Let me get out of your way so you get everything done on time."

A moment later she was gone. "How much you want to bet our buddy Virgil has another photography shoot in his future?" Bucky said. "And what was she trying to suggest anyway? That there's a chance we wouldn't get everything done on time without him? We've been staging state dinners since she was in diapers." He looked at me and at Cyan. "Well, at least I have."

Cyan jostled his shoulder. "Diapers, Bucky? Come on. You're not that old."

A smile curled one end of his mouth. "High school, then." He shrugged. "Okay, maybe college."

Bucky left for the day shortly after Virgil

handed dinner off to the butlers to serve. While Virgil cleaned up his area, Cyan and I made notes about what we'd spent the afternoon working on. Not only would these notes help us remember where we left off when we consulted them in the morning, they would be critical as we prepared dinner Wednesday night. Cyan and I planned to go over everything meticulously, no matter how long it took.

"Good evening," Valerie said from the doorway.

The White House was always quieter at night and her voice, a sudden high pitch in the soft silence, made me jump. She must have realized it, because she spoke in more subdued tones as she continued. "How much later do you plan to stay this evening, Virgil?" she asked.

He glanced at the clock. "Ten minutes."

She tilted her head. "Could you stick around just a bit longer?" she asked. "We need to ask you something."

He put down the bowl and spoon he'd been holding and wiped his hands. "Go ahead."

"No, no," she said, "this is a very special request. And we need you to stay for just a teensy bit longer." She put up her thumb and index finger to indicate just how "teensy" she meant.

"Sure," he said absentmindedly. "I'll be here."

A half hour later, Virgil was pacing the kitchen, clearly annoyed. The constant looks at the clock, his watch, and the door weren't my only clues. His deep, resigned sighs came at intervals so regular I could almost predict them.

"How much longer do you think they'll be?" he asked.

Cyan and I shared a glance. "No idea," I said. "But I'm sure they wouldn't have asked you to stay if it wasn't important."

He grumbled.

"Abigail wanted you to come out to Camp David to cook for her sleepover. Maybe it has to do with that."

"I hope not."

"I thought you wanted to go. After all, Camp David is beautiful," I said. "You'd really like it there."

He stopped pacing long enough to join us at the computer station. "I would enjoy it if I were preparing a feast for the president and his wife," he said, keeping his voice low. "Their children are fine as far as kids go, but they don't have cultured palates. They would be happier with store-bought chicken wings than they would with any of my specialties." He gave me a pointed look. "It was a mistake for you to refuse to serve those wings to the kids, if you don't mind me saying so. I think that if you'd have let the kids have their treat, their mother wouldn't have been so insistent about me coming here." He affected a sad look. "She'd approached me right after the election, of course, but after the chicken wing incident, she was positively adamant."

Cyan looked as miserable as I felt. Why hadn't I dumped the box the moment it showed up in my kitchen? Because I'd wanted to give the giver time to make himself or herself known. What I wouldn't give to be able to go back in time and handle the situation differently. Of course, if I had, Secret Service would be unaware of the threat against the First Family. Had all this played out for a reason? Maybe the added protections Tom had implemented and that Gav was now overseeing were doing exactly what they were designed to do: Protect President Hyden and his family.

Slightly less vexed with myself after my reasoning, I said, "It is what it is."

"Yes," Virgil agreed, "but just think about it: If Mrs. Hyden hadn't absolutely insisted that I come here, we would both be a lot happier right now." Virgil wandered into the refrigeration room. "I'll be in here checking inventory if anyone needs me," he called.

"Oh, Ollie," Cyan said. She kept her voice low. "This really is all my fault."

"No one died, remember," I whispered back, adding, "This may have ultimately been the best thing to have happened."

She shot me a skeptical look and I shared my theory about how all this may have happened for a reason. How we wouldn't have known about the threat if the chicken wings had been disposed of.

"You always know how to put a positive spin on things," she said when I was finished.

I was about to answer her when Valerie returned to the kitchen, accompanied by Mrs. Hyden and Josh. "Good evening, Ollie," Mrs. Hyden said. "Is Virgil around?"

Cyan was already heading to the refrigeration area and in moments returned with Virgil, who greeted our visitors with more warmth than I'd ever seen the man display. "What can I do for you?" he asked Mrs. Hyden.

"It's what you can do for Josh," she said. Nudging her son, she prodded, "Go ahead, honey. Ask him your question."

I anticipated another request to work in the kitchen. I hoped it wouldn't be for this week because we would be swamped. But Josh's eyes were so bright that I knew it would be hard to turn him down no matter what the request. Still, I was unprepared for what came next.

"Chef Virgil," Josh said solemnly, "my school is having career day on Wednesday. All the kids have to do a project on what we want to be when we grow up. I want to be a chef, just like you."

"Thank you so much, Josh," Virgil said. "I'm very flattered."

Mrs. Hyden nudged Josh again. The little boy continued. "We're supposed to bring in a person to school who does the same job. I want to bring you."

Virgil's bottom lip dropped. He shifted his attention to Mrs. Hyden with a "This is a joke, right?" look, but she was smiling down at her son and missed it entirely.

"I don't know what to say, Josh," he began.

Valerie seemed to be the only other person in the room besides me and Cyan aware of Virgil's exasperation. "I think the best thing to say is that you would be delighted to participate," she said.

"But . . ." Virgil stammered. "You mean to tell me that every child in your class is bringing in a professional of some sort?"

Josh nodded enthusiastically.

Mrs. Hyden continued to smile. "Josh's class is small, and this school provides a very forward-thinking environment. That's part of the reason we chose it. They've run this particular program for the past ten years with great success. Which is why we support Josh's request."

Her words were soft, but her message was clear. Virgil had no choice.

"I would be delighted," he said. Turning to Josh, he added, "Thank you for asking me."

Josh was all smiles. "Great," he said. "It's on Wednesday. And because I have all kinds of bodyguards and stuff, my teacher said I could go last that day. You don't have to be there until kinda late." To Valerie, he said, "Did we get the time from my teacher yet?"

How young kids learn the power of power.

She nodded to Josh and smiled at Virgil. "I'll send you the schedule as soon as I get back to my office."

"Thanks," Virgil said as they left.

The moment they were gone, he uttered an expletive.

"Be quiet, they may hear you," I said.

"This is ridiculous," Virgil said.

Cyan and I returned to our note-making. Virgil started pacing again, but this time right next to where we were working. There was no way I was going to put up with his growling and muttering behind us for who-knows-how long.

"Listen," I said, turning to him, "Josh looks up to you and that's pretty special. You should look at this opportunity as a gift. You can do some good here, and if you stop complaining for half a minute, you'll see that maybe you can do yourself some good, too."

"You don't understand," he said. "I am not comfortable around kids."

Cyan held her hands up, "You took this job — why?"

He gave her a "Duh!" look. "For the prestige, the glamour." Pointing at me, he went on. "Remember, I expected to have her job. I had all sorts of wonderful events planned. But no." To me, he said, "You get to do all the big events with printed menus and big coverage in the society pages." Throwing up his hands, he went on, "What am I talking about — society pages? You have big coverage on *front* pages. That's what I wanted. Not to play nursemaid to some kids. And certainly not to be brought in for show-and-tell."

"It's career day, not show-and-tell," I said.

"Can't *you* do this for me?"

"No."

324

"Why not?"

"Because he asked you. And Mrs. Hyden wants you. And," I added, just because this once I couldn't resist being snotty, "I'm busy. I have one of those big front-page events to work on that day."

I called Gav on the way home, but his phone went right to voicemail. After our discussion last night and Tom's cryptic "He'll be fine" this morning, I was worried for him. I couldn't quite understand how Gav had gotten under my skin so quickly, but he had. Plus, there was nothing wrong with a friend calling to check up on another friend.

Over the past couple years, he and I had chitchatted now and then, but it was seeing him again last night that had made my heart flip-flop. I didn't know what kind of investigative work he was doing right now. For all I knew, he was in a meeting with the president and top staffers and had, understandably, turned his phone off.

But I couldn't shake the worry.

I alighted from the elevator on my floor, not terribly surprised to see Mrs. Wentworth waiting for me. "Did James tell you I was on my way up?" I asked her.

"Of course he did. You have an interesting

life, Olivia Paras. I expect you to share it with us."

I laughed.

"Want to come in for a little bit? Stan's busy downstairs and I've got *Jeopardy!* on my DVR."

"Some other time, Mrs. Wentworth."

She'd inched out into the hall. "Who was the new fella?"

Not wanting to get into specifics about Gav's role at the White House, I said, "I introduced him to you . . ."

She wiggled her cane impatiently. "That's not what I mean."

"He's just a friend."

"Yes," she said, suddenly seeming more like Yoda than a sweet old lady, "but there's more to that one, isn't there?"

I didn't have an answer.

"How old is he?"

This one I could answer honestly. "I'm not sure. A little older than I am."

"My first husband was seven years older than me." She nodded, clearly pleased to be imparting wisdom. "Perfect age. Too bad he died so young." Shaking her head, she said, "My second husband was ten years older." Making a so-so motion with her hand, she said, "Not so good. We had different experiences growing up, different outlooks. I divorced him."

"And Stan?" I asked, referring to our building's electrician and her near-constant companion.

She winked. "Seven years. Perfect again."

"I'll remember that."

"That fella from last night looks about seven years older. Ask him next time you see him."

"Will do," I said.

I let myself in and tried Gav's phone again. Straight to voicemail again. Mrs. Wentworth's words bounced around in my brain, making my stomach curl in on itself. Why was I so worried for Gav's safety? He'd been out of the country for nearly a year and I'd only given him the occasional passing thought. Now I wondered where he was and when I'd have the chance to talk with him again.

CHAPTER 23

Monday blew by in a blur — with Bucky off, Cyan and I barely had time to breathe, and before we knew it, it was Tuesday. I'd called Gav's cell several times over the past day and a half. I'd even left a couple of messages.

On Tuesday, Virgil's complaints about his upcoming commitment to Josh ramped up several notches. His nonstop whining made me wonder how he'd ever made it to adulthood without someone beating him up. I glanced over during one of his rants. Maybe they had.

Bucky worked next to the giant mixer across the kitchen from us. When Virgil stomped by him for the fourth time, Bucky snapped.

"Get over it already," he said over his shoulder. "You work here, you check your ego at the door. It's about time you understood that."

Virgil stopped in his tracks. I probably should have intervened at that point, but right about now I was thinking that Virgil deserved whatever he was about to get.

"My job here is too important for me to leave it . . . to spend time away . . . at . . . at a grammar school, for heaven's sakes. What do they expect me to do? Answer a bunch of boring questions from kids who have no idea what a real chef does for a living?"

"This is your chance to enlighten them," I said.

"I still think you should take my place. You're better with kids."

Chopping shallots while Cyan kneaded bread next to me, I shook my head. "Not a chance. This one is all yours."

He folded his arms across his chest. "Well then, if I'm stuck spending the afternoon at school, I'm taking tomorrow off."

"Whoa," I said. "You can't."

"What do you mean? Bucky wasn't here yesterday."

"Don't even go there," Bucky said. "This is our sandbox. You have to learn to play by our rules."

"Yesterday was Bucky's regular day off, Virgil," I said in an attempt to quell the rising tide of anger in the room. "We *planned* for him to not be here. We've got this week scheduled down to the minute. All days off need to be requested ahead of time. Paul went over this with you when you first started, remember? Except for regular days off, we require a week's notice. In a pinch we can probably work with less time, but not on a day when we're hosting a state dinner."

His mouth agape, he tightened his arms. "You're just playing favorites now."

"Sorry," I said, though I wasn't sorry at all. "If you would have told us last week, we might have been able to work it in." I snapped my fingers, feeling a little justifiable meanness take over where my good sense usually resided. "But wait, you *did* take an extra day off last week. You were playing golf . . . in Florida."

"With the president," he added.

Like I didn't know that. "No matter. You have to live by the same rules we all do. We're going to need you here all day tomorrow."

"You mean until it's time for me to go be Josh's show-and-tell project."

"Yeah. Until then." I looked up at the clock. "Are you going to have everything done in time for lunch?"

Virgil pouted, but went back to work. I was getting used to his little hissy fits.

Maybe one of these days he'd start acting like an adult.

Cyan stopped kneading as though she suddenly remembered something. She hurried over to the computer. Consulting our schedule and then checking e-mail, she looked at the clock, then turned to me. "Secret Service hasn't gotten back to us about that extra order I placed. I probably should have followed up sooner, but they're always so reliable. Do you think they forgot?"

"It's worth checking," I said. "Let me call over there now."

I asked for our regular contact, Agent Flora Scott. She wasn't in. I tried a couple other agents, but came up empty. "Argh," I said.

Cyan looked on in sympathy. "Always something, isn't it?"

"I'm going over there to see who's around. We have to make sure this gets done."

I walked over to the nearby Secret Service office where Bost and Zeller had attempted to corral and question me, but the only person on duty had no idea about any grocery orders, nor where Flora might be. He apologized profusely. I told him I'd check with the other office.

On my way to the West Wing, I tried Gav's

cell again. Still no luck. If he was ignoring my calls, I was going to be pretty angry when he finally answered. At least that's what I kept telling myself. I also kept reminding myself that he and I had no commitment to one another. He had made that clear. There was no reason why I should expect him to check in with me. None whatsoever.

My brain waged war with itself. Half of me argued that after our conversation, Gav would keep in touch. If he wasn't answering, there had to be a really good reason. The other half of me argued that I just wasn't that important to him. That didn't square with my feelings from the other night — or the feelings I believed I'd read from him — but it was still a possibility.

Tom was in his office when I got there, but the agent in the anteroom asked me to wait. "Agent MacKenzie is on the phone."

I sat on the edge of one of the sofas, looking around the room, trying to keep my mind on preparations for Wednesday, yet fingering the cell phone in my pocket, just in case. I often turned my phone off because I couldn't afford to have it ring at an inopportune time. Maybe that's what Gav had done.

But he hadn't had it on last night in his

hotel room. That is, if he'd made it back to the hotel room at all. Maybe he'd gotten in very late and decided not to wake me. Or maybe he hadn't thought of me at all.

"Agent MacKenzie will see you now."

I stood and walked in to Tom's office while the other agent held the door, and then closed it behind me. "New guy?" I asked, pointing toward the anteroom.

"One of many. What can I do for you, Ollie?"

I told him about the order we'd placed with Flora Scott, and he said he would look into it right away. "She's usually very conscientious," he said. "I'll find out what's going on." He held up a finger and in moments had her on the line. He handed me the phone. "Tell her what you need."

I did. "And I just wanted to be sure we're on target to get those items tomorrow morning."

Agent Scott apologized for not getting back to me sooner. "We had some trouble with a few ingredients."

"Which ones?"

She named several items I hadn't requested and I said so.

"Your chef Virgil added these to the list."

"Oh, did he?" That man was a growing thorn in my side. "Thanks for letting me know. Would you be sure to get separate receipts for his purchases?"

She said she would.

"Thanks." I handed the phone back to Tom. "I appreciate it. You saved me a lot of time."

"Glad to help."

I started to leave.

"You came all the way down here for that?"

I held up my hands. "No one in the other office had any idea. And I didn't want to wait for an e-mail reply. Time's tight and if we run late on this order, it could really throw us off. The sooner I was sure we were still on target, the more efficient we could be."

He nodded. "Okay."

I started to leave again, but just as I reached for the doorknob, I turned back. Casually, I said, "Gav hasn't been around much the past couple days."

Tom folded his arms. "No, he hasn't."

"Has he been reassigned again?"

The look on Tom's face was at once, hurt, curious, and sad. "Wouldn't you be the first to know if he was?"

"No," I said honestly. "I don't think so."

He took a moment to straighten his blotter. "I'm surprised," he said softly, then

looked up again and met my gaze without expression. "I haven't heard from Special Agent in Charge Gavin since our discussion in the hall Sunday."

My face must have given away my reaction because he held up a hand.

"That doesn't mean anything bad. I knew there was a chance we wouldn't hear from him for a while."

"A while meaning . . ."

"A while." Tom sighed. "Don't push me, Ollie. This is hard enough."

"I understand," I said, even though I didn't.

"I'm sure he's fine."

CHAPTER 24

Unable to sleep, I got in to the White House kitchen early Wednesday morning. Ridiculously early, even for me. State dinners were among the most important events that went on in this house, and although we occasionally had to deal with unexpected mishaps, I was determined to be prepared for anything.

By 5:30 A.M., I'd gotten almost everything done that Cyan and I had slotted to have completed by 8:00. I was confident that this would be a magnificent state dinner and as I took a long look around the quiet kitchen — my kitchen — I felt a calm settle over me. There may have been issues I felt unsure about since the Hydens arrived, but one thing I knew how to do was throw a party at the White House. Over the years we'd gotten the process down to a science, and I looked forward to showing Mrs. Hyden exactly what the cook she'd inherited from the prior administration could do.

I thrust my hands into my pockets and my fingers encountered my cell phone. I still hadn't heard from Gav. Maybe he'd felt awkward after the evening in my apartment. Maybe he preferred to maintain radio silence until he sorted things out for himself. Maybe I'd read him wrong and he wasn't interested in me at all.

I felt a hard lump in my throat. Or maybe he was in trouble somewhere and couldn't call. As uncomfortable as it might be, I decided that I would find time to ask Tom again about what was going on. Until I knew, I wouldn't be able to fully concentrate. And I had to be at my best today of all days.

Gav once told me I had a sixth sense. Not ESP or clairvoyance, he'd explained, but an awareness that allowed me to anticipate things before they happened. Right now, I was feeling as though all the hairs on my arms and the back of my neck were tingling, trying to send me a signal that I couldn't quite make out. All I could determine was that today was make or break. For me, I wondered, or for Gav?

I couldn't think about it.

"How long have you been in?" Cyan asked as she pulled off her jacket. "And where's Virgil?"

"Not in yet," I said with an absentminded glance at the clock. "He should be here by now, though." I consulted the day's schedule behind me. "Looks like he has breakfast going up at seven this morning for Josh and Mrs. Hyden. Abigail is at Camp David, and the Navy Mess is taking care of the president. He's got time."

"Whoa," Cyan said, looking around. "Look at all you've gotten done already. Were you here all night?"

"Couldn't sleep, so I figured I might as well come in and get started."

Cyan touched my forearm. "What's wrong, Ollie?"

I wanted to tell her, but speaking my concerns out loud would make them real. Keeping silent seemed like another way to offer protection to Gav. I wrinkled my nose. "Nothing, really."

"I don't believe that," she said, "but I won't push you. Too many other pressures today."

Fifteen minutes later, Bucky rolled in, but Virgil still hadn't shown up. "Do you think he's working from the residence kitchen?" I asked.

"Better call up there to find out," Bucky said. "The guy said he wanted the day off. What if he doesn't show?"

"He's too much of a professional for that,"
I said, but my stomach started to crawl with
concern. I lifted the receiver and dialed the
upstairs kitchen. A butler answered. "Is Virgil up there?" I asked, wishing my voice
hadn't risen two octaves. There was no
reason to be nervous.

"No ma'am," the butler answered. "I have
not seen Mr. Ballantine this morning."

"Thanks." I hung up.

When I turned to tell Bucky, my heart
sank. Paul and Valerie approached, looking
somber. I could read it on their faces. "Virgil's not coming in today, is he?"

Paul shook his head. "He called in sick.
And you know the rules, Ollie. No one feeling under the weather can be allowed to
work in the kitchen."

I gritted my teeth. "Okay," I said. "This
puts a crimp into today's plans. But it's
nothing we can't handle." I turned to
Bucky. "Why don't you get started on
breakfast? Cyan and I will keep moving
forward on tonight's dinner."

"Good thing you got in extra early this
morning, Ollie," Cyan said from behind me.
"All that prework is really coming in handy
now."

She was right. "This is only a small set-
back," I said to Paul and Valerie, feeling a

certain joy in knowing we could handle whatever they threw at us. "We'll cover Virgil's responsibilities and still be in great shape to deliver a phenomenal state dinner tonight."

I expected Paul to nod and smile. I expected Valerie to cheerfully check something off on the clipboard she carried, then pivot and run off to put out some other fire.

Neither moved. Neither smiled. In fact, they both looked a little pained.

"What aren't you telling me?" I asked.

"Josh's school project," Paul said. "Virgil was supposed to go."

"Right," I said slowly. The creepy, crawly stomach bugs were back. "But if he's sick, he can't go."

Valerie and Paul exchanged a look.

"No." I held my hands up and backed away. "No, no."

"This is very important to Josh," Valerie said.

I held up a finger. "He wanted Virgil. Not me. I'm sure the teacher can reschedule him."

"Do you have any idea how much work it is to coordinate an event like this?"

I shook my head.

"Security," she went on, "is on special alert. There are plans and protocols and timing issues. If we cancel today, we'll have to set all this up again another day."

That really wasn't my problem, though I refrained from saying so. "Every day Josh goes to school is a major security maneuver. Adding a chef shouldn't really complicate matters."

Valerie sighed. "You wouldn't think so, but the Secret Service informs me that adding a second subject makes coverage more difficult. They strongly suggest you take Virgil's place."

When the White House PPD "strongly suggested" anything, you complied. I was losing ground here, and quickly. I had one more argument left and it was a doozy.

"The state dinner," I said, as though that explained it all. It should have. "I need to be here. All day. This is a huge event and we can't leave anything to chance."

"You would only be gone for about two hours," she said. "We expect to have you both back here by three-thirty at the latest. The state dinner isn't scheduled until eight." Valerie gestured toward Cyan. "As she said, you've already worked ahead. Knowing how well you're organized, I bet you could easily leave the kitchen in your staff's capable hands for two hours."

I bit my lip. She'd effectively painted me

into a corner. To argue now would be to claim that Bucky and Cyan couldn't handle the extra work.

"This isn't right," I said in a last pathetic attempt to get out of it. "Josh will be very disappointed."

"According to the First Lady, Josh originally asked for you because you were so nice to him the other day when he came down here." Valerie smiled. "But because the state dinner was the same night, she knew you would be busy and she talked Josh into asking Virgil instead."

Speechless, I could do nothing but acquiesce. "What time should I be ready?"

Valerie and Paul straightened and smiled. "A Secret Service agent will arrive here at one to escort you to the school," she said. "Thank you, Olivia."

She turned to leave and Paul leaned back to whisper, "I knew you'd come through for us, Ollie. You always do."

The go-to girl. That's me, all right.

When I turned to face Bucky and Cyan, they looked exactly the way I felt. "You tried," Cyan said. "There was nothing else you could have done."

Bucky scowled and returned to his pasta making. "You're the executive chef. Not a babysitter. I wish more people around here would start realizing that."

Coming from Bucky, that was remarkable moral support indeed.

At precisely 1 P.M., a female Secret Service agent arrived in the kitchen. "Ms. Paras?" she asked.

I had cleaned up, changed my tunic, and grabbed a fresh toque — I figured the kids wouldn't actually believe I was a chef without the hat — and was ready to go. "Bucky, Cyan?"

"Go," Cyan said. "You've been running nonstop all day. We're in great shape now. Don't worry about it."

Bucky waved me off. "You'll be back in a couple of hours. Heck, we're so far ahead, maybe I'll take a nap."

"Ha, ha," I said. "Okay, wish me luck."

"Luck!" Cyan called.

The agent assigned to me introduced herself as Brenda Notewell. She was taller than me — although most people are — and slim. She wore a black leather jacket over her gray suit, and I wondered, idly, if every Secret Service agent shopped at the same store. They sure all dressed alike.

She escorted me through the Diplomatic Reception Room outside into the blustery February afternoon, where I ducked my head to keep the cold from nipping at my ears. The wind bit at my nose even on this quick walk to the waiting limousine. "Really?" I said, when she held the back door open for me. "I can't imagine I necessitate this level of security."

She smiled — unusual for an agent, so I figured she must be new — and climbed in next to me. "Things go more smoothly if we operate at a higher level than is required."

I'd been in the backseat of government-issue limos a few times. Mostly under unpleasant circumstances. Our driver didn't speak. Agent Notewell, in contrast, was positively chatty.

"Are you bringing me back, too?" I asked.

"I'm only your escort to the school. From there, you will be covered by the agents protecting Scamp — er — that is, Josh."

"Scamp is a good name for him," I said.

She smiled again. "I agree with you. Fits in with the rest. You've heard them all?"

I had. The Secret Service always came up with code names for the First Family. These nicknames no longer served as a function of security, but the tradition of naming the family members continued nonetheless. President Hyden was Scholar, his wife Symphony. Abigail was Sparkle and

Grandma Marty was Sage.

We arrived at the school less than twenty minutes later. The stately brick structure, castlelike in appearance with turrets and tall peaked corners, sat deep behind giant trees. The school was completely fenced in by black wrought iron, looking more like a posh boarding school from 1800s England than a grammar school in the twenty-first century. I would bet that once the trees bloomed and the grass grew green again, this would be a most welcoming environment. Today, under the gray sky and with the wind whistling through the bare branches, it looked positively spooky.

The car slowed and the driver announced our arrival. I finished consulting the notes I'd prepared for my presentation, and shoved them into my pocket, next to my cell phone. With no need to bring a purse, I'd instead packed a bag of items to use as visual aids when talking to the kids: measuring cups and spoons, a few spatulas, examples of paperwork an executive chef might regularly handle. No knives. I also brought along one of my favorite easy recipes for chicken strips — and made enough copies for every kid in the class.

Brenda told me to wait a moment before getting out. She spoke briefly into a small microphone, listened for a response, then nodded. "Clear," she said.

Two other agents emerged from the school and as they came through the front gates, Brenda finally let me get out. I shouldered my bag, tucked my hat under my arm, and followed her. She handed me over to the two agents, wished me luck, and returned to the limo.

The two agents, both male and young, kept their eyes on our surroundings as they shuttled me through the gate held open by a school security guard. This place was as tight as Fort Knox. Maybe tighter. The security guard welcomed me to Dolorosa Academy with a smile, then shut the massive iron gate behind us with a *clang*. I heard the solid *snick* of an automatic lock and turned to watch the guard amble over to a small windowed structure just inside the grounds.

"Are the two of you on duty here every day?" I asked.

The one on my left answered, "We rotate."

Not that I expected a full-blown conversation, but I tried again as we headed up the stone steps. "How do the kids react to Secret Service always being around?"

The guy on my right shrugged. "We become part of the landscape," he said.

346

"That's good."

"Are there more agents inside?"

Lefty answered this time. "Scamp has a personal bodyguard who does not leave his side."

Righty opened the school's front door and nodded to me once we were inside. "Agent Johnston will take you to the classroom. I will remain here."

"Thanks," I said.

Agent Johnston checked his watch. "We are right on time," he said.

The school's exterior may have resembled a castle, but inside, I felt magically transported back in time. I knew we couldn't be far from the gym — despite all the upgrades over the years, that peculiar aromatic combination of sneakers and sweat didn't change. A wide corridor spread before us, its floor tiled in grammar-school green with a center ribbon of white. At the far end was a wide staircase backed by a wall of windows, which allowed in what little light the day had to offer. The entire area was quiet except for the squeak of our shoes against the tile and the occasional burst of young voices urging teachers to call on "Me, me."

I felt small. Sure I probably wasn't much taller than some of the fifth graders enrolled here, but I also worried about letting Josh down. Had he truly requested me first, or was Valerie just feeding me that line to encourage my participation? Either way, I hoped to make him glad to have me here.

Johnston came to a crisp stop outside the third door on the left. "The teacher's name is Mrs. Fosco. She is expecting you."

The closed door was an indecipherable red wood, alligatored by decades of varnish. An opaque window in the top half of the frame offered only indistinct shadows, and I could hear very little of what was being said. "I just go in?" I asked.

Johnston nodded and grabbed the door-knob.

"Hang on a minute."

He waited while I placed my toque atop my head and took a deep breath. "Okay," I said.

He opened the door. "Good luck."

CHAPTER 25

Twenty heads swiveled to see who was coming in. Twenty pairs of eyes, bright with alert curiosity, watched as I nodded to the teacher and said hello.

Mrs. Fosco was a tiny woman of about fifty with a cheerful expression and powerful voice. "Welcome to our classroom, Ms. Paras," she said, indicating that I should join Agent Nourie until she was finished with the current lesson. To Josh, Mrs. Fosco said, "Why don't you take your guest's coat and hang it up for her? You can help her get ready for the presentation." Josh was up and out of his seat by the time I made it to the back of the room, where a whiteboard had been decorated for Valentine's Day.

After assisting me with my coat, Josh returned to his desk. I joined Agent Nourie in the back corner where he maintained a view of the entire classroom, and stood within a three-step reach of Josh.

Nourie smiled and stepped aside to give me space in the crowded back corner. With the windows to our left and a row of computer terminals to our right just below the whiteboard, I again felt a rush of nostalgia.

"So Virgil called in sick, huh?" he whispered.

I nodded. Nourie shook his head, but said nothing further.

As I stood there, I became aware of the kids' occasional glances my way. Pure curiosity. I'm sure it was the hat. Fortunately, less than five minutes after my arrival, Mrs. Fosco instructed all the children to put their math books away.

"Josh," she said kindly as soon as the scuffling was over and the kids had quieted, "I think it's time."

Josh boosted himself from his desk and ran to the front of the room. I wasn't sure if I should join him yet, but I didn't have to worry long. He waved me forward right away. "Hi," he said to the class as soon as I joined him. From up here, the kids all looked so small. So young.

"Today is my career day presentation," Josh said. He stopped abruptly, ran back to his desk, and shuffled through his books. I waited up front with those twenty pairs of eyes fixed on me, looking as though they expected me to start tap dancing. "Okay," Josh said, evidently finding whatever it was he was looking for. He proudly held up note cards and announced, "I almost forgot these."

Back up front next to me, he held the cards in both hands and read from hand-written notes. "When I grow up I would like to be a chef. Not just somebody who makes food at a regular restaurant, but like a chef on television." He looked up. "I want to be famous."

I thought it was sweet that he seemed oblivious to the fact that he already was — and always would be — famous.

Continuing, he said, "I know that if I work hard and study, I can be anything I want to be. I have some experience in the kitchen already, but I still have a lot to learn. We have two main chefs at our White House and some extra assistants."

Wouldn't Cyan and Bucky be thrilled to hear themselves referred to as "extra assistants"? Still, I smiled. Little Josh was quite charming as he shifted his weight from foot to foot. "The two main ones are Chef Virgil and Ollie." He pointed to me. "This is Ollie." Looking down, he read what his mother must have added, "Olivia Paras is the first female executive chef in the White

House." Looking up again, he added, "And she's really nice and lets me help all the time. I'm even going to work on a big state dinner we're having tonight."

I caught Nourie's amused look. That's all we needed. Josh helping in the kitchen today, after my being gone for so many hours.

"Ollie is here today to tell us about being the executive chef and to talk about her career."

Josh scampered back to his seat, then remembered the final part of his speech. "Thank you for joining us," he said to me.

I placed my bag of props on the table the teacher had cleared up front. Taking a deep breath — I'd never really interacted with children that much and wasn't quite sure how to get them to like me — I started with a question. "Who here likes food?"

All hands went up.

"Have any of you ever made any of your own lunches or dinners? How about breakfast?"

Some of the kids kept their hands raised. I invited a few of them to tell me what they'd made. Most of the children admitted to having professional cooks at home, and not really paying attention to where their meals came from. I talked a little about nutrition,

farmers, and growing our own vegetables —
I told them that Josh's family had plans to
start a big garden in the spring.

I held up my utensils and asked who knew
what they were for — several of the kids
had their hands up right away — and I
passed out my recipe sheets to take home.

Once they were warmed up with basic
information, they started jumping in with
commentary and questions. To my surprise
and delight, the banter didn't stop, and the
kids really seemed to enjoy themselves for
the duration of the presentation. I kept an
eye on the clock, and when we had about
two minutes left I answered a final question.

A little girl raised her hand and said, "My
mom says that I should eat carrots because
bunnies don't need glasses." She pointed to
the frames on her own face. "She says if I
eat a lot of carrots maybe I won't need these
anymore either."

I smiled. "My mom used to tell me the
same thing. Carrots have something called
beta-carotene in them. It's very good for
you, and helps provide vitamin A, which is
very important," I said. "I don't know if eating a lot of carrots will help you get rid of
your glasses, but some people believe that
vitamin A does help." I pointed to my own

eyes. "Carrots are very good for you, but there are other things you can eat that are good, too. Bananas, apples, green peppers, strawberries, spinach . . ."

At the word *spinach,* they all made "ugh" and gagging noises.

I laughed. "If you tasted my spinach, you might change your mind."

Josh made a face.

"Don't you like my spinach, Josh?" I asked him.

He frowned. "I liked yours that you made the other night for the tasting. But Virgil does something different. He puts something weird in it that I don't like at all."

I seemed to remember that Virgil had prepared his spinach with beets and kalamata olives. I winked. "I'll have to share my recipe with him."

Josh nodded.

"Thank you very much," Mrs. Fosco said when our time was up. She had the kids give me a round of applause. I thanked them for allowing me to be a part of their career project and looked to Nourie for guidance. He held up a finger and pointed to the door.

In the hall just outside, I could hear the sounds of all the classes of kids getting themselves ready to leave for the day — teachers' voices raised to combat chaos —

and just as everything quieted again, a distant bell rang.

Doors swung open, and kids filed out in double lines. I wondered how the Secret Service agents assigned to Josh dealt with this every single day. With so many kids, so many variables, there had to be a constant fear of something going wrong. There were two agents stationed at the end of the hall to my right and two to my left.

A moment later, Josh's class was dismissed. I stood close to the wall as they processed out past me toward the school's front door. I looked for Josh, but he wasn't among the chattering, cheerful students.

"No talking until we're outside," Mrs. Fosco admonished.

As the kids dispersed and the line diminished, Josh finally appeared, accompanied by Agent Nourie, who had brought my coat out for me. He waved me to follow. "We exit through the back," he said. Gesturing with his eyes, he continued, "There are lots of cars out front with parents and nannies picking up kids. There's no way to know if there's a vehicle out there that does not belong. So our team pulls up in the back parking lot." He smiled. "Less chance for trouble."

Josh was used to the routine. He skipped

next to me. "The kids really liked you, Ollie," he said. "You were funny."

"Thanks," I said. "I enjoyed meeting all your friends."

He made a so-so face. "I'm still the new kid," he said. "But when we were getting our coats, a few of them came over to say they liked what you said."

"I'm glad."

The two agents at the end of the hall fell into step with us as we took a narrow stairway to the school's back door. One of the agents went first. He opened the door, stepped outside, and spoke into his microphone before waving us out. "Clear," he said.

Poor Josh. He lived in this bubble every day of his life.

Nourie stayed close to his charge, and I followed. The other agent brought up the rear. The back of the school was set up like a giant U, with a parking lot just beyond a small courtyard. Josh's limo cleared the grassy center strip and swung into the driveway that skimmed the back edge of the school. Great for deliveries or for quick, secure exits like this one. Our little group followed a bricked walkway to the waiting limousine. The first agent raced ahead to open the car door for us.

About three hundred feet away, the school's back gate remained open in anticipation of our departure. With the castle structure surrounding us, the giant iron gate in the distance, and all the security, I felt quite out of place. Almost like the unnamed narrator in *Rebecca*. Everything was so grand, so precise, so large.

I followed Nourie and Josh along the walkway, fascinated by how closely Nourie guarded his charge. Secret Service agents were posted to our right and to our left — and every single one of them was brightly alert, ready for anything. I was convinced we were as safe as anyone could be.

At that moment, a black car swerved through the back gate. Big, and government-issue, it barreled at us. Fast.

I heard shouts, and shots fired in the distance, but couldn't tell which direction they came from. The agent behind me pushed me to the ground.

"Down! Down!" Nourie shouted. He lifted Josh off his feet and sprinted to the waiting limousine, covering Josh's small body with his own and reaching the door in two strides. Pushing myself to my feet, I followed, and the agent behind me shoved me forward until I tumbled into the back of the limo, right behind Nourie and Josh. I was about to ask what was going on, but the agent outside slammed the limo door shut and then slapped the back of the car twice.

Nourie shouted to the driver, "Go, go!"

The driver didn't need a second prompting. I heard the car doors lock as the limo leapt forward, its engines revving like jets on a plane. Above that, I heard the sound of more shots fired.

Heart pounding, I struggled to right myself, looking from side to side. The mysterious black car screeched to a halt. Someone who looked a lot like Bost bounded out. I gasped.

The Bost-man began to run after our car, but he was quickly surrounded by agents. The car he'd jumped from made a giant U-turn, clearly intending to follow us, but we were gaining speed. As soon as we cleared the iron gate, it lurched into action behind us and slowly closed them in.

Josh buckled up. Smart kid. I did the same.

"What happened?" I asked. For Josh's sake, I tried to keep the panic from my voice. "What was that? What's going on?"

Nourie ignored me. He spoke into his microphone. "Shots fired. Attack at Dolorosa Academy. Subject is safe. Repeat: Subject is safe. Implementing plan Delta. I

358

repeat, Delta."

Nourie practically leapt over the back of the front seat. He yanked the GPS monitor so that he could see where we were headed. He pointed. "Initiate Delta maneuver," he told the driver tersely.

The driver kept his eyes forward, but he blinked. "Sir?"

"Delta," Nourie repeated, this time with more authority. He glanced back at me. "Are they behind us?"

I looked back. "Not yet," I said.

Nourie ordered the driver, "Hurry."

"Yes, sir." The driver shook his head, but didn't seem nearly as rattled as I thought he should be. But then again, they were the professionals, not I. "I'm not familiar with Delta, sir," he said.

Nourie swore as he expelled a breath of frustration. "Whose idea was it to replace all the seasoned agents with you new guys?"

The driver had no answer. Nourie ordered him, "Turn left. Here. Now."

The driver complied.

Nourie muttered under his breath. "Get to 495."

"The expressway?" the driver asked. "That's the wrong direction."

"We aren't going to the White House." Exasperated, Nourie said, "Plan Delta has us rendezvous with a special team north of the city. We will have cover and reinforcements there. Go." He glanced behind us again. "They will assume we're headed back to the residence. They're going to be looking for us on Woodmont Avenue. We might have lost them. Take a circuitous route to 495. I'll let the team know where we are." He spoke again into his microphone.

I couldn't hear the reply, but I did see Josh. His eyes were wide and his bottom lip trembled. "What's going on?" he asked.

"Here," I said. Some reflexive maternal instinct caused me to put my arm around him. "We're okay. We'll get back to the White House really soon. It's okay." When he wiggled closer, trusting me, I felt my own panic abate. Helping console him helped me calm myself. A little.

Our limo raced through side streets, going north and west toward 495. We were bounced and flung sideways by the driver's erratic choices. Josh whimpered and snuggled closer.

"Faster," Nourie shouted.

"Who's after us?" I asked.

Nourie didn't answer. He spoke so quietly into his microphone I couldn't hear what he said, but whatever he heard in reply made him startle. He sent me another panicked look, then used both hands to gesture me to stay calm.

That made me worry even more.

"Driver," he said. "Pull over."

"But . . ."

"Pull over. Now."

The driver complied. "But, sir, the other car . . ."

The moment the car was in park, Nourie was over the backseat, plunging a syringe into the driver's neck.

I screamed, and covered Josh's eyes.

"He's with whoever's after us," Nourie explained, his eyes flashing. "He didn't know Delta. Even the new guys know Delta."

I didn't know what to say, what to do. Josh wriggled his face free from my protection. "What happened?"

"Don't worry," Nourie said, reading the alarm in my eyes. "I got word that we lost that other car. At least temporarily."

"But . . ." I was shaking as I pointed to the driver, who was writhing and convulsing. "What did you do to him?"

"Knocked him out. That's all." With that, he unlocked the car doors, jumped out, and climbed into the driver's seat, shoving the now-unconscious young man to the passenger side. "We need him alive for questioning." Putting the car in drive, Nourie checked the rearview mirror and sped off. "What I wouldn't give to put a bullet in his head right now."

I didn't think that was appropriate for Josh to hear, but I was too shocked to come up with a reply. "Where are we going?"

"There's a safe house where we'll meet up with another team," he said.

"Wouldn't we be better off at the White House?"

Nourie started fiddling under the dash. "That's where they expect us to go." He yanked something free and sat back, satisfied.

"Who?"

He met my eyes in the mirror. "Armustan. That's who's behind this." He shot a look of pure hatred toward the man in the passenger seat. "And they almost had us."

"Who's Armustan?" Josh asked. "Why are they after us?"

I didn't want to have to explain how the individuals who had taken people hostage at the hospital were part of a larger group — and that group was after us now, but I also didn't want Josh to think this situation was anything but serious. These were the same people who had targeted him and his sister with the chicken wings. We'd been warned that they were relentless. "Some very bad people. They tried to get their way once before, and it looks like they're trying again."

"You mean the people who want their leader to be let out of jail?"

I nodded.

Josh spoke confidently. "My dad told me all about that. He won't give in to them. He says he won't negotiate with terrorists."

Nourie met my eyes in the rearview mirror again. I doubted the president would be so secure in his policy if his own child's safety was at risk. I stared outside at the landscape zipping by. "How far is the safe house?" I asked, glancing behind us. No one followed.

Nourie didn't answer.

I stole a look at the GPS monitor. "What happened?" I asked.

Concentrating on his driving, Nourie still didn't answer.

"The GPS," I said, "it's not on. Did we lose signal?"

We took a hard left, making the tires screech. We were staying on side streets and avoiding any busy roads, veering different directions at almost every intersection. I assumed that made it more difficult for the Armustan operatives to follow us. "The

GPS," I said again.

"Don't need it," Nourie said. He pulled hard to the right this time, and studied the next intersection before zipping past. I hated traveling this fast — we had to be doing more than 40 miles per hour — down residential streets.

"Watch out!" I screamed.

Blowing through a stop sign, we narrowly missed hitting two bicyclists. They veered sideways just as Nourie swerved around them and one of the cyclists toppled to the ground. "Is he okay?" I asked.

Josh twisted to stare out the back windshield. "He's getting up, I think," he said. Turning to me, he asked, "What's going on?"

"Why is the GPS off?" I asked again.

"We have to assume our GPS has been compromised," Nourie said. "This is all part of Plan Delta. Disengaging the signal will make it that much harder for the Armustan soldiers to know where we are. We don't want to lead them to our safe house."

After a moment, I said, "But then the Secret Service can't track us either."

"That's why we've initiated Delta," he said. "The Secret Service knows exactly where we're headed. Now hold tight and keep an eye on Josh; it may get bumpy."

He wasn't kidding.

We swerved right to take a frontage road alongside one of the expressways. Sheltered from sight by a row of trees, the road was unpaved and caused us to jiggle in our seats. Good thing we were belted in. Even with the monstrous vehicle's heavy shocks, we were getting bounced around pretty badly. Josh's voice was uneven. "I'm scared, Ollie," he whispered.

"It's going to be okay."

I glanced up at Nourie. His expression was hard and his eyes remained focused on the road ahead.

My cell phone vibrated in my pocket against my leg. I had ensured the device was on silent before I went into the classroom but had not had a chance to turn the ringer back on. I was holding on to the door handles so tightly, I couldn't answer it right now. It was probably Bucky or Cyan calling, wondering where I was. I glanced at the dashboard clock. We'd been due back at the White House about ten minutes ago.

Not a sixth sense, but a *sick* sense — the "awareness" that Gav had talked about — was causing my stomach to wriggle with fear. On impulse, I slipped the phone out of my pocket and shoved it into the top of my knee-high hose. I had no reason to do so, but I trusted my gut. We were bouncing so hard, Josh didn't even notice my sleight of hand. I wanted to know who had called me, but I didn't want to risk checking right now.

"Okay," Nourie said after turning down another small unpaved road. Just ahead was an old barn that looked as though it had been abandoned twenty years ago. The barn's wide doors were open, and the inside beckoned like a giant, gaping mouth. Nourie pulled in and jammed the car into park. "We're here."

"This isn't a house," Josh said. "And it doesn't look safe."

"Hurry up." Nourie opened the door. "Come on, come on."

We scrambled out of the car and out of the barn. "Where are we?" I asked as the cold afternoon wind hit my face. In the middle of nowhere, the gray day seemed even darker. Trees surrounded us, but — as Josh had noted — there was no actual house.

"Around this bend," he said.

We followed him about twenty steps past a grouping of trees and shrubs to a silver sedan with dark-tinted back windows. "Get in," Nourie said.

"Where are we?" I asked again. "Why are we changing cars?"

"Delta," he reminded me. He reached to open the driver's side back door. "Hurry."

Josh got in first. As I followed, Nourie stopped me. "Your bag," he said, pointing.

I'd kept it tight since we left the school. Instinct, maybe. Security blanket, probably. "What about it?"

"Give it to me."

Terror raced up my spine. "Why?"

"I need to make sure you're not carrying anything dangerous."

This was wrong. Wild, panicked tingles flushed me head to toe. And, if I was to be honest with myself, I'd felt panic rise ever since Nourie had drugged the limo driver. I pulled the bag's canvas straps closer. "I'm not carrying anything dangerous."

"Your cell phone," he said. "It can be traced. They're probably tracing it right now."

"I'm not carrying a cell phone," I lied. "What about the driver? You said we needed him for questioning."

"Nobody goes anywhere without their cell phone. I know you've got it. Give me your bag." He yanked it away and dumped its contents on the cold ground at my feet. "Where is it?" he asked.

I did my best to look terrified and co-operative. The cooperative part was tough.

"I left it in the kitchen," I lied again, "at the White House. I didn't want it to go off while I was at Josh's school."

He pointed to my tunic and apron. "Empty your pockets. All of them."

I did. I had nothing but notes in my pockets. Nothing at all in my pants pockets, which he made me turn inside out. "The Armustan people wouldn't know to trace my cell phone," I said. "Why do you really want it?"

Nourie gave me a shrewd look. "Don't play dumb. If I didn't need someone to keep the kid in line, I'd leave you here," he said.

Wind whipped around us and any hope I held flew fast away with it.

"Get in," he said and this time he pulled out his gun.

I got in.

Starting the car, Nourie peeled out from behind the trees and took another, smaller side road, which he navigated as though he'd driven this way before. Josh looked ready to throw up.

I pulled him close and whispered that everything would be okay. He didn't believe me. I wouldn't have believed me either. I knew, at least, that as long as Josh was safe, Armustan called the shots. That's what they wanted. They couldn't risk him without giving up their trump card. Josh was not expendable. I was.

"No matter what happens, you just remember that your dad will come get you, okay?" I whispered, as we sped along in the gathering dark. "He's got armies and police and lots of powerful people who will help him." This car didn't have a dashboard clock, so I chanced a look at my watch. There had to be an all-out search going on by now. There had to be blockades, an all-points-bulletin, and air surveillance. Where was it? Where *were* we?

As if in answer, I heard the *whup-whup-whup* of a helicopter above. Nourie had been smart to park the limo in the barn. There was no way they'd spot it from the air. "Where are we going?" I asked.

"I told you. We're going to a safe house," he said. "But it's to keep us safe. Not you."

Chapter 26

We finally did reach the expressway. We took it heading north and west, farther away from the White House. The helicopter noises became ever more distant. Josh and I couldn't flag down any passing motorists because the windows were tinted and reflective.

"There are going to be roadblocks," I said. "You'll never make it out of here."

"You forget that I know all the security protocols," Nourie said over his shoulder. "I know what I'm doing."

But by now, I thought, *they know it's you.* The Secret Service should be able to get one step ahead of this guy.

We exited and followed another small road that connected to yet another. We had taken so many curved and angled streets that I no longer had any idea where I was or how far we were from the White House. We took a drive down a residential lane, followed up by a long stretch where there were no houses whatsoever. Nourie turned right down yet another uneven road. "Is he awake?" Nourie asked.

Josh had been quiet since we'd changed cars.

"He's awake," I said.

"Good." Nourie drove deep into a wooded area, finally pulling up to the side of a one-story frame home in a small clearing. About a hundred feet from the front door was another barn — this one slightly bigger than where we'd left the limo. This time, however, we were surrounded by dark, ominous, and — if the long drive in was any indication — deep woods. Just like last time, Nourie eased the car into the barn and shut off the engine. He turned, perching his elbow atop the seat. Addressing Josh, he said, "You remember what your dad told you? About not negotiating with terrorists?" he asked.

Josh nodded.

Nourie smiled. It was a scary sight. "That's only because the terrorists haven't had the proper tools to negotiate with." He pointed at Josh and winked. "We do now."

As he ushered us from the car into the house, Nourie warned: "See for yourself, there is no one nearby. No one to hear you yell. The closest house is over two miles away." He whispered near my ear, "I know you wouldn't take off without him, and *you* know I would catch up very quickly. Don't give me any reason for target practice. Trust me. I'm very good."

I shivered, more from the cold look in his eyes than the surrounding chill. "Got it," I said quietly.

The door was unlocked and Nourie made us enter first. We found ourselves inside the home's kitchen. Barren, its linoleum floor was coated with dust. Cobwebs filled the sink and stretched between cabinets. It was as though whoever owned the place had moved out quickly and been unable to sell. Instinctively I reached for a light switch, but all I got was a hollow click. "We cut the power here so nobody would see lights on in an abandoned home," Nourie said. "We've got heat and running water, but don't expect creature comforts." He locked and double-dead-bolted the door behind us, pocketing the key.

He herded us into the living room. About twenty-by-twenty, the low-ceilinged space smelled of mold and was devoid of furniture except for a couple of folding chairs and a bent card table in the far corner. A giant stone fireplace took up the long wall and a cardboard box sat in front of the hearth.

Heavy drapes were closed across the front windows. I stumbled over the bumpy, carpeted floor.

"You okay?" Josh asked.

I nodded.

Nourie checked the locks on the front door. "These are the only two ways in and out," he said.

"How long will we be here?" I asked.

"Until it's time."

"For what?"

No answer. The place was small, the tension in the air thick. Nourie pointed to the chairs. "Sit," he ordered.

We took off our coats and sat.

The rear of the house was dark, but I held out hope that there might be a window back there to crawl out of. Getting past Nourie to get to that window would be tough. I knew he was right about there being little chance to get away. Maybe, though, once it got really dark . . .

We had to try. Staying here, under Nourie's control, was the worst thing we could do.

"I have to go to the bathroom," Josh said.

"This way," Nourie said brusquely. He made us walk ahead of him down the back hall to the two back bedrooms and small bath. Josh held my hand. In each of the bedrooms, the day's waning light filtered through metal bars that had been installed inside, preventing escape. The bathroom had glass block windows. No hope there. "This is it," he said. "Hope you can manage in the dark."

Josh nodded solemnly and closed the door.

"I'll wait in the living room," I said.

"Don't even think about it," Nourie said. "We know how you are. You will wait right here."

"Why are you doing this?" I asked. "What's wrong with you?"

Nourie's eyes were like steel. Even in the dim hallway I could see them glitter with anger. "There is nothing wrong with me. Everything is finally right."

"What are you talking about? You're a Secret Service agent. You pledged to —"

"You know nothing of what I pledged."

"What are you saying?"

"You're stupid, you're female, and you're weak. That's all you need to know," he said. "Now shut up."

In a minute or so, we heard the water running. "There isn't any soap," Josh said from behind the door.

"Life's rough, kid. Time you learned to be less of a fancy-pants."

In a moment, the door opened and Josh came out wiping his wet hands on his pant legs. "No towels either," he said.

I had to give the kid credit. He was holding up extraordinarily well. Better than I would have at that age.

Nourie ushered us into the living room again, forcing us back onto the chairs. He settled himself on the raised fireplace hearth and dragged the cardboard box over. Arranging it on the floor in front of him, he lifted the flaps and pulled out crackers, water, and a radio.

Turning the device on, he glanced at his watch and frowned with such displeasure that I got the impression we were running late. Or that someone else was. "Be quiet," he said unnecessarily, and started fiddling with the radio controls.

Josh eyed the crackers and water.

"May I?" I asked, reaching for them.

Nourie yanked the box away from me. "Don't touch."

The look on our captor's face was enough to make me wither, but I refused to back down. "He's a kid, okay? Let him have a couple of crackers and some water. It isn't going to kill you, you know."

He shoved the box at Josh, then handed him a bottle of water. "You have some. Not her," he said, pointing to me. "Got it?"

Josh looked too afraid to touch either one. He stared up at me, terrified. I nodded to him and he accepted the proffered food.

Nourie tuned the radio. "We figured on having Virgil here, not you. But then that fool had to call in sick today."

Nourie stopped as the announcer's voice came through. "Breaking news. Shots were fired this afternoon in an attack at Dolorosa Academy, where President Hyden's son, Joshua, is enrolled. It is believed that the president's son was the target of the attack, but no students were harmed. Secret Service agents were on hand and prevented Joshua Hyden from being injured. At this point we do not know who is responsible or what their objectives were. Joshua has been taken to a secure location and we expect updates shortly. Stay tuned."

"Perfect." For a split second Nourie seemed to relax, but when he consulted his watch again, his agitation returned.

"Waiting for somebody?" I asked.

"Shut up."

Nourie bent his head to dig through the box again, and I felt my phone vibrate against my calf. I stood up quickly, hoping he hadn't heard the hum. "I have to go to the bathroom," I said.

Nourie looked up. "You can wait."

I stepped backward and shifted from foot to foot, as though I really needed to use the facilities, but what I wanted most was to mask the quiet vibration running up my leg. Exhilaration thrilled me with giddy energy — if my phone was receiving a signal out here, I could use it to call for help. "I only need a minute," I said.

"Sit down, woman," Nourie shouted. "What is wrong with you?"

Josh cowered in his seat.

"We're cooped up here," I said. I paced in a circle, moving away from him as I did so. I raised my voice to cover the muted sound of the phone. I couldn't hear it myself, but I could feel it, and I didn't want to risk anything at this point. Every time it buzzed against my leg, I hoped to heaven it was the last ring. Why had I programmed it for *five* rings before the phone went to voicemail? This thing was taking forever to shut off. "We're scared," I said, raising my voice. "What do you think is wrong with me?"

I stopped at the sound of a lock turning. Nourie leapt to his feet. He strode to the door, forgetting me entirely — which was fine. The pulsation against my leg had ceased. I wanted to grab my phone and send out texts begging for help, but I couldn't do anything until Josh and I were alone.

By the time Nourie reached the kitchen, the back door had opened. I heard another man's voice as he and Nourie greeted each other in a foreign language. I didn't recognize it specifically, but I decided it must be Armustan. The new man's voice was louder, deeper, but I couldn't understand a word he was saying. I moved closer to Josh, who had begun to whimper. "What's going on, Ollie?" he asked.

"I don't know," I said. "But we're going to be okay."

"You promise?"

I couldn't promise, but I put my arm around him. "They can't hurt you, Josh. They need you to negotiate with your dad."

His eyes were clouded with worry. "What about you?"

I hugged him close. "They need me here to take care of you."

"Did you really have to go to the bathroom?" he asked.

"No."

"Good. I was worried about that." He pulled out the crackers he'd taken for himself. "Want some?"

I shook my head.

A split second later, Nourie and his companion came into the living room. Although the ambient light wasn't enough to make out crisp details, I could see that the new man was older than Nourie — close to fifty — and had a full head of hair. He was about six feet tall and had to weigh more than 250 pounds. "Has my friend explained what we need from you?" he asked in accented English.

"No," I said. "Nourie . . . or whatever his name is . . . didn't tell us anything."

"You foolishly placed yourself in the wrong place at the wrong time," the big man said to me, stepping closer. "Women are so much less valuable than men, and we had hoped to make our point with your male counterpart."

Terror made me flippant. "Gee, thanks," I said.

"Women are weak. You crack too easily," he went on, as though terribly disappointed. To Nourie, he added, "We discovered a traitor among the brotherhood."

"Who? What happened?"

The older man shrugged. "He is no longer a threat. But this operative was one of your Special Agents. We knew him only as Galen."

Nourie didn't react, but my mouth went instantly dry as the weight of his words settled on me. Gav? Could they be talking

379

about Gav?

"I killed him myself," the man said, as though it were nothing. Turning his attention back to me, he said, "We had planned to extend our broadcast. Because of you, we will now have to cut it short."

I couldn't find the words to speak. Fear paralyzed me. Fear for Gav, for Josh. For myself.

"Broadcast?" Josh asked. "You mean like TV?"

"How else to get your father's attention?" he asked. "We will take you both to a location where, even now, our brothers are preparing for our arrival." He took a long look around the small area. "You will stay here until it is time."

Coming to stand right in front of me, he stared down. Shadows played along the lines of his face, sinking his cheeks and deepening his eyes. I felt as though I were looking straight up into the face of death.

"We do not want to subdue you because subjects are much more sympathetic when they are alert. But I warn you to cooperate, or we will administer drugs."

"Where is this other place?"

He shook his head. "We know it was you who thwarted our original plan. If it weren't for you," he pointed to Josh, "the children

380

would have been our hostages over a week ago. We would have achieved our objective. Our illuminated one, Farbod, continues to languish in prison. We must now settle for only one child, but at least we have the opportunity to exact our revenge upon you." When he smiled, it shook me to my very core. "We will do so on American soil. On camera. This is what would be called poetic justice, yes? Fear not. Your name will go down in history for having died in service to your country." He held his hands out and stared upward. "So many men would count themselves fortunate to die in such a way. A shame it will be wasted on a woman."

Josh went completely still. There was nothing for me to say even if I were capable of talking.

"I am your enemy," he said, even though I had no doubt about that fact at this point. "What is wrong with the men in your country? They force me to deal with that other female . . . the congresswoman who controls Cenga Prison." Spitting on the floor, he glared at me. "It is because of that woman I was late." He chucked Josh under the chin and winked. "Be brave, little man."

In English, Nourie asked his boss how much longer we needed to stay in the house. The boss, who Nourie called "Sami," reverted to his native language. From their tone, I could gather very little beyond the fact that Sami was upset about something — the delay, perhaps? — and that they were both annoyed with having to deal with women. They remained close enough for me to see them point and cast derisive looks in my direction.

Josh began to cry. "I don't want them to hurt you," he said.

"I'll be okay," I said again, although I was beginning to doubt it. I needed access to my phone, but as long as the two men stayed so close, I couldn't very well pull it out and start dialing. Who would I call? I swallowed, hard.

I couldn't think about what they'd said about killing a special agent. I couldn't let myself believe it was Gav. Not now. Not yet. I had to think about Josh.

Planning my next move, I decided if I could access my phone, I would try to text Tom.

The two men's conversation grew heated, but they quieted when Nourie apparently acquiesced to whatever Sami told him to do. They gesticulated and Sami occasionally paced. Neither one paid us any attention.

Tempted as I was to skim my fingers down my leg to reassure myself that my phone hadn't moved from its spot in my sock, I held off. Any movement I made could telegraph my intentions. I watched the two men argue and tried to understand — if not the words — the gist of their conversation.

Josh's whimpers grew into sobs. Visibly angry, Sami stopped talking with Nourie and came to stand over the little boy. He shouted at him to stop crying. That just made it worse.

Josh tried to bury his face in my shoulder, but the sounds of his wretched fear were too much for the men. Sami pointed to the back bedrooms and asked Nourie a question I had to assume was a query about how likely it was we might escape. Nourie pointed to the bathroom as he answered. I wondered what that language's word for glass block windows was.

We heard a knock at the kitchen door. Nourie grabbed at me. Whatever he said caused Sami to grunt approval.

I pinched Josh lightly and whispered to keep crying. He obliged. Sami roared for silence and Nourie shuttled us off to the bathroom. "Keep it down," he said, and shut the door.

The moment he was gone, I silently directed Josh to sit with his back to the door. I pantomimed that he should keep crying.

He understood, and upped the sobs. I pulled my phone out from my sock. Surprised, Josh gasped and stopped crying. I shook my head and encouraged him to continue. He started back up, right away.

Even when programmed to vibrate, my phone always made musical beeps when I pressed the keypad. I figured there must be some way to shut that off, but right now was not the time to go searching for those commands. I sat on the edge of the bathtub and opened my phone. I had two missed calls and two missed text messages. I didn't have time to access my voicemail, not now. All I could do was text. I was about to try to reach Tom and Cyan when I saw that my missed messages were from Gav.

My heart leaped. He was alive.

His first message read: *All is well. Will call soon.*

His second message, time-stamped just moments ago, read: *Where are you?*

I whispered a tiny prayer in thanksgiving. Gav was okay. But *we* weren't. Quickly, I hit reply. Josh had gotten interested in what I was doing and had inadvertently quieted. I glanced up quickly to remind him to keep up the noise. He nodded and restarted the flow.

I typed: *Help. Nourie traitor. Far north and*

west. Remote small house, barn. Silver sedan. Leaving soon.

I held the little phone in my hot hand and waited for a reply. What if he didn't get it? What if there was a dampening field in this bathroom? I stared down at the phone, willing it to buzz. I had two signal bars. Should be enough for texts.

I composed another. *J okay. Plans to broadcast demands soon. Brothers at secure location. Moving out. Can you GPS me?*

Rocking back and forth on the bathtub's edge, I knew I couldn't wait for a reply. I texted Tom as well. *Nourie is kidnapper. Help. Use GPS?*

Who else could I reach? Who else had the power to help us?

I dialed 9-1-1 and waited until the dispatcher answered. I couldn't risk talking to her, but I whispered "help" just the same. I listened as she asked me, again and again, what the emergency was. I hung up and tried again, this time dialing *9-9-9. It seemed so pointless, so lonely — a little voice in the dark crying for help when I had no idea where we were.

My phone vibrated. Gav. The text was blank, but the message was clear. He'd received and understood. But he couldn't reply.

Would he be able to find us here? I had no idea how GPS worked with regard to cell phones. One of my favorite TV shows featured a female FBI cyber-genius who could nail down a location for the bad guy the very moment his cell phone went live. Did analysts like her really exist? I glanced over to Josh, who had his ear to the door now. I hoped so.

I wanted to text Gav again, even though I knew he couldn't let me know what they were planning for fear of my phone getting confiscated. I started to type: *I hope,* but suddenly Josh spun and waved his hands. They were coming. I hit "send," and snapped the phone shut. I was just shoving it into my sock when the door opened, banging into Josh, and making him cry out for real.

"Get away from the door," Nourie said. He caught me lowering my pant leg and crossed the bathroom in two strides. "What's going on?"

He jerked my pant leg up and found the phone. Swearing loudly, he called out. A new man who looked vaguely familiar ran in. He swore, loudly.

"We have to get out of here," Nourie said.

"But it isn't time yet," the new guy protested in English. "Sami said to wait an hour." He glanced at his watch and pressed a button to make the display light up. "He only left a couple minutes ago."

"Too bad," Nourie said, grabbing my arm and dragging me to my feet. "Call Sami and let him know we're on the way."

"Sami said no phone contact," the other guy said. "I'm not calling him."

"But we're going off script."

"He doesn't know that. We'll drive slow."

Nourie lifted the toilet lid with the edge of his shoe, dropped my cell phone in, and flushed. "They'll be coming. But we'll be long gone."

"Where are we going?" I asked.

The new guy grinned, and I suddenly remembered where I'd seen him before. "Smile, sweetheart. It's time for your network debut."

CHAPTER 27

"A shame we have to leave. This would have been a great location for the broadcast," the new arrival said to Nourie. Devon Clarr — the man Congresswoman Sechrest had been concerned about, the man who had been released on a technicality and whose face had been plastered on the TV after the hospital siege — spoke in unaccented English. He increased the pitch of his voice to make it sound creepy. "Where nobody can hear you scream . . ."

"That's enough," Nourie said, pulling me next to him. My shoulder bumped against the bathroom doorjamb and I cried out in pain, but Nourie didn't slow.

My gut was tied up in knots as Josh and I were hustled back into the living room. "Get your coats," Nourie ordered. To the new guy, he said, "I don't want to leave any evidence behind. Sami wants this done to the letter."

"No screwups, you mean?"

Nourie looked at me. "She screwed things up already."

Clarr shook his head. "This one's all on you, man."

Nourie ignored that. "We're still far out of reach — even for local authorities. Even if the FBI can pinpoint our location, it's going to take time. We need to get out before anybody gets here."

"You should have checked who she called," Clarr said. "Before you flushed the thing."

"What does it matter?" Nourie said. "That would have taken more time. Now quit talking. If we don't get out of here . . ."

He let the thought hang.

Every second I could keep us here would work in our favor. Leaning close to Josh, I said, "We need to stall. Try to get away. Don't let them catch you."

I took my time donning my coat. So did Josh. "Hurry up," Clarr said. "Why did you bring her, anyway? I thought we planned for the guy."

"Yeah well, things change. Just get them out," Nourie said. "I'll pull the van up."

He let himself out as Clarr shouted for Josh to get his jacket on. Exasperated, he finally said, "Just forget it," and reached for the boy's arm. Josh ducked his grasp. "What the . . . ?"

Clarr tried again, but Josh ran behind one of the chairs and dodged right and left as Clarr tried to reach him. In the dark, it was difficult for me to make out where one of them began and the other one ended, but I could hear Clarr's grunts of disgust and I launched myself onto his back, doing my best to wrench him away from Josh.

Clarr threw me off, and I landed with a *whump* on the floor. Josh yelped, and I could tell from Clarr's shallow breathing and satisfied grumble that he'd finally grabbed the boy. "Get up," he said to me. "And don't try anything stupid again."

We'd bought ourselves a minute, maybe two. "I'm not going out there and neither is Josh," I said.

"Yeah, right."

Clarr started for the door, pulling Josh along behind him. I ran up and wrapped my arms tightly around his little chest, and dropped to the floor. "Sorry, Josh," I said as Clarr yanked him forward. "This is going to hurt."

The boy was crying, but I heard him say it was okay.

"Let's move," Clarr said, tugging at Josh's left arm.

I sat on the floor, arms still wrapped around Josh, refusing to let go. We tangled like that until Nourie stormed back in. "What is taking you so long?"

I can't imagine what it must have looked like. Nourie swore and moved quickly to peel my arms off of Josh. "Get the kid into the van," he said. "I'll handle her."

And handle me he did. He threw me over his shoulder and carried me out the door. I was hoping to make a break when he turned to lock the deadbolts, but he was unconcerned about securing the premises at that point. A white cargo van sat outside in the pitch dark. I couldn't make out the logo or lettering on the van's side, but as Nourie threw me in, I saw that the vehicle had no side or back windows. The side door had been pulled open, and a dim dome light revealed that the entire back of the van was bare metal. Josh was curled into a tight ball in the cargo portion's far corner. I felt the cold of the van's floor and walls. This would be a rough ride. In more ways than one.

"Do you have a blanket or something?" I asked.

Nourie shut the door. Clarr had already climbed into the passenger seat. "Hurry up," he said, and jerked his thumb backward toward us. "She's a real fighter, that one."

"She wasn't part of the plan," Nourie replied.

Clarr said, "Well, we're stuck with her now," and shut his door.

Nourie ran around the front of the van. "You know where we're going, right?" he asked as he slid in behind the wheel.

Clarr had opened the window and adjusted the sideview mirror as he answered. "Yeah, head back to the expressway." He switched on a handheld GPS. "Go north."

"That's not traceable, is it?"

"Not in a million years."

Nourie put the van in gear and eased forward. "Let's do this." Tires crunched against the gravel, sending little pings as rocks bounced up to hit the van's undercarriage. Once we were on the road, I would have no way of telling Gav where we were. And he would be looking for a silver sedan, not a white cargo van. Why had I told him that?

I positioned myself directly behind the two men so that I could see out the front window. So that I could hear every word they said. Maybe there was some way to signal an oncoming car . . .

"Back off," Clarr said. He'd drawn his gun and had it pointed at me. "This will kill your eardrums in such close quarters," he said.

"To say nothing about what a bullet would do at point-blank range."

I moved farther back. "Who are you, anyway?"

"One of the loyalists," he said. "One of the many who will not sleep until justice is served."

"Justice?" I said, nearly spitting the word. "This is terrorism."

Nourie said, "No more talking." He shot a warning look at Clarr. "Keep your mouth shut."

This far back in the van, I couldn't see the GPS display, couldn't see anything of our surrounding area. I couldn't hope to do anything without telegraphing my objectives. We were at the men's mercy . . . and from what it seemed, there was little to be had. My heart sunk so deep in my gut that I nearly lost myself in despair. I didn't notice Josh sidle up next to me. He had to tug at my sleeve before I realized he was talking to me. "What happens now?"

"I . . ." My voice caught in my throat. "I don't know."

Nourie drove with his headlights off and slowed as we reached the end of the long gravel road, which had brought us to the house. I remembered that Clarr had told him to head back to the expressway. Peering over Clarr's shoulder at the GPS, I was determined to memorize every turn, every single landmark so that if the opportunity presented itself, I could jump on it.

Nourie eased off the brake, preparing to turn left. "Hang on," Clarr said, placing his hand on the wheel.

"What?"

He gestured to the right with his chin. "Car coming."

Hope rose in my chest, but a moment later, I saw that it wasn't a cavalry of thirty government vehicles; it was one lone car trundling up over the rise. With its headlights low to the ground and its over-loud bass beat causing my heart to shudder with every syncopated throb, I knew no one was coming to save us. Just as the sports car was about to pass, another car came around the bend from the left, speeding.

"Busy street," Clarr said.

"Yeah, all of a sudden. What's with this place? Sami said nobody ever comes down this way."

"Teenagers, probably. You know how it is. They find all the local deserted places. Good thing that house is so far off the road. Otherwise we might've had company."

"That would have been their mistake," Nourie said. He switched on his headlights and pulled out onto the paved road. There would be no chance of anyone finding us now.

For the next mile or so, Nourie and Clarr talked softly between themselves. My mind raced, but I could come up with nothing that even resembled a plan. I had to do something, but I didn't have anything to work with. Just wacky, disjointed ideas, most of which were too ludicrous to even attempt. Josh was quiet, too quiet. I turned to find him curled up, nearly asleep. Part of me wanted to let him stay that way, to forget, for a while, the peril we were in.

"Josh," I said, shaking his arm.

For one second, he looked just like any nine-year-old might who suddenly finds himself jolted awake. Puzzled, yet drowsily content. A split second later, however, reality washed over him with an electrifying effect I could actually see. "Are we there?"

"No, but I need your help," I said. "Make noise. Keep them busy. Be pesky and annoying but don't get them mad."

"Why?" he asked, rubbing his eyes.

"Just try it. Give me a little time."

He boosted himself to his knees and scuttled forward. "I have to go to the bathroom," he said, affecting a whiny tone.

"You just went," Nourie said.

"But I had all that water."

Clarr half-turned. "You're just going to have to wait, kid."

"But I'm hungry and I'm tired and I . . . I want my mom." The moment he said the words, pretending went out the window. Josh's overwhelming sadness came bubbling up and he began to sob.

"Stop it," Clarr shouted.

I didn't pay attention to the rest. I'd been moving quietly to the back of the van. Thank goodness they'd opted for such a bare-bones model after all. I bent a plasticy piece of covering to expose the back of the vehicle's driver side taillight. Positioning my right foot behind it, I waited until Josh's cries crescendoed, then kicked with all my might.

The light didn't fall out, but I thought it budged. I kicked again.

"What's going on back there?"

"I'm getting sick," I lied. "I'm going to throw up."

Josh must have known I needed more cover because he ramped up his complaints and started crying, loudly, again. "Please take me home," he said between sobs. "Please."

I kicked one more time. Success burst through in a thin rush of cold air as the taillight went flying. Pulling off my apron, I stuffed it through the opening. Then, thinking fast, I tore off my shoe, and wrapped the apron strings around it, tying a quick knot. The shoe was too big to fit through the opening, but the apron should be flying free behind the van, like a white flag of surrender.

Which it was anything but.

Nourie shouted, "What's going on? The dash says one of my taillights is out."

He started to turn, but Clarr said, "Just drive," almost as loudly. He tried to see what was going on but I blocked his view of the back of the van.

"One of my taillights is out," Nourie said again. "Did she do it?"

"We can't stop now."

Josh had silenced his complaints and turned to me. He gave me a thumbs-up. *Oh, if it were only that easy,* I thought.

"Nobody is around. Just drive."

"What if some hick cop decides to pull us over?"

"Just drive," Clarr repeated.

By my estimation, we'd traveled about five miles from the "safe" house. All hopes of Gav swooping in to save us were gone. I'd been holding on to the belief that he was just waiting for the right moment to pounce on the van, but every minute since we'd left made me realize how slim those chances were.

There were no oncoming headlights and I couldn't tell if anyone was behind us. Would anyone report an apron flying out from the back of a cargo van or would they just think it was a weird advertising gimmick? An observant cop might see it and pull us over, but what then? Would the unsuspecting officer then be shot just for doing his job?

Guilt almost made me want to pull my flag back in, but fear for Josh stopped me. I shivered as the temperature in the back of the van dropped with each passing mile. My body tensed — the cold of the frigid metal and the ruthlessness of our abductors made it difficult to think. But I had to. Josh was depending on me.

"How much farther?" Nourie asked.

Clarr consulted the GPS. "The expressway's just ahead. Ten miles on that, then maybe about five miles north."

My heart soared. Somebody on the expressway was bound to see us.

"We're going to be too early. Sami's not going to be happy."

"Okay, fine. We can avoid the expressway," Clarr said. "Side roads will take longer."

Disappointment nearly made me snap. I

had only fifteen miles to do something, yet no idea what that should be.

Josh stared up at me with such trust in his eyes my heart broke. For both of us.

Well, I reasoned, *if I've already done every-thing in my power, maybe it was time to do something that was* not *in my power.*

"Take a right, here," Clarr said.

I pointed, telling Josh to move back. He did. I had no real plan. My only plan was to foil their plans. Create chaos. And then jump on any opportunity that presented itself.

As we completed the turn, and Clarr consulted the GPS again, I saw a car coming toward us. Praying that no one would be injured, I launched myself between the two men's seats, intending to grab the steering wheel and shove it far to the left into the oncoming car's path.

Deaf to Clarr's and Nourie's shouts, I heard our tires screech and the other car's horn blare furiously. We skidded sideways and Josh tumbled around the back of the van, crying out in pain. But I held tight until we ground to a halt. No impact. The other driver was out of his car in seconds, running over, shouting and raising his fist.

Nourie didn't hesitate. He spun the wheel right and hit the gas. We fishtailed as Clarr fell sideways off his seat, shouting. Josh screamed. Nourie swore but gripped the wheel with both hands and had the car righted in seconds. We sped away.

With a murderous look in his eyes, Clarr climbed into the rear compartment of the van with Nourie bellowing about tying me up.

Clarr looked around the van's dark interior. "With what?"

"Improvise."

It was then that Clarr spotted the open taillight. "What have you done now?" He yanked the shoe upward, but the apron outside caught tight and wouldn't give. He pulled again, finally bringing the fabric inside. "I'll use this," he said, but Nourie wasn't paying attention.

"Should I stay on this road, or do I head north again?" he asked.

"Just stay on this road until I get back up there." Clarr ripped the apron's strings off and used them — twisted and cold from being outside — to bind my hands behind me. "I need to find something for your feet," he said. Turning to Josh, he said, "Give me your shoelaces."

Josh pointed to his shoes. "These don't have any."

He looked to me. I shook my head.

"Don't move an inch," he said, sitting on the floor of the cargo van to remove his own laces. To Nourie, he said, "This has got to be the worst planning I've ever been involved in. Nothing is going right."

"You want to be the one to tell Sami that?"

"He planned this?"

"How much farther do I take this road?" Nourie asked again. "It looks like we're getting into a town up ahead."

Clarr finally got his laces free and used them to bind my feet together. He pulled the laces tight across my ankles — as tightly as he'd tied the apron strings around my wrists, making the cords bite into my skin. As he got back to his feet and stared out the window, I tried to find wiggle room. There was none.

Clarr got into his seat. "We should have turned a while back."

"I asked you."

"I'm telling you now."

"Fine." Nourie was at his breaking point. He spun the van around in a tight U-turn and headed back the way we'd come. "This is ridiculous."

"You're telling me."

We traveled about two miles before Clarr told Nourie to go left. "You're sure?" he asked.

Clarr didn't bother to answer.

My wrists hurt and my ankles chafed; when Josh tried to loosen my bindings, Clarr yelled at him to get away from me.

"We put up a good fight," I whispered to him. "And we're not done either. These men are going to put you on camera. Think about anything you can say that might tell your parents where we are, without these guys knowing."

Totally confused, Josh stared up at me panic-stricken. "What do you mean?"

"When we get out, look around. If you see anything unusual that can help them find us, say it on camera. Maybe talk about a family vacation that you remember that is like the place they take us."

"A vacation?"

I was losing him. "Anything at all, Josh. Think about any clues you can give your parents. I know it's hard, honey. I know it's a long shot, but we have to keep trying and never give —"

"Shut up back there," Clarr said.

We rode the rest of the way in silence.

CHAPTER 28

"Turn left here?" Nourie asked.

"No, next left," Clarr said. "I keep forgetting you've never been at headquarters before."

"And I shouldn't even be here now." Nourie turned as instructed. "If the hospital plan would have gone the way it was designed to . . ." He let the thought hang. "Now my cover's blown and there's nothing for me to do but get out."

"If you can," Clarr said. "It's going to be tough."

The two were quiet for a long moment.

"Just about a mile more," Clarr said. "Turn right at the next intersection." He waited a beat, then asked. "So why didn't you bring the kid up here right away? Somebody else could have given you directions. Why go all the way out to that house and have to deal with transporting the two of them?"

Nourie made a noise of impatience. "If anything went wrong with taking the kid, Sami didn't want headquarters to be compromised. He thought this was the only way to make sure everything stayed separate until the last minute."

"Makes sense." Clarr glanced back at me. "Too bad we had all the trouble with her. What a feisty one. Who gets to do the honors?"

The pain in my hands and feet evaporated as I processed his words. *Do the honors?* As in, kill me?

"That's Sami's call," Nourie said. "But if it were up to me . . ."

"Turn left here."

Nourie turned. "This is pretty remote."

"It's supposed to be."

After another five minutes down another road with no lights, Clarr told Nourie to slow down. "Pull up to that gate," he said. "We have to wait here for a guard to meet us before we're let in."

The fence was cyclone with barbed wire wrapped in spirals up top. I couldn't see much in the pitch-dark beyond the glow of our headlights. These were the gates of hell.

Nourie pulled up and placed the car in park. After a minute he asked, "What's taking so long?"

Clarr lit up his watch again. "They're not expecting us for another twenty minutes."

"Great," Nourie said, banging the steering wheel. "How far up is the building? Can one of us get past the fence and get someone's attention?"

"You want your head shot off?" Clarr asked. He sat back. "We'll wait."

Less than a minute later, a sentry approached the door. I'd managed to position myself to be able to see out the front, and when the young bearded man trotted forward, I gasped. He motioned for Nourie to cut the headlights, but not before I saw his camouflage outfit and the giant machine gun across his chest. Josh sat up at my exclamation, but by the time he looked out the window, the lights were out.

Nourie rolled down the driver's-side window. The man with the machine gun asked him some questions in a foreign language. Clarr looked lost. At least we had that in common. The man at the window stepped back. The moment he was gone, Nourie put the car in gear and we eased forward through the now-open gate.

"Which way?" he asked Clarr.

"About two hundred feet to the right."

We pulled up to a double-sized prefab house. Every room inside was lit up like there was a party going on. I supposed in some ways, there was.

"Home sweet home," Clarr said. He jumped out of the passenger seat the moment the van stopped.

Nourie turned off the engine and alighted. "I'll take the boy."

"Sure, you bring home the prize," Clarr said. "Leave me with the she-devil." He opened the side door.

"Don't let them separate us," I whispered to Josh.

Nourie reached for the boy, but he squirmed away into the cargo area's far reaches. "Get back here," Nourie said and climbed in to get him.

I was still bound but I had flipped onto my back and used both feet to kick him as hard as I could.

Nourie went sprawling sideways, banging against the open door. Clarr shouted, "Hey!" and reached in to stop me. He tried to grab my feet, but I called upon every ounce of energy I could muster to fend him off. I didn't know what I hoped to accomplish. At this point I just knew I had to fight. As I kicked, the laces around my ankles loosened and I hammered Clarr with one-two foot punches.

He grabbed hold and yanked me out of

the van. Airborne for a heart-pumping moment, I fell to the ground with a *whump.* Nourie wrestled Josh down and came out the side door with a squirming, screaming nine-year-old burden in his arms.

At that very moment, the world exploded.

At least that's what it felt like.

Lights burst around us like a giant blue sun had suddenly erupted over our heads. I blinked against the glare and the noise. Megaphones blasted with men barking orders. Sounds of people running, shouting, and sharp-edged silhouettes against the hot, bright blue combined to make me wince, but I scrambled sideways to my knees. "Josh?"

I couldn't make out what was happening. "Josh?" I called again. I couldn't find him, but I thought I heard him cry out. Squinting against the brightness, I tried to see.

Then out of the din I heard a familiar voice on a loudspeaker. "Put the boy down."

Crouched between Clarr to my left and Nourie to my right, I spotted Josh, still in Nourie's strong hold. Whether he was unconscious or terrified, I didn't know. Nourie took a step back.

Clarr pulled me to my feet and placed the barrel of a gun against my right temple. "Don't tempt me," he shouted to the surrounding group. "Believe me, it won't take much." Although he still conveyed that sense of bravado he'd shown since his arrival, I noticed his voice quivered just a bit. There had to be fifty men and women — possibly more — silhouetted around us. I couldn't see into the dark, but I felt the presence of an army poised to strike.

"Put the gun down," Gav ordered. "You can't get out of this. Don't try."

Nourie squeezed Josh so hard he yelped. "We've got what you want right here. No way we're giving up."

"Don't be stupid," Gav said. "There is no way out. We've arrested everyone. There is nowhere to go. Nowhere to turn. Your 'brothers' are in custody."

The use of the term *brothers* seemed to shake Nourie. His face was pale in the bright light, but his eyes glittered. "Let us go and we'll release the boy."

Gav didn't have a chance to answer. Clarr pulled me closer and pressed the gun harder against my head. "Want to know how serious we are?" he shouted.

I *didn't* want to know. Ducking my head, I kicked hard backward against Clarr's left knee. The gun in his hand went off with a deafening crack next to my ear and I stumbled sideways. I heard another *pop,* and

Clarr spun against Nourie, causing him to lose his balance and his grip on Josh. The boy fell to the ground. I took heart from the fact that all this awareness meant I was still alive. I dropped to my knees and scooted next to Josh. "Stay down," I said, attempting to cover him. I heard another *pop,* then another, and from my position in the dirt, I wondered if these were echoes or if there really was a firefight going on.

It couldn't have taken longer than thirty seconds, but the adrenaline coursing through my beaten body made everything feel like it was in slow motion.

The quiet came suddenly. Then a shout, "Clear."

There was scuffling around us and then we were surrounded. I was still on the ground, draped over Josh's trembling body when a female agent knelt next to me. "Are you okay? Are you hurt?" Unable to speak, I shook my head. She untied my wrists and helped me to my feet. "Medic!" she shouted.

"I'm okay," I said, pulling away from her and rubbing circulation back into my hands. "Josh?"

Another agent crouched next to him on the ground. The kid was scratched up and dirty, but he shook his head vehemently when the agent asked if he was hurt. "Ollie saved me," he said. He scooched closer to me. "You said we would be okay. You were right."

I sat on the ground and put my arm around him. "I couldn't have done it without you."

The female agent urged me to stand up. "We need you to come with us."

Another agent was trying to talk Josh into going with him. "I'm staying with Ollie," Josh said.

The young, male agent tried coaxing him. "We need to get you back to the White House," he said. "Back to your parents."

Josh wavered, but only for a moment. "Okay," he said. "But only if Ollie comes with me."

The two agents looked up toward Gav, who was issuing directives with regard to Nourie and Clarr. Clarr had been shot and paramedics were working on him. I would find out later how everything had gone down, I was sure. For now I was just happy that Josh and I were alive and unhurt.

"Keep that guy away from his partner," Gav said as agents handcuffed Nourie. "I want to interrogate them separately."

As the team followed his orders, he turned to us. He didn't look at me directly — and for that I was grateful. Had I seen one ounce of concern in his eyes, my tenuous hold on bravery would have broken down right then and there. All business, he consulted with the agents around us. "Take them both back to the White House." Still without looking at me, he said. "I will debrief Ms. Paras later."

The two agents nodded, totally unaware of the emotions swirling around us right now. I was glad of it.

Josh and I were trundled into a waiting limousine. I wanted to ask our escorts a hundred questions, but within two minutes of settling into the soft leather seats, security enveloping us with its comforting arms, Josh fell asleep against me.

CHAPTER 29

The president, Mrs. Hyden, and Abigail ran out the south doors as our limo pulled up. Josh had been roused by our slowdown at the White House checkpoints and now sat up, as eager to see his parents as they were to have him home. Our driver stopped the car and two agents stepped forward to help us alight. Josh was out of the backseat like a shot, racing into his mother's waiting arms.

I felt a hot bubble of emotion work up the back of my throat at the sight of their obvious joy. Having had a nice nap, Josh was full of energy. "Mom, you should have seen Ollie. She was amazing. She kicked out the back light of the car all by herself and . . . and . . . called in the bathroom for help . . . and made the car swerve. I thought we were going to get hit. And then she shot one of the kidnappers."

I cringed at his description. I hadn't shot anyone, but things had gotten a little crazy there and Josh was confused.

Mrs. Hyden looked as though she wouldn't ever let her son go. "Oh my God," she kept saying, over and over. She buried her face in the top of his head and held him close. "Oh my God."

President Hyden's eyes were shiny, but he nodded as he stepped over to me. "Ms. Paras . . ."

"Ollie, please," I said.

He smiled. "Ollie. I can't thank you . . ." Emotion tugged his mouth downward, and he struggled to speak.

"It's okay," I said. "I understand."

He nodded again. "We'll talk later."

Two agents stepped up. One of them took my arm. "Ms. Paras, we need to debrief you."

All I wanted was to get away from agents, to relax just for one solitary minute before being called upon to rehash the day's events. My disappointment must have broadcast across my face because the president placed his hand on the arm of the agent who had stopped me. "Ms. Paras has been through enough. Don't you think this can wait until morning?"

"Yes, sir, Mr. President." The two agents stepped back.

"Thank you," I said and began to make

my way back to the kitchen.

Josh broke away long enough to ask, "Where you going, Ollie?"

I winked at him. "I have a feeling my family is waiting inside."

Bucky and Cyan jumped to their feet when I walked in. "Ollie," Cyan cried out and rushed to hug me.

Bucky groused, "Why is it always you?" He swallowed, and I swore I saw him blink back his reaction. "Why can't you stay safe once in a while?"

"Good to see you, too, Bucky."

Cyan released me. "I'm so glad you're okay. The news said that Matt took you and Josh to safety. Is he okay?"

Matt? Then it dawned on me. Agent Nourie. Cyan didn't know.

I hesitated.

"Is he okay?" she asked again, this time more frantically.

"He's alive and unhurt as far as I can tell," I said. "But . . ." To buy time, I dragged a chair over and sat, right in the middle of the kitchen. The two of them stared at me, waiting for all the details. "You guys know the drill," I said. "I can't tell you anything until I know what's classified and what's not. Half of it I don't even understand myself yet."

"Like what you're not saying about Matt?" She waited, her innocent fear for him so palpable I couldn't bring myself to say the words. But she would have to find out sooner or later.

"He's . . ." I hesitated again, not knowing how much I should say. "He's . . . a bad guy."

Cyan's hand went to her throat. "What?"

I stood and pulled her into a hug so I could whisper, "He's been behind this all along. I'm sorry." I'd had time to think on the drive back here. Time to piece things together. But Cyan hadn't.

As I pulled away from her, her eyes grew red and shiny. "What are you saying, Ollie?"

"We'll find out more soon, but it was Nourie behind everything. All along."

"No . . ." Cyan said, "not Matt."

I knew we would find out more when the time was right, but until then we had to be patient. I hoped Cyan understood that, too.

I sat back in my chair as weariness engulfed me. I wanted to change the subject for Cyan's sake, and to help me have something concrete to talk about. "The state dinner was canceled, I assume?"

"What a fiasco," Bucky said. "That agent

you got to be friends with — Gavin — he was here for a while. Thank God he showed up. The guests started arriving right on time, and nobody wanted to tell them the real reason why dinner was canceled. So, they just made up an excuse about a 'situation.' Everybody understood —" He and Cyan exchanged a meaningful look. "That is, everybody but the guests of honor. When Paul explained that an emergency had arisen and the dinner was canceled — holy! You should have seen the ruckus the president of Armustan and his people caused. Your friend Gav and his team escorted them out."

"Uh . . ." Cyan interrupted. "I heard a bunch of them were detained."

"Arrested?" I asked.

Bucky shrugged. "I don't think you can arrest dignitaries, but I got the impression they took them to a safe house."

"Safe house." I shuddered involuntarily.

Cyan watched me warily. "I don't think Armustan's diplomats are going to be welcome here anytime soon."

"Yeah, I don't think so either."

Cyan's and Bucky's eyes widened in the same unspoken question. I held up my hand. "I'll tell you what I can, when I can."

"Why," Bucky asked, "why is it always

you?"

I was asking myself that same question an hour later as I prepared to leave. I'd marshaled whatever energy I could muster after Cyan made me eat something for strength. "We have lots of wagyu beef and potatoes left over," she said. "Protein and carbs are good for you right now." I refused coffee. It would be hard enough to sleep tonight. Finally, bolstered by the calories Cyan had forced me to consume, I felt ready to embark on my trip home. The Secret Service had informed me that they would escort me, but the prospect of facing the empty apartment was, at the moment, too much to bear.

"You're taking the day off tomorrow, aren't you?" Cyan asked.

"I'd much rather be here. I always feel better when I'm doing something." I sighed. "But yeah, I'll take the day."

"I'll stop by after work and see you," she said. "How does that sound?"

Cyan was trying so hard to cheer me up when I knew her heart had to be breaking because of Nourie's deception. I wondered what Cyan might have inadvertently shared with him — believing him to be trustworthy — that helped his group with their plan.

417

And how did someone like Nourie ever climb so high in the Secret Service ranks?

These were questions to be pondered. But not tonight. My head hurt.

I recognized the agent waiting for me in the hallway — Brenda Notewell. "Ms. Paras," she said.

"Call me Ollie."

"Ollie." She gestured toward the back of the residence. "We're going to get you home safely."

I nodded.

We walked across the hall to the Diplomatic Reception Room. Outside, at the waiting limo, she asked if there was anywhere I needed to stop along the way — or anything I would like to pick up. I thanked her and said I was fine.

She handed me her card. "Once you're home, if you change your mind and need anything, just give me a call. We will be happy to get you whatever you need."

"What I need most right now is a hot shower."

"I'll bet," she said.

If I were being perfectly honest, I needed much more than that. I didn't want to be alone tonight. I climbed into the backseat wondering if maybe Mrs. Wentworth wouldn't mind a visit. Not that I could tell her anything. Brenda shut the door to the back and started toward the front passenger seat. I rolled down the window. "Would you mind?" I asked pointing to the seat across from me. "I could use some company right now."

She smiled again and joined me in the spacious backseat. We sat facing one another. "How much do you know of what happened?" I asked her when we were on the road.

"Not a lot," she said. "But I've been apprised of some of the basics."

"How much does the media know?"

"They know there was a scuffle at the school . . . of course. What the media doesn't know is that we've determined that the disturbance was set up by Agent Nou— er — a renegade agent. He arranged to have shots fired so that it would look perfectly reasonable for him to take charge of the president's son and get him to safety. In fact, he had everyone convinced of that for a little while. That's why there was a delay in finding you."

"*How* did you find me?"

"That, I don't know," she said. "But one of our other agents started to suspect Nourie."

"Who?"

"Bost," she said. "He was shot in the skirmish, but he's going to be okay."

"That's good." I blew out a breath of relief. I'd been suspicious of Bost from the start. Maybe I should have paid attention to what he'd been trying to tell me. Maybe Nourie could have been stopped sooner.

Returning to my question, she said, "The media knows about the scuffle. They know that you and Josh were taken away, but everyone believes you were sequestered in safety all this time. No one knows what really happened."

"So no one knows about Nourie?"

"No," she said, "and this is a huge hit for our department. The Secret Service will suffer for a long time if word gets out. Nobody suspected Nourie. Ever. Now we have to go back and find out what we missed. And how we missed it. The last thing we need right now is for the media to get hold of this."

I nodded. "Lots of meetings all night tonight, I'll bet."

She nodded. "Special Agent in Charge Gavin is organizing a major investigation into the Secret Service and the PPD. We've already been warned that heads will roll. Nobody's getting out of this unscathed."

At the mention of Gav's name, my heart

skipped a beat. He was okay. I was okay. I should be happy enough with that tonight. But I felt as though I needed to talk with him. Right now. Brenda didn't seem to notice my attention waver. I worried for Gav. I knew it would be a very long time before I saw him again. I knew that deep down, and it hurt.

She finished by telling me about the press conference planned for tomorrow morning to discuss the "precautions" taken on Josh's behalf and for the White House to divulge the "real" reason for the canceled state dinner.

"Real reason?" I asked.

"That's part of what's being decided in all these meetings tonight."

We traveled the rest of the way in silence.

When we arrived at my building, I waved off Brenda's offer to walk me up to my apartment. "I don't know," I said. "I somehow feel stronger doing at least this much on my own."

"I understand."

I was sure she did.

James waved to me as I walked past him toward the elevators. "Little excitement today, huh?" he asked. "You okay?"

"Just fine. No big deal."

"The news is saying now that it was all a

big misunderstanding. Some agent's gun accidentally went off and it scared the bejezus out of the agent watching you and the president's son." He looked at me shrewdly. "That how it happened, Ollie?"

"Close enough," I said. "Good night, James."

The elevator dinged when it reached my floor, and I was relieved to see Mrs. Wentworth's door completely shut. As much as I had wanted company earlier, I realized now that what I needed most was sleep. Too bad I still felt so alone.

CHAPTER 30

I peeled off my clothes and left them in a pile on the floor, stepping into the hot shower I'd promised myself. When my skin was bright pink and the room fully steamed, I pulled on a pair of flannel pajamas and fuzzy socks, climbed into bed, and closed my eyes. Lying there for twenty seconds, I started to feel as though my skin was itching from the inside. I sat up. Then tried again.

This wasn't going to work.

Two minutes later, I was back on my feet, way too charged up to relax.

Wandering into my living room, I sat on the sofa and picked up the paperback I'd started last week. Three paragraphs in, I realized I had no idea what was going on, and I couldn't even remember what had happened in the prior fourteen chapters. No idea whatsoever.

I turned on the TV and switched to a news

channel. Since I couldn't expect updates — because the real news hadn't been released — I hoped that the anchors' soft drones would put me to sleep.

An hour later, I was still buzzing with energy. I considered pouring myself a glass of wine. Maybe I'd even have two. That would knock me out in a hurry.

Resigned, I rolled off the couch and headed to the kitchen. With all this lack of sleep it was a good thing I had tomorrow off after all.

I had a bottle of cabernet sauvignon I'd been saving for a special occasion. "What better to celebrate than being alive?" I asked aloud as I grabbed my corkscrew.

From the other room, I heard my phone register a text. I dropped the corkscrew and ran to find out who would be messaging me at this hour of the night, but I already had a feeling I knew.

Flipping open my phone, I read Gav's text: *You awake?*

I typed back: *Wide.*

Figured, he wrote. *Either that or you're sleeping with all your lights on.*

You're here? Come up.

There was a soft knock at my door three seconds later. I ran to open it and said, "How?" but he didn't answer. He pulled me into his arms and held me so close I could hear his heart beating.

"Ollie," he said, "I thought I'd lost you."

"I was worried about *you*," I said.

I felt a chuckle rumble up in his chest. "You would," he said.

We stood there in my doorway for a long moment, both of us silent. He felt so good, so strong. So alive. "I missed you," I said at last. "Where were you?"

"Let's talk."

As I closed the door behind him, I thought I heard Mrs. Wentworth's door click shut. What a character she was.

"I was about to pour myself a glass of wine," I said. "Want some?"

He shook his head. "I'm back on duty at six."

"That's only four hours from now," I said. "When are you going to sleep?"

He took my hand and led me to the sofa. "We need to talk," he said again. "Sit next to me."

I did.

"I know you're off tomorrow." I didn't even bother to ask how he knew that. "But we will need to debrief you, to see if there's anything we're missing. Your captors may have spoken more freely in front of you . . ."

"Because they thought I'd be dead tonight," I finished.

Gav's eyes clouded. "Yeah."

We talked for a long time. Gav wanted to know everything that had happened, and he encouraged me to remember sounds and smells. "This will help you tomorrow when you're being questioned."

"You make it sound like I'm the guilty one."

He sighed. "Your friend Tom is leading the investigation. He's not pleased."

"Not pleased? About Nourie turning out to be a terrorist?"

"He's most definitely not happy about that. But he seemed just as upset that it was you involved." Gav gave me a pointed look. "He was very worried about you."

I decided to ignore that. "It wasn't supposed to be me," I said. "This time it was supposed to be Virgil. I was a last-minute replacement."

"We know that. And I think that tonight, Mrs. Hyden is thanking God that it was you and not Virgil who was there for Josh."

I stared at the ceiling. "The whole time I was out there I was wishing it had been Virgil. But now that it's over, I guess I'm glad it was me, too."

"You saved that kid."

"I didn't really," I said. "They planned to

426

use him to negotiate. They never planned to harm him."

"Those kind of men don't play fair. They promise only when they believe it will help them achieve their objective. I guarantee you, once Farbod was released from prison, they would have disposed of Josh."

I shuddered. "I think I'm going to be sick."

We were silent a long moment. "The main guy, Sami, said that they'd killed one of our special agents." It was hard for me to speak the words. "I thought it was you."

Gav's mouth tightened. He took a breath before answering. "You probably didn't know Agent Schumann."

I shook my head. "I'm so sorry."

"He was a good man who died in service to his country. We probably couldn't have found you without his help." He rubbed my back. "You're very brave, Ollie. Not many people could have held up the way you did."

"How did Nourie get so high up in the Secret Service? How did he even get in? Don't you guys do background checks anymore?"

"Nourie is one of a whole new breed. And I mean that literally. Our enemies are birthing and breeding terrorists in secret. Nourie's family is as clean-cut, all-American as you can find. Only now, when we know where to dig, are we discovering that his family has ties to Armustan. Nourie's path was set from the time he was born. These people grow the kids in happy, suburban settings, where the parents are model citizens. Not one of them has a hair out of place. Their connections to the terrorist cells are buried so deeply underground that the links are impossible to track."

"I don't understand," I said.

Gav sighed. "Take Nourie, for instance. His background, education, career? All squeaky-clean. His parents are also squeaky-clean. We checked them thoroughly before we accepted him. Right? But maybe his father gets his car fixed by a mechanic who frequents a bar where the bartender 'knows' some people."

"And that's how they communicate?"

"It isn't very efficient, but it is effective. It's a scary world, Ollie. And the terrorists are getting smarter every day. Bost started following up on a lead for me. That's part of why he was chafing at Tom's orders. We didn't suspect Nourie, not until the last moment. And Bost decided to move — on his own — when he started to put pieces together. He inadvertently messed up Nourie's plans. Good man."

"Oh God, I have a hundred questions.

Probably more than that."

"You know you won't get them all answered."

"I figured as much."

Gav's hand was still on my back. I liked it there.

One thing still bothered me. "How did you know where to find us? Once we left that house . . ."

"One of our teams found the location. Obviously too late. It was your text that saved you. You said they were getting ready to broadcast." His hand skimmed down my back and dropped to his lap. "Agent Schumann was our operative in that cell. He was new to them, so he remained low on their totem pole. That is to say he knew nothing of the cell's infiltration of the Secret Service and he knew nothing about the arsenic poisoning. We hoped, in time, he would bring us back the kind of intelligence we needed to save lives. We had no idea that time would come so soon."

I still didn't understand.

"He was one of their drivers, taking midlevel bad guys where they wanted to go. He had seen and reported the cameras and equipment for a broadcast, but he had no idea what they were planning, or when. Nothing he'd seen was illegal, but his information proved invaluable. When you texted, telling us what they had in mind, we knew exactly where to go. And I just thank God you were there."

"I was so worried that I'd told you the wrong kind of car."

Gav chuckled. "You did good, kid. Again."

We sat facing each other on the sofa, our knees so close they almost touched. "You have no idea how happy I was to hear from you," I said softly. "When we were stuck in that bathroom and I saw that you were okay . . ."

He smiled so gently it nearly broke my heart.

"Ollie," he said, taking both my hands in his, "your last message . . ."

I couldn't remember what I'd sent last. I shook my head.

"You wrote, 'I hope.' What were you going to say?"

"Ah . . ." I said softly, remembering. I stared down at our joined hands. Looking up, I wondered if his eyes were actually blue. I'd always thought they were gray. Right now I couldn't quite tell. But maybe I would have time to find out. "I was going to say that I hope if we got out of all this, you could stop thinking of yourself as a jinx. And maybe . . ."

"Maybe?"

I didn't finish.

He brushed hair out of my eyes. "You're beautiful."

I laughed.

"But you're tired," he said. "I can see it in your eyes."

"I couldn't sleep," I said, "but now I'm finally starting to relax."

"Shh. Come here." He put his arm around me and tucked me in, close. "Sleep a little. I'll watch over you."

As I nestled in, I felt exhaustion wash over me like an old friend. Just as I started to doze, I remembered something. "Gav?"

His chin rested on top of my head as he stroked my hair. "Yeah?"

"How old are you?"

He told me. Even in my blissful half-asleep state I could do the math. "Seven years," I said.

"Yep."

"Mrs. Wentworth says that's just perfect."

I don't know if he responded, or if I just fell asleep and missed his reply.

WELCOME TO YOUR NEW HOME, MR. PRESIDENT

Getting to know a new First Family is not without its challenges. When a new president takes over the West Wing, life changes for everyone in the country, and for everyone here on staff. What most people don't realize, however, is that the biggest adjustment is made by the family moving in. Think about it: Despite the fact that they've had a couple of months to get used to the idea, no one realizes the pressures of living one's life in a fishbowl until they're actually in it.

This can be particularly difficult when kids are involved. The Campbells' grown kids had been on their own for years, and we only saw them from time to time. But the Hydens brought two youngsters to the White House — kids who had to leave their friends and normal lives behind because their dad just happened to become one of the most powerful people in the world.

Our first duty in the kitchen has always been to provide the president and his wife with the best possible meals — all the time, and every time. As the White House chef, I had provided elaborate meals for world leaders and I had designed sophisticated and lavish events for the Campbells for as long as they were able to entertain.

But bring kids into the equation and things change. Quickly.

The Hydens are young, with young kids. They bring a new vibrancy, new energy to the house. And that means no small measure of complexity.

What I mean is that we now face the challenge of feeding individuals whose choices are not necessarily their own. If Mom insists on certain veggies at each meal, you can bet we'll provide them. Our goal, however, will be to make these good-for-you offerings appealing enough to tempt even the pickiest eaters.

The moment the results of the last election were known, Bucky, Cyan, and I understood that we needed to brush up on our kid-friendly fare. We worked up a number of specialties in anticipation of life at the White House with Abigail and Joshua. I hope you like them. I hope the kids in your life do, too.

And just so you don't think we forgot the fancy-schmancy stuff, I've included recipes for the Hydens' first state dinner. It's a darned excellent menu, if I do say so myself. I particularly recommend the spinach, which is so good I prepare a simplified version of it at home all the time.

Enjoy!
Ollie

BUFFALO WILD WEST WINGS WITH HOMEMADE RANCH DRESSING AND CELERY STICKS

Buffalo wings can be made two ways. The original style is fried and unbreaded. The newer version is breaded and baked. Both are good, so I present both here for you to experiment with.

Chicken Wings

TRADITIONAL FRIED RECIPE
4 lbs. raw chicken wings (approximately 20)
Vegetable oil to fry, held at 375 degrees F
4 tablespoons butter, melted
1 12-oz. bottle Wing Sauce, or homemade wing sauce
Homemade Ranch Dressing

Serves 4

Traditionally, Buffalo wings are deep-fat fried, and not floured. If you prefer to fry your wings rather than bake them, rinse the chicken wings and pat dry with paper towels. Cut each wing at the joints into three sections. You can discard the wing tips, or save them for use in making chicken stock later, as you prefer. Personally, I put them in a resealable bag and collect them in the freezer until I have enough to make stock. But you won't be using them here. Take the two top wing portions, and drop the cut up wings naked into vegetable oil in a deep fat fryer at 375 degrees F. Do this gently — spattering hot oil on yourself is painful. I find frying 8 to 10 pieces at a time keeps the oil temperature from dropping too low — you want to maintain it high so that the wings are crisp rather than rubbery. Once the chicken is browned and cooked through, about 8 to 10 minutes, remove with slotted spoon, drain on paper towels. Keep cooking until all wings are fried. Put the cooked chicken wings in a large bowl with the hot sauce and melted butter and stir to coat. Serve with celery sticks and Homemade Ranch Dressing on the side.

BAKED RECIPE

4 tablespoons butter
4 lbs. raw chicken wings (approximately 20)
1 cup flour
1 teaspoon salt
2 teaspoons garlic powder
Freshly cracked black pepper, to taste
(about 1/2 teaspoon for me)
Wing Sauce
Homemade Ranch Dressing

Preheat oven to 400 degrees F.

Place the butter in a 13 × 9 cake pan, and put in oven to melt butter.

Rinse chicken wings and pat dry with paper towels. Cut each wing at the joints into three sections. You can discard the wing tips, or save them for use in making chicken stock later, as you prefer. Personally, I put them in a resealable bag and collect them in the freezer until I have enough to make stock. But you won't be using them here.

Place the flour, salt, garlic powder, and cracked pepper in a sturdy gallon-sized plastic bag. Close the bag and shake to mix the contents. Drop 4 pieces of chicken at a time into the bag. Shake to coat with the flour mixture. Remove and set aside. Keep coating pieces until all are coated.

Remove pan with melted butter from the oven.

Roll floured chicken pieces in the butter. Spread evenly in the pan. Place in oven and bake for 25–30 minutes, until chicken is cooked through and juices run clear.

When chicken is cooked through, remove from oven. Pour chicken, melted butter and all, into a large bowl with the wing sauce; stir until chicken is well coated.

Serve with celery sticks and dressing on the side.

WING SAUCE
1 cup ketchup
4 tablespoons red wine vinegar
1 tablespoon sugar
Tabasco sauce to taste

Whisk the ketchup, vinegar, and sugar together, then stir in Tabasco sauce one drop at a time, tasting after each drop, until the heat is exactly what you like.

Instead of making your own, you can also

try Texas Pete's, Frank's RedHot, Defcon 2, Anchor Bar Original Buffalo Wing Sauce, or whatever suits your fancy. The average supermarket now carries several kinds to choose from. Whatever you use, you'll need a cup and a half, or 12 fluid ounces of wing sauce.

Homemade Ranch Dressing

1 head celery, washed, leaves and roots removed, sliced into 4 inch sticks

DRESSING
1/2 cup buttermilk
1/4 cup mayonnaise or Miracle Whip
1/2 teaspoon garlic powder
1/2 teaspoon salt
Freshly cracked black pepper, to taste (roughly 1/4 teaspoon for me)
1/4 cup flat-leaf parsley, finely chopped
1/4 cup fresh chives, finely chopped

Place all dressing ingredients in a medium bowl. Whisk to incorporate. Chill. If you're in a hurry, you can substitute a good store-bought dressing, either ranch or blue cheese. I just like to make my own.

SPRING GREENS SALAD WITH MANDARIN ORANGES AND BERRIES

DRESSING
1/4 cup fresh basil leaves, finely chopped
3/4 cup honey
1 clove garlic, smashed, peeled, and finely minced
1/4 cup apple cider vinegar
1 lime, zested and juiced
1/4 teaspoon salt

Serves 4

Place all ingredients in a blender container. Blend to incorporate. If you don't have a blender, whisk together. Chill.

SALAD
1 container mixed spring greens, preferably organic
1 can mandarin oranges, chilled and drained
1 pint fresh berries, rinsed, and picked over to remove bruised fruit (If berries are out of season, substitute 1/4 cup Craisins)
1/2 cup pecans or walnuts

Wash and spin the salad greens dry. Place in a large bowl. Toss with orange slices, berries, and nuts. Serve with dressing on the side.

KID-FRIENDLY RECIPES
GREEK NIGHT

This is a traditional Mediterranean meal, with a lovely selection of easy-to-make Greek dips, pita, and bread to scoop them up, traditional chicken kabobs, and a Greek salad to add some veggie crunch. Mediterranean diets have been found to be tremendously heart-healthy, as well as tasty enough for any family, kids included, to enjoy. One favorite feature of this meal is that the whole thing — with the possible exception of the salad — can be eaten as finger food.

HUMMUS

1 16-oz. can garbanzo beans or chickpeas (they're the same thing)
2 tablespoons tahini
Juice of 1 lemon
4 cloves garlic, smashed and peeled
1/2 teaspoon salt
Paprika (optional but very pretty), olive oil, and parsley, to garnish

Serves 6

Drain chickpeas, reserving liquid for later use. Place chickpeas, tahini, lemon juice, garlic, and salt in a blender. Blend until mixture is smooth and all ingredients are fully incorporated. While blender is running, slowly add juice from chickpea can until the mixture has a soft and easily scoopable consistency. The amount of liquid you need will vary, depending on how much juice you got from your lemon. Adjust seasonings as needed.

Place in a bowl, use a spoon to smooth the top of the hummus, then create a well in the center of the dip with the bottom of your spoon. Sprinkle dip lightly with paprika, pour a little olive oil in the well, and top with sprigs of fresh parsley. Serve.

TZATZIKI

2 cups Greek yogurt (If you can't find Greek yogurt, make your own version from plain regular yogurt. Take a large bowl. Place a strainer or colander inside it. Line the straining device with a double layer of cheesecloth. Pour in regular plain yogurt. Let it drain in the refrigerator for at least 12 hours. Discard the liquid. Use the thick yogurt in the cheesecloth in place

of the requested Greek yogurt.)

3 cloves garlic, smashed, peeled, and finely minced

1 small cucumber, peeled and grated

1/2 teaspoon salt

1/4 cup fresh dill and chives, rinsed and chopped finely (optional)

Fresh dill sprig to garnish (optional)

Serves 6

Place yogurt, garlic, cucumber, and salt in bowl, stir to combine. Add chopped dill and chives. Stir in. Taste and adjust seasonings as necessary. Garnish with fresh dill. Serve.

BABAGANOUSH

2 large purple eggplants

1/4 cup olive oil

1/2 teaspoon salt

1/4 cup tahini

Juice from 1 lemon

1 cup Greek yogurt

1/4 cup fresh herbs (chives, parsley, or dill) loosely chopped (optional), to garnish

Serves 6

Set oven to broil.

Cut eggplants in half. Brush the cut faces

with a little olive oil. Place facedown on a cookie sheet and broil, watching carefully, 10–15 minutes, until eggplant darkens and softens. Remove from oven. Let cool until safe to handle.

Peel. Place eggplant in a bowl. Add remaining olive oil, salt, tahini, lemon juice, and yogurt. Whisk. Taste and adjust seasonings as necessary. Chill. Top with herbs to garnish, if using.

Serve these dips accompanied by a platter of sliced warm French or Italian bread, and warmed pita rounds sliced into quarters.

CHICKEN SOUVLAKI (CHICKEN KABOBS)

These are traditionally done with lamb, but chicken is far more kid-friendly. If you want to go vegetarian on this menu, simply eliminate these kabobs.

1 lb. boneless, skinless chicken breasts, cut
    into 1-inch cubes
Juice from 1 lemon
1/2 teaspoon salt
1/4 cup olive oil
2 teaspoons fresh oregano, chopped (or 1
    teaspoon dried)

4 cloves of garlic, smashed, peeled, and finely minced

Serves 6

Place all ingredients in a sturdy gallon-sized plastic freezer bag. Shake to mix and coat.

Place sealed bag in refrigerator for 1 hour to marinate, turning halfway through.

Place meat cubes on 6 skewers (more if needed). Discard liquid.

Grill skewers over medium-high heat for 4 minutes per side, either on a stovetop grill, in a grill or skillet pan coated with cooking spray, or over a propane or charcoal fire.

Serve.

SIMPLE GREEK SALAD
1 pint cherry or grape tomatoes, washed and halved
1 red onion, peeled and loosely chopped
1/4 lb. feta cheese, cubed or crumbled
1/2 cup Kalamata olives, drained and pits removed
2 cucumbers, peeled and cut in half lengthwise

1/4 cup balsamic vinegar
1/4 cup extra virgin olive oil
1/2 teaspoon salt
Freshly cracked black pepper, to taste
1 clove garlic, smashed, peeled, and finely
  minced

Serves 6

In a large bowl, place tomatoes, onions, feta
cheese, and olives. Take halved cucumbers,
run a spoon firmly along the seeded side to
remove the seeds. Discard the seeds. Slice
the cucumber halves into C-shaped slices.
Add to bowl.

In a smaller bowl, whisk together balsamic
vinegar, olive oil, salt, pepper, and garlic.
Pour over salad, toss to coat.

Serve.

KID-FRIENDLY CHICKEN MEAL

This is another kid-tested family meal that has the virtue of consisting mostly of finger foods, but it's surprisingly healthy.

"FRIED" CHICKEN STRIPS

2 eggs
3 cups cornflakes
1 tablespoon garlic powder
1/2 teaspoon salt
1/4 teaspoon paprika
1 lb. boneless, skinless chicken breasts, cut into finger-sized strips

Serves 4

Preheat oven to 375 degrees F.

Crack the 2 eggs into a medium bowl. Whisk until golden and foamy.

Place the cornflakes, garlic, salt, and paprika

into a sturdy gallon-sized freezer bag and seal. Smash with a rolling pin, the smooth side of a meat tenderizer, or the bottom of a tumbler, until the cornflakes are turned into crumbs. Shake to mix crumbs and spices together. Dip the chicken strips into egg, then place into bag of cornflake crumb mixture, and shake to coat. Place coated strips onto a cookie sheet. When all strips are coated, place the cookie sheet into the oven. Bake for 25–30 minutes, until chicken is firm and juices run clear.

HONEY-MUSTARD DIPPING SAUCE
1/2 cup Dijon mustard
1/4 cup mayonnaise
2 tablespoons olive oil
2 tablespoons honey
2 tablespoons orange juice

Whisk ingredients together. Serve.

RUSTIC FRENCH "FRIES"
2 tablespoons garlic salt
2 tablespoons Mrs. Dash — original flavor
Freshly cracked black pepper, to taste
4 potatoes, scrubbed and each sliced into 8
  wedges lengthwise
Cooking spray

Serves 4

Preheat oven to 375 degrees F.

Place garlic salt, Mrs. Dash, and cracked pepper to taste into a sturdy gallon-sized plastic bag. Spray the potato wedges with the cooking spray. Drop them into the bag of seasonings. Shake to coat. Lay the potato wedges, peel side down, on a cookie sheet and bake until wedges are cooked through and crispy outside, about 15–25 minutes. Serve with ketchup.

CORN ON THE COB WITH HERBED BUTTER

4 ears corn on the cob, shucked, strings removed, and washed
1 stick butter, melted
1/4 cup chives, rinsed and finely chopped

Serves 4

Place a large pan of water on the stove on high. Bring to a boil. Drop the ears of corn gently into the hot water. Boil until cooked to taste, roughly 7–10 minutes. Remove and serve warm.

Place melted butter in a pitcher. Drop in chives and stir. Pour over cooked corn ears. Serve.

GREEN BEANS WITH BACON BITS AND BLANCHED ALMONDS

1 tablespoon Real Bacon Bits
1 tablespoon olive oil
1/4 cup sliced blanched almonds
3 tablespoons water
1 lb. green beans (fresh or frozen), washed, ends and strings removed
Salt, to taste

Serves 4

Place Bacon Bits, olive oil, and the almonds in the bottom of a heavy skillet or saucepan over medium heat. Stir until the bacon is warmed through and the almonds smell toasty, about 2 minutes. Add the beans and toss to coat. Add the water, cover. Cook until beans are bright green and warmed through, but still slightly crisp, about 7–10 minutes. Salt to taste. Serve.

WHITE HOUSE STATE DINNER

This menu is set up to feature American ingredients at their finest. You can always substitute if you have trouble finding the right ingredients. A lot of these recipes call for experienced chefs and unique ingredients, but I've provided shortcuts and cheats that make it easy for a home cook to come up with a reasonable approximation.

The menu:
Chesapeake crab agnolottis with basil oil
Wagyu beef on a bed of garlic mashed potatoes
Nantucket sea scallops
Creamed spinach with olive oil and shallots
Mixed berry cobbler

CHESAPEAKE CRAB AGNOLOTTIS AND BASIL OIL

Serves 6

Agnolottis are stuffed pasta squares that look and taste like little square raviolis. They are made from a very rich egg dough pasta. I'll tell you how to do this the hard way, and then the easy way.

THE HARD WAY

4 cups bread flour

7 egg yolks, plus 1 egg white, beaten just enough to break egg yolks and mix together

1/4 teaspoon salt

Pile the flour in a mound on a clean and dry kitchen countertop with a lot of room to work with dough. Make a well in the center. Pour the egg mixture into the well, and sprinkle the salt over the eggs. Working with your fingers, mix the eggs gently into the flour, a little at a time. Pull a little flour from the edges of the hill into the liquid; mix. Pull a little more flour into the eggs; mix. Do this until the flour and eggs are formed into a dough. Knead dough for 15 minutes, until it is smooth, golden, elastic, and slightly stretchy. Divide the dough into two parts. Cover with a damp towel and let rest for a few minutes.

Take one portion of the dough. If you have a pasta machine, follow directions for the machine from here to roll one portion of dough into a thin sheet. If you don't, you can roll it out by hand using a rolling pin: Roll the dough out, flip it over, and roll it out again. Keep rolling and flipping until the dough is almost thin enough to read through. (It should be about the thickness of a dime if you can manage it, or even thinner if you're good at this.) Cut the dough into 2-inch squares. Fill with filling below (or filling of your choice — once you have the hang of dough-making, you'll never go back to store-bought pasta again.). Place a scant teaspoon of filling in the middle of a pasta square. Wet your fingers. Dampen the edges of the pasta square. Place a second square of dough on top of the filled square of pasta. Use your fingers to stick the dough edges together, so that you have a little sandwich of pasta dough around the filling, with the edges firmly glued to each other. Repeat with second ball of dough.

THE EASY WAY
2 packages wonton wrappers (look for them in the produce section)

453

Place a heaping teaspoon of filling in the middle of a wonton-wrapper square. Wet your fingers. Dampen the edges of the wonton square. Place a second wonton square on top of the filled square of wonton wrapper. Use your fingers to stick the dough edges together, so that you have a little sandwich of wonton dough around the filling, with the edges firmly glued to each other.

FILLING
1 cup ricotta cheese
3/4 cup grated Parmigiano-Reggiano cheese
1 egg yolk
1/2 cup chopped fresh basil leaves
1 lb. lump crabmeat, preferably fresh Chesapeake crabmeat, carefully picked over to remove any shell fragments
1/4 teaspoon salt
1/4 teaspoon freshly ground pepper

Place all filling ingredients in a large bowl and mix well.

Once your agnolottis are stuffed and ready to go, drop them into a heavy pot filled two-thirds with salted boiling water. Stir the water gently with a wooden spoon to keep the pasta from sticking together. Boil until pasta is cooked al dente, roughly 3–6 minutes. (Fresh pasta cooks a lot faster than dried pasta.) Remove to a warmed platter with a slotted spoon. Drizzle with basil oil. Garnish with fresh basil leaves, if desired. Serve.

BASIL OIL

1 cup extra virgin olive oil
1 cup loosely packed basil leaves

Place the olive oil and basil leaves in a blender container. Pulse until leaves are finely chopped but not yet a paste. Transfer the mixture to a skillet over medium heat. Warm through until the oil smells fragrant. Place a fine-meshed strainer over a glass bowl. Line with two layers of cheesecloth. Pour the warm oil through the strainer to remove the basil leaves. Pour the filtered oil into a cruet or a bottle. Keeps in the refrigerator for 3 weeks.

WAGYU BEEF STEAKS

Wagyu beef is an American version of the fantastic Japanese delicacy Kobe beef. It can be hard to find either Kobe or Wagyu beef, so a really nice porterhouse, T-bone, New York strip steak, rib eye, or top sirloin will do the job here if you can't turn up the gourmet stuff.

Approximately 8 oz. steak per person, brought to room temperature. To do this, remove steaks from the refrigerator about 45 minutes before you plan to cook them. Leave on the counter covered in plastic wrap. If your steak is cold, as you cook it, it can burn on the outside while remaining too rare on the inside.

Salt
Freshly cracked black pepper
2 tablespoons canola oil
1 teaspoon butter

In the White House, we broil these in our commercial ovens. But for home chefs, these steaks can be handled in a number of ways. They can be grilled, broiled, or pan-seared. The real trick is starting with a hot surface, and using a good meat thermometer to determine the internal temperature of the steak so you bring it to the desired doneness that you prefer.

Preheat oven to 450 degrees F. The easiest technique to handle a steak, and the most universally available, regardless of season and weather, is to pan-sear it. You will need a sturdy cast-iron skillet or equivalent. I am particularly fond of enameled cast-iron cookware. You want something with a heavy bottom that will evenly distribute the heat from your cooktop, and not have hot spots that might burn the meat. Place the pan on a burner set on medium-high heat. Place oil in the bottom of the pan and heat until hot but not smoking. You can test the surface to see if it's hot enough by carefully dropping a drop of water into the pan. If it sizzles and dances across the surface, the oil's hot enough.

Pat steaks dry. Season both sides of the meat to taste with salt and pepper. Using tongs, (forks pierce the meat and allow those delicious juices to escape) gently place the steak in the heated oil. You should hear a sizzling sound from the pan if it is the right temperature. Slide the steak around on the pool of oil for a few seconds, to keep the meat's surface from sticking to the pan.

Let continue cooking in the skillet for approximately 2 minutes for a medium-rare steak.

At the end of 2 minutes, using your tongs, turn the steak over. Place a pat of butter on top of the steak. It should bubble and melt immediately. Let the steak sit in the skillet, cooking the other side, for an additional 2 minutes.

Using your meat thermometer, place it in

the steak with its tip firmly seated in the middle layer of the meat. Take the temperature of the inside of your steak. For rare, the internal temperature should be 115 degrees; medium-rare, 120 degrees; medium, 125 degrees; medium-well, 130 degrees; and well-done, 140 degrees.

If you are looking for more doneness than you've got, using a pot holder, carefully move the steak to the hot oven. Keep an eye on the meat thermometer. When the internal temperature matches your doneness temperature, remove it from the oven.

Using a set of clean tongs (The old ones could transfer germs from the original raw steak you handled to the finished meat. That's bad. Very bad.), move it from the skillet to a warmed clean platter, and tent with aluminum foil.

Why, do you ask, can't you just serve these things? They smell fabulous! One of the biggest secrets of handling steaks is that they continue to cook after you remove them from the oven. In fact, the internal temperature of the meat will typically rise between 5 and 10 degrees after you remove your meat from the heat source. After you've cooked the meat, you need to set it aside, tented with foil, so the meat rests, reaches your preferred doneness, and the juices redistribute evenly through the steak. If you serve it right off the grill, you're missing the mark on perfection. The outside will be too hot, and the inside too cool.

Let rest 5 to 10 minutes, then serve on a bed of warmed Garlic Mashed Potatoes.

Note — the following recipe originally appeared in State of the Onion. *But for those of you who haven't got a copy handy, I repeat it here.*

GARLIC MASHED POTATOES

2 lbs. peeled and diced potatoes (I like to use traditional Idaho russets, but just about any variety of potato will do)

6 tablespoons butter

1/2 to 1 head garlic cloves, peeled and mashed

1/2 to 3/4 cup milk, warmed

1 tablespoon salt, or to taste

1/2 teaspoon freshly cracked pepper, or to taste

1/4 cup fresh chives, chopped, for garnish, optional

Serves 6

Place potatoes in a large, heavy-bottomed pan. Add water sufficient to cover them. Put lid on pan and bring to a boil over medium heat, watching to be sure pan doesn't boil over. Once the water is boiling, reduce heat slightly and simmer until potatoes are fork-tender, about 25 minutes.

Drain cooked potatoes and set aside. Return empty pan to heat and add butter. When butter melts, add garlic. Cook until tender. Return cooked potatoes to pan. Mash or whip with immersion blender until nearly smooth, gradually adding warm milk until potatoes are the desired consistency. Add salt and pepper, to taste. Place in warmed serving dish and top with chives, if using. Serve.

Note: Some people salt the water the potatoes are boiling in, which raises the temperature and lets the potatoes cook faster. I prefer to add salt after cooking, when I have more control over the amount the dish has. I think it leaves the potatoes more tender, too — but either method works.

NANTUCKET SEA SCALLOPS

Cooking scallops is easy. Cleaning them is hard. And finding good fresh scallops is the real secret for making this into a food fit for feasting.

In most cases, you can get your supplier to clean the scallops for you. If you can, go for it. But, just in case you can't, here are the instructions for dealing with live scallops and getting them ready to eat.

Place the scallops on ice. This makes the animal inside relax and open up its shell.

Hold the scallop firmly in your palm, with its hinge side toward your fingertips and its rounded side toward your palm.

Place a sturdy paring knife in between the two halves of the shell. Twist and cut against the top of the shell, opening the scallop up and severing the muscle from the top shell half. Discard the top shell. Scrape the dark meat away from the scallop by running a spoon over the bottom scallop shell from the hinge toward your palm. Discard the dark stuff. You should be left with a gorgeous, pearly white scallop muscle on the bottom shell. Cut beneath the muscle to release it from the shell. Remove any tough tendon from the outside edge of the scallop. Your scallop is now cleaned and ready to cook.

2 tablespoons of canola oil

4 tablespoons butter

3 cleaned scallops per person for an appetizer portion. 6 cleaned scallops per person for a main course

1 clove garlic, smashed, cleaned, and finely minced

Salt and pepper, to taste

You will need a sturdy cast-iron skillet or equivalent. I am particularly fond of enameled cast-iron cookware. You want something with a heavy bottom that will evenly distribute the heat from your cooktop, and not have hot spots that might burn the scallops. Place the pan on a burner set on medium-high heat. Place the canola oil in the bottom of the pan with the butter. Mix together as the butter melts. Toss in the minced garlic and give the pan a stir. Let the oil heat up until it is hot, but not smoking. You can test the surface to see if it's hot enough by carefully dropping a drop of water into the pan. If it sizzles and dances across the surface, the oil's hot enough.

Using tongs, transfer the scallops to the prepared hot oil in the pan. Let brown for roughly 2 minutes, then turn to brown the other side. Remove cooked scallops from skillet onto warmed plates. Season with salt and pepper, to taste. Serve on a bed of

Creamed Spinach with Olive Oil and Shallots.

CREAMED SPINACH WITH OLIVE OIL AND SHALLOTS

2 tablespoons olive oil
1/4 cup shallots, finely minced
10–12 oz. fresh spinach, washed, dried, and trimmed to remove tough stems
2 tablespoons butter
1 tablespoon flour
1/2 cup liquid — milk, chicken broth, or white wine, depending on personal taste
1 pinch fresh ground nutmeg
1/4–1/2 tablespoon salt, or to taste
Freshly cracked black pepper
1/4 cup grated Parmigiano-Reggiano cheese

Serves 6

Put olive oil in a sturdy cast-iron skillet or equivalent over medium-high heat. When oil is hot, add shallots, stirring until they are clear, about 1 minute. Add spinach, and continue stirring until mixture is heated through and reduced and wilted, about 2–3 minutes.

Remove from heat. In a large skillet, melt the butter over medium heat. Add flour and whisk vigorously until a smooth bubbling paste forms, about 1 minute. Slowly whisk in the liquid. Keep stirring until you have a thickened sauce. Add the nutmeg and salt and pepper, to taste. Whisk. Add in the spinach mixture. Stir to coat. Plate. Top with grated cheese. Serve.

MIXED BERRY COBBLER

4 cups berries, fresh or frozen
1 tablespoon cornstarch
11/2 cups sugar, divided
1/2 teaspoon salt
2 cups flour
2 teaspoons baking powder
1/2 teaspoon salt
4 tablespoons butter, melted
1 teaspoon vanilla
2 teaspoons milk
1 egg, beaten
1 tablespoon sugar, for sprinkling

Serves 8

Preheat oven to 350 degrees F. Toss the berries with the cornstarch, 1/2 cup sugar, and salt. Place in a large casserole dish and set aside.

In a medium bowl, mix together flour, remaining 1 cup sugar, baking powder, and salt. Whisk to incorporate smoothly. Make a well in the center of the dry ingredients. Add butter, vanilla, milk, and egg. Stir until ingredients are just mixed. Batter will be lumpy. If you work this batter too much, the topping of your cobbler will be tough.

Pour over the berries. Top batter with a sprinkling of sugar. Bake for 45–50 minutes, until berries are bubbling hot and the cobbler top is golden and cooked through. Serve warm.

Of course, adding a scoop of good vanilla ice cream to hot cobbler is always appropriate.

ABOUT THE AUTHOR

An Anthony and Barry award-winning author (for *State of the Onion*), **Julie Hyzy** also writes the Manor House Mysteries for Berkley Prime Crime, beginning with *Grace Under Pressure*. Please visit Julie's website at www.juliehyzy.com.

We hope you have enjoyed this Large Print book. Other Thorndike, Wheeler, Kennebec, and Chivers Press Large Print books are available at your library or directly from the publishers.

For information about current and upcoming titles, please call or write, without obligation, to:

Publisher
Thorndike Press
10 Water St., Suite 310
Waterville, ME 04901
Tel. (800) 223-1244

or visit our Web site at:

http://gale.cengage.com/thorndike

OR

Chivers Large Print
published by AudioGO Ltd
St James House, The Square
Lower Bristol Road
Bath BA2 3BH
England
Tel. +44(0) 800 136919
info@audiogo.co.uk
www.audiogo.co.uk

All our Large Print titles are designed for easy reading, and all our books are made to last.